THE BEASTS OF WINTER

ALSO BY J. C. CERVANTES
The Daggers of Ire

THE BEASTS OF WINTER

A DAGGERS OF IRE NOVEL

J. C. CERVANTES

STORYTIDE
An Imprint of HarperCollinsPublishers

HarperCollins Children's Books, a division of HarperCollins Publishers,
195 Broadway, New York, NY 10007

HarperCollins Publishers, Macken House, 39/40 Mayor Street Upper,
Dublin 1, D01 C9W8, Ireland

Storytide is an imprint of HarperCollins Publishers.

The Beasts of Winter
Text copyright © 2026 by J. C. Cervantes
Illustrations copyright © 2026 by Paula Zorite
All rights reserved. Manufactured in Harrisonburg, VA, United States of America. No part of this book may be used or reproduced in any manner whatsoever without written permission except in the case of brief quotations embodied in critical articles and reviews. Without limiting the exclusive rights of any author, contributor, or the publisher of this publication, any unauthorized use of this publication to train generative artificial intelligence (AI) technologies is expressly prohibited. HarperCollins also exercises their rights under Article 4(3) of the Digital Single Market Directive 2019/790 and expressly reserves this publication from the text and data mining exception.
harpercollins.com

Library of Congress Control Number: 2025939403
ISBN 978-0-06-331213-5

Typography by Joel Tippie
25 26 27 28 29 LBC 5 4 3 2 1

First Edition

For those who believe in freedom

Chapter One

Fetch was no ordinary fox.

An obvious fact to anyone who had seen him soar across the sky wearing the coat he had created with his enchanted threads. He was a Zindero, a weaver of magic with an endless supply of spools, each with a different and magnificent power.

Some might call him peculiar. Others, extraordinary.

But on his first day back home in Ocho Manos, he didn't feel extraordinary. He felt nothing but exhausted from his recent journey to the Otherworld.

It had been a death-defying adventure in which he'd performed a great service to human witches, one that would inspire the kind of tales that would be told for eons. Maybe his story would even make it into a book that would sit on the shelves in Los Misterios—a library that housed countless spellbinding books. The library had once been his favorite place . . . but that was before.

Still in his bathrobe, Fetch plopped onto the wooden stool in his workroom and began opening the mail that had arrived while he'd been away.

A catalog of bargain spells—cheap little charms that did things like make someone sneeze five times in a row, or glue someone's mouth shut for ten seconds. No real or significant magic. He tossed the catalog into the trash and picked up the next bit of mail: a note from his fairy friend Garzo. The paper, a light blue linen, smelled like poppyseed and spun sugar.

Fetch's stomach grumbled as he read.

> Is my superpowered vest ready? It had better be magnificent (PERFECT!) with all the time you've taken. Your customer service is rather lacking, to be honest, and not at all what I expected from a FRIEND. I'd hate to leave you a one-star review. (Insert grumble here.) I'll be by the day after Winter's Eve to collect. Do NOT disappoint me.
>   G (for GREAT)

Fetch smirked. Garzo really was the most dramatic, self-absorbed fairy he'd ever met. With a sigh, he dragged a paw down his furry face. He didn't want to think about how behind he was on his sewing orders. Nor did he want to think about winter only a day away. After all, winter was the time of year when everything had changed—

Bzzz. Bzzz.

Fetch scanned his workroom, a small dusty space with worn wood floors and dozens of shelves that housed his magical spools in every color and shimmer.

A spool of rainbow thread trembled as if it had heard the sound too. Or had Fetch only imagined it?

This is what happens when you're so tired you start seeing and hearing things, he thought. He'd been home a day, slept through most of it, and was still so tired all he wanted to do was fall into his cozy bed for an entire season.

A ghastly odor floated into the air just then—like a murky, slimy swamp on a hot summer afternoon.

As a fox he was quite excellent at picking up scents. And this one was not only foul but incredibly old. Had he left some food to rot while he was away?

"I'm definitely not imagining *that*," Fetch said, covering his nose.

His ears pricked as he reluctantly sniffed the air, walking over to a side table that was stacked high with scraps of fabric and heaps of tangled thread. His enchanted trench coat was tossed next to the mess.

Bzzz. Bzzz.

Whatever was making that sound was buried beneath the rubble. Or maybe it was inside his coat. He knew better than to reach into one of its limitless pockets—what if some venomous insect had stowed away in there and was just waiting to bite or sting him?

It was also entirely possible that it could be a vampiric beast waiting to suck his blood. There were all sorts of strange and monstrous insects in Ocho Manos, his island home, but with winter approaching, most had already died out or gone into hibernation.

Fetch snatched a spool of chocolate-colored thread used for its ability to create a temporary armor. He unraveled and wound the string around his paw, where it tightened on contact.

With a wince, he reached into a coat pocket. Empty. He reached into another.

But all he found was the magical flower he'd taken from Esme's hair when they'd said goodbye yesterday. A reminder that he had a friend out there, even if she did live in another dimension.

There it was again—that horrid buzzing sound. A shiver climbed up Fetch's spine as the tangle of threads on the table shifted.

The swampy smell of death floated up like a northern wind, and he nearly gagged. Covering his nose again, Fetch slowly began to untie the tangle. One layer at a time.

Then he saw it.

The little culprit wasn't like any insect he'd ever seen. It was a sort of spidery wasp with red spotted wings, six hairy legs, and a face that looked a bit like a scrunched head of cabbage with narrow eyes and a very angry mouth.

A scream climbed up Fetch's throat only to die when he saw one of the creature's back legs was caught by a thread.

"So you're stuck," Fetch said, feeling a bit bad for the feisty thing, but secretly grateful it couldn't get liftoff and attack him.

The insect flailed its legs, then opened its mouth. Out came an earsplitting shriek.

Fetch jumped back, but he didn't have the heart to smash the thing. How had it even gotten in here? His underground home was a very well-secured labyrinth of tunnels.

He rushed back to his worktable, emptied a small jar of buttons, and grabbed a pair of scissors. Then just as quickly (before he lost his nerve) he clipped the length of thread tied to the creature's trapped leg as he set the jar on top of it.

There was a moment of stillness, when Fetch thought perhaps the beast was appreciative. But then it glared at him and began buzzing furiously around inside the glass, releasing itty-bitty trails of pea-green smoke.

Fetch shrugged off his robe and tugged on his coat before turning back to the caged beast. "I'm going to go to the market, and when I get back, if you've calmed down, I'll set you free. Got it?"

The beast said nothing, just kept glaring.

But what Fetch didn't tell him was that he was going to

research what the insect was before he ever set it into the wilds of Ocho Manos.

After Fetch left, the trapped creature clicked its hairy legs against the glass.

Clickety click click.

And then it smiled.

Chapter Two

The air was chilled, a crisp *almost* cold that felt as blue-gray as the sky. The trees' leaves had lost their golden luster as they clung to the skeletal branches.

But the market stalls were brimming, overflowing with fruits and breads and jars of golden syrups and shimmering jams.

Fetch loaded his basket with apples, blackberry buns, a dozen eggs, three cans of sardines, and half a smoked ham.

Shoppers milled about, preparing for winter as the scent of pipe smoke and ash bark filled the air.

"Beg your pardon," an old woman in a tattered sweater huffed as she muscled past the fox and through the crowd of magical creatures. There were fairies, and witches, and sprites. There were shape-shifters, goblins, and golden-winged crows.

Fetch's last stop was at the entomologist's stall. The bug expert was a tall, balding man with thick glasses and a bushy silver beard that touched his broad chest. "What bugs you, son?" he asked. "Ha ha. Get it? Bugs?"

Son. That's what Fetch's grandfather used to call him.

Fetch smiled, forcing a polite chuckle. "I just need to ask a question," he told the merchant.

The man pushed his spectacles up his bulbous nose. "Shoot."

Fetch quickly described the insect he'd found, down to its foul temper and fouler odor. "Have you ever heard of anything like that?"

The man stroked his beard, thinking. "Can't say that I have. Sounds like the critter's possessed."

Fetch frowned. "Possessed? By what?"

A small laugh rolled out of the man. "Well, not exactly possessed, but I have heard of creatures who run straight into evil like it's a cloud, and it sticks to them long after it's gone."

"Sticks to them?"

"Although evil often has a hard time perceiving such a small creature. Heck, big evil often can't even perceive a small act of magic, never mind a bug. You say you imprisoned it under glass?"

Fetch nodded. "I . . . I don't think I could kill it."

"Tell you what," the man said. "You bring that jar to me. I'll see what I can learn. You could also try a reveal spell. They aren't too expensive. Of course," he said, still stroking his beard, "it could make things worse."

Fetch's pulse picked up speed. He could certainly try a reveal thread. But he didn't want to muck things up. "Worse how?"

"Throwing good magic after bad isn't always the best plan. Best to just bring it to me."

Fetch nodded, although his mind was already busy thinking about his enchanted threads. Each had a different power, so surely there was one that might work. The problem was that there were so many, he hadn't even begun to learn them all. His grandfather, who had raised him, had spent countless hours instructing Fetch, showing him the delicate nature of magic, but all that stopped five years ago when he took his last breath. Fetch had only been nine years old.

"Thanks," Fetch said. "I'll figure something out."

"You'll bring me the jar?"

"Sure," Fetch said before turning down the winding cobblestone road toward home. On the way, he stopped in front of the bronze clock tower in the open square. Others had gathered in its shadow, drinking apple cider and hot cocoa, waiting to ring in the winter season.

At midnight, the fall queen, Pria, would fall into a deep slumber and the winter queen, Celeste, would wake from hers. This arrangement—an agreement made by four enchantresses hundreds of years ago to avoid squabbles that could lead to war—maintained harmony and balance in Ocho Manos.

"Long live the winter queen!" someone shouted.

More like the thief queen who stole my little sister, Fetch thought with a scowl.

One terrible night five years ago, Fetch and Violet had gone to Los Misterios, and while he had been busy reading a book, Violet wandered off and Celeste swept in and took her. Then she'd cursed him into this fox form. Days later he received a message that Violet was dead, but he never believed it. He'd immediately wanted to storm the palace to prove it and to rescue his sister, but the place was heavily spelled against intruders, and if Fetch failed (a likely scenario) he knew his sister would pay the price. Never mind that the queen had promised to tear him limb from limb if he ever tried, and what good would he be to his sister then?

Even through all the chatter and commotion, Fetch could hear the clock tick-ticking away, counting down to winter. The moment Celeste opened her eyes, Ocho Manos would be cast in shadow. The days would grow shorter and darker, and the world would fade from red and gold to silver and white.

And tomorrow it would be Violet's tenth birthday. Though Fetch didn't want to think about that. It hurt too much. Plus, he had more pressing things to consider, like the creepy little cabbage-faced beast trapped in his home.

When he returned to his labyrinth, he set the basket down and rushed into his workroom, hoping he could find the thread that would reveal what or even *who* the creature was.

But the moment he got to the table, he froze. His tail swished wildly. For there was nothing under the glass. The little monster had escaped. But how? Where?

Fetch's eyes darted about, listening for any sound, any

movement. His senses were on high alert. Every shadow seemed deeper, every creak of the floorboards louder.

But then . . .

He heard the buzzing before he saw the little beast. Before he felt the burn of a sting at the back of his neck.

Fetch clutched at the spot where the pain flared. As the beast's venom worked its way into his bloodstream, it left a burning trail that made him grimace. But before he could react fully, he saw the deadly invader tumble to the floor.

Its wings twitched, and then the beast went completely still.

Malvada

The Malvada stirred.

Hungry. Vicious. Prepared.

But weak.

It was the fault of that wretched girl, Esmerelda Santos. The same girl the fox had helped. After she had expelled the Malvada from the witch Escarlata, the darkness had been damaged—but *not* defeated, as the fox believed. It had been difficult, but the Malvada had managed to reduce itself to the form of a lowly insect and stowed away in Fetch's pocket as the fox made his journey back home. It was the new beginning the darkness needed, but for its plan to succeed, it would require more than this scrawny, weak, half-cursed fox could offer.

A momentary disappointment, the Malvada thought as it observed the world through Fetch's eyes, breathing in the magic that hung in the air like thick honey. It needed a more powerful vessel, one that would allow it to take a permanent form—one that would give it unyielding power.

Until then, the Malvada would watch, and it would learn. It would feed on the fox's magic until he was an empty sack.

The fool has no idea what's in store for him.

Chapter Three

Fetch slept through the turning of the seasons. He wasn't sure if it was the insect bite, or maybe the healing ointment he'd used on it, but his sleep was far deeper than usual. The good news was that when he woke, the wound was healed, as if he'd never been stung at all.

The bad news was, today was Violet's tenth birthday.

Which meant that her Zindero powers would awaken fully. But without the enchanted threads that were a part of her inheritance, and without Fetch to teach her, she'd never truly command her magic. Which made it all the more confusing why the queen had taken her. Fetch had once thought that maybe Celeste just needed a servant, maybe one who was a naturally good sewer. But then why not take him?

Fetch shook loose a long exhale, wondering what Violet

looked like now—did she still have unruly red hair? Were her eyes still as blue as the summer sea?

He grabbed a memory thread from his collection and, as he did every year on her birthday, he tied the piece around his wrist and made a wish for Violet. That she was safe. That she was warm. That she was loved.

The pink-and-gold thread shimmered, and the sound of Violet's laughter, a soft mischievous giggle, floated into the air. Fetch's heart ached. If only her joy could fill the house again for real.

"I miss you," Fetch said as the thread vanished with a spark. "Today you're ten, a true Zindero. I'm sorry I'm not there to teach you."

The silence was so thick it felt as though it could swallow him whole.

Then, out of the corner of his eye, he caught a sudden movement. He turned to the rack where his enchanted coat hung.

He stared for a moment, then just as he shifted his gaze, the hem of the coat fluttered again. "That's odd."

He went over to inspect the thing. It went still at his approach.

Twisting his furry mouth, Fetch removed it from the hook and slipped it on. It felt the same as it always had.

Then, just as he began to remove the coat, the buttons buttoned themselves and the collar tightened. He clawed at the garment, tearing off the buttons, gasping as the collar cinched tighter and tighter. And then, as suddenly as it had come to life, the coat fell perfectly still.

Panting, Fetch threw the thing off. He'd never heard of a murderous coat and he most certainly hadn't designed it that way!

Maybe it had gotten damaged during his travels, a missing stitch or a torn hem. Something to explain why his coat had gone haywire.

But though he inspected every inch, there was no defect that he could see. He sat hunched over his scratched mahogany sewing table and tugged his wool sweater tighter as the cold reached its long bony fingers down into the labyrinth of tunnels, expertly carved by his grandfather, that made up his home.

He glared at the mountain of orders that had piled up while he was away. They certainly weren't going to stitch themselves, and he needed the coin, so he forced himself upright, groaned, and got to work.

First up, a fairy vest.

Fetch truly hated working on fairy garments. The little creatures, also known by names like alasinders and hadas, were always his most demanding clients.

"The stitching must be perfect," they'd squeal. "Extraordinary. Remarkable in every way!"

"It's just a hem," Fetch muttered to himself as he inspected the velvet vest's *remarkable*, perhaps even *perfect*, stitching.

He had been sewing for three hours with an iridescent purple thread known for its properties of invisibility, when—

Gong!

Fetch startled, glancing at his pocket watch. With a grumble, he stood and headed down his home's main tunnel toward the late-afternoon visitor.

Fetch pulled the periscope closer and peered through the glass.

"I know you can see me!" Garzo practically roared. "Open up! I'm cold and getting colder by the second." He stomped his little foot on the doormat. "And soon I'll be frozen over, closing my eyes forever to this wretched world all because—"

Huffing, Fetch tugged on the thick rope to open the hatch fifteen feet above.

With a hoot, Garzo slid down the pole.

Fetch stepped back, eyeing the two-foot-tall creature, who had lavender eyes and silvery hair that stuck up in great tufts, framing his round, cherubic face.

"You could have just flown down here," the fox said.

"Didn't you hear the part about me freezing?" Garzo argued. "My wings are delicate filaments of beauty, yes, but very susceptible to the cold. And thanks to your slowness, they are now brittle sheets of ice, thank you very much."

"You're welcome."

Garzo's face bloomed red with anger. His nostrils flared as he tugged a tiny notepad from his vest pocket and, using only the tip of his finger, began to scrawl words onto the page. "Slow," he repeated. "Indecisive . . . rude."

"Are you seriously taking notes on me?" Fetch asked, his eyelids heavy with exhaustion.

"You know I take notes on everything! Why do you think they call me Spy the Magnificent?"

"I thought *you* called yourself that."

Garzo scowled, pocketing the notebook. "Did you get my note? Do you have the merchandise? Is the hem perfect?"

Fetch nodded.

"Extraordinary?"

"Remarkable in every way," Fetch said. "What's your obsession with vests anyway?"

Garzo's face brightened and a tiny smile tugged at his lips. "Pockets!" he sang, sweeping past Fetch and into the sewing room as though he owned the place.

Violet had loved pockets too. *Hiding places for marvelous things*, she'd called them.

The fox entered behind the fairy, who was already examining the vest eagerly.

Fetch said, "I used thread with invisibility powers and as a bonus I added another thread that will mask the spell of strength—"

"So no one will see me coming!" Garzo did a little leap. "How strong are we talking? Will I be able to bend iron with my bare hands? Because I've got my own magic for that."

"It will be more like you're the iron."

Garzo sniffed, then smiled. "Iron Spy the Magnificent!"

"But every time you wear the vest," Fetch added reluctantly, "that power will get weaker."

"So not remarkable magic."

Fetch gave a light shrug. "No magic is forever." Wasn't that what his grandfather had always said? He extended his paw. "That'll be two silvers."

Garzo huffed as he reached into his vest pocket and retrieved two coins, both engraved with Queen Celeste's image, her narrow jaw and penetrating eyes.

Beaming, Garzo said, "This will be the perfect vest to wear to the festival."

"Festival?"

The fairy raised a single eyebrow. "Didn't you hear? It was announced at the turning of the seasons. Or did you sleep through the festivities as usual?"

"You know I hate winter," Fetch grumbled. "But tell me about this festival."

With a snort, Garzo flitted into the air and perched atop the desk, crossing his little arms over his chest. "Well! It appears that Queen Celeste is hosting a winter festival in ten days' time. Can you imagine? It's been several decades since the last soiree at the palace."

"I thought she throws a big party every year," Fetch said. "To choose a few magical creatures to give up their magic."

"Really, Fetch, you shouldn't fall for such gossip." The

fairy leaned closer, his voice low and conspiratorial. "I think she likes such wicked stories circulating because it creates fear, and fear creates control." In a burst of energy, Garzo swooped across the room and back again, his wings shimmering.

"But *this* party is real! Think of the splendor, the glittering opulence—a fairy's paradise, I tell you!" He tilted his head close. His messy tuft of hair fluttered. "Do you think I'll get an invitation?"

Fetch's mind stumbled over Garzo's words as if each was an exploding bomb. A festival. At Sterling. The highly guarded winter palace, which was protected by spells so strong no unauthorized intruder could ever get in—or out—alive.

The very place where Violet was.

Garzo took to the air again, flapping his hands in front of Fetch's face. "I can see the wheels turning, and they are dangerous wheels indeed. Best to forget I said anything."

But the words had been spoken and Fetch's mind wasn't just turning, it was *spinning*. *For one night, there will be no spells protecting the palace. Could this be my chance to save Violet once and for all?*

Fetch's heart raced, skipping around his chest as if to say, *yes, yes, yes*.

"Garzo," he whispered, "this is my chance."

The fairy whipped his head from side to side. "I don't like that look on your furry face, and before you even ask—which

I know you're going to—I will not participate in any treachery or treason. Well, unless it benefits me tremendously, and this does not."

A horn sounded, so loud it shook the walls.

"Eep!" Garzo exclaimed.

Fetch's eyes went wide. "Is that what I think it is?"

"That horn can only mean one thing."

The winter queen's army was approaching, calling on the citizens of Ocho Manos to assemble. Fetch's fur bristled and his heart raced.

Shrinking back, Garzo squeaked, "Let's hide down here and pretend we didn't hear it."

"You'd risk the queen's wrath?"

"If it means keeping my head and my precious wings, yes."

"I don't think they're here for those things."

The last time the winter queen's army came through this quadrant of Ocho Manos, Fetch had been a toddler. He recalled only bits and pieces, like his grandfather whisking him into his arms as they headed outside. "Pretend you're asleep," he'd whispered to Fetch.

He didn't remember what had happened next.

"We should go," Fetch said.

"Fine, but if anything happens to me it will be all your fault, and you'll have to live with the guilt all the days of your woeful life."

"What are you worried about? You're wearing a very fine vest that gives you strength," Fetch said, hoping to make the fairy feel better.

"Well, maybe that strength doesn't work against zombies."

The army's horn sounded again.

Garzo had a point. Because this army wasn't like any other. This one was made up of the walking dead.

Chapter Four

The air was crisp and gray, ringing with the hollow sound of winter.

Stone buildings with green tiled roofs slanted this way and that, crammed together along the narrow road. Fetch felt queasy as he and Garzo fell into the rhythm of the moving crowd of duendes, fairies, and brujos, all looking just as terrified as Fetch felt. Well, maybe the witches *appeared* less terrified, but that was only because they hid their emotions better than most.

The horn sounded again, long and deep.

The crowd picked up their pace. Murmurs and whispers twisted all around them.

"This had better be good."

"What could they possibly want?"

"Do you think the queen will make an appearance?"

When they got to the town square, Fetch's gaze landed on the twelve soldiers representing the queen. The Legión Inmortal stood like neatly lined-up gravestones. Twisted, knobby trees cast odd shadows on the ghostly figures, which were at least seven feet tall, with ashen skin so thin Fetch could see the muscles and bones beneath. Hanging from their necks were chainlike threads that reached the length of their arms, which dangled nearly to their knees. Their eyes were slits of black, empty and terrifying.

One of the soldiers, taller and more intimidating than the others, stepped closer to the frozen crowd. His tangled white hair hung around his face like spiderwebs.

"Greetings," he said bitterly. "I am Ernesh, capitán of the guard."

The capitán spoke slowly, spacing out each word. The chain around his neck made a sharp clanking sound as he turned his head from one side of the crowd to the next. Black mist rose from the links.

"As you are aware, winter is Ocho Manos's longest season," he said. "The darkness swallows the light after only a few hours, and this winter the light will be even briefer."

Why? Fetch thought. *And how brief—an hour, two?*

Ernesh paused as if to read their reactions, or maybe he just liked being the center of attention. "It is for this reason"—his cold, vacant eyes scanned the crowd—"that new rules have been put in place. By royal decree, the use of magic is now prohibited during the hours of darkness."

Shock rippled through the mob in gulps and wheezes, but no one dared question aloud why the queen would do such a thing. Did it have to do with the festival? Fetch could feel the tension expanding, the confusion and anger growing. Ocho Manos was a vast island where magic ran wild. Limiting people's magic was like telling the sky to limit its rain.

The capitán snarled, revealing icy fangs. The air quieted almost immediately. "The new law takes effect," he said, "tomorrow. Invitations to the festival will be delivered then as well. Of course, not everyone will be graced with one."

"Why not?" someone asked.

"If everyone were invited, it wouldn't be special, would it?" Ernesh emphasized *special* in a tone that told Fetch the capitán didn't really care about the festival. "The queen herself has chosen who will attend," he added.

Garzo was digging his bony little fingers into Fetch's leg, but the fox didn't so much as flinch. It was best to remain unnoticed.

Ernesh added, "I need not remind you that we have hunters of magic. And if you are caught breaking royal law, I will hunt you down personally." His voice hung on the threat for several beats, as if reminding everyone of what they already knew—that such a crime meant a slow and painful death, or having your magic ripped away.

At once, the soldiers turned as a single unit. Ernesh surveyed the crowd one last time as if looking for something.

A trail of black smoke floated toward the crowd, twisting

and hissing as it drew closer. As the smoke reached Fetch, he realized it wasn't smoke at all, but more like the dark threads of a spiderweb.

Fetch stepped out of the way as Ernesh smiled, then turned and led his army out of the square in a silent ghostly march.

Chapter Five

As soon as the army was gone, the crowd erupted in an uproar of *what*s and *how*s and *why*s.

Heart pounding, Fetch turned to Garzo, but the little fairy was nowhere in sight. He'd probably flown to his stone cottage and was already sitting by a fire warming his toes, waiting for his invitation to the Winter Festival.

The fox ran all the way home.

Once he was tucked safely inside, he darted into the sewing room, skidding to a halt in front of his worktable. His tail twitched and his spine tingled with the cold.

Magic is now prohibited during the hours of darkness.

Fetch's heart thumped to the rhythm of *tomorrow tomorrow tomorrow*.

This was the first real chance he'd had in five years to

rescue his sister, and now this ridiculous new rule could ruin it all. How would he ever rescue Violet if his magic was on a leash! A feeling of uselessness threaded between his ribs. *No.* He'd been afraid for too long, made excuses for even longer.

I'll find a way.

Somehow he would slip into Sterling during the festival when all eyes and spells were elsewhere, then he'd find Violet and escape before the ghostly guards caught them.

But the palace was vast. How would he locate her?

The queen's voice rang in his memory: *If you ever try to find her, I'll know, and I will tear you limb from limb. There will be no end to your suffering.*

Fetch paced. His bushy tail swished restlessly. Doubt began to burn holes in his resolve.

Then an idea sparked. What if he could *see* Violet? Maybe gather some clues as to her precise location. The idea reminded him of what the entomologist had said: *big evil often can't even perceive a small act of magic.*

Well, the queen was evil, so maybe she wouldn't notice such a minor spell, right? It didn't matter—Fetch had to risk it.

Determinedly, he took a deep breath, closed his eyes, and called on his Zindero magic. A familiar humming began in his stomach, then rose to his chest, swirling around his heart. A spool of pale blue thread floated into the air as a spool of gray rolled toward him.

Meticulously he knotted together the two threads, then reached into his coat pocket and pulled out the handkerchief

Violet had shown him right before she disappeared. On it, she'd sewn a crooked heart with twelve stitches.

"What's this for?" he'd asked.

"It's my heart."

"Oh?"

"I'm going to carry it in my pocket, so it never gets lost."

And before Fetch could ask for an explanation, she continued, "In the book I just read, the princess had a best friend, a dragon, and . . ." Here she paused, bottom lip quivering before she added softly, "He died. It was so sad, Fetch. The princess said she lost her heart that day and never ever found it again." Violet looked up at him with wide blue eyes. "Do you get it now?"

"Got it," Fetch had said, his mind elsewhere as usual.

The hankie had once belonged to their mother, who Violet had never known because she'd died along with their father in a boating accident when Violet was a baby.

She had never been without the handkerchief. Not once.

Fetch set the woven threads on top of the stitched heart. Then, for good measure, he placed Esme's magical flower petal there as well. Maybe it held no power, but it made him feel less alone.

Fetch floated his paws before him. "Show me where Violet is."

The air crackled and shimmered. The threads floated up, waving back and forth, creating sparks of soft blue light.

Fetch held his breath. His jaw clamped tight. His paws shook with the weight of magic and hope.

Please work.

Just then, the spot where the wasp had stung him began to throb.

He touched his neck, but there was no proof he'd ever been hurt. Something began to rise in him. Something hot yet cold, terrifying yet inviting. Something dark and brilliant. He felt dizzy.

His body grew heavy, and his eyes even heavier, and soon he was pulled into a world of mist and shadow.

When his vision cleared, he saw himself in Los Misterios, standing in a dark row of shelves, cradling a leather-bound book—just like he had that horrible night.

This was all wrong. Fetch didn't want to relive this memory. He wanted to find Violet's location in Sterling.

Still dreaming, Fetch stared at himself, the last time he had been a human boy. He'd been lanky, with red hair and a lopsided smile. His hand casually in his coat pocket as if he had no worries in the world.

Well, that was all about to change.

"So that's what you looked like as a boy," a familiar voice said.

Fetch turned to find his friend Esme standing next to him. Her dark, wavy hair hung around her face, each strand laced with enchanted flower petals.

"Esme?" He was so elated to see her he practically leaped into the air. "Are you . . . are you really here?"

"Apparently," she said. "But why am I in your dream?"

"Maybe because I used one of your flower petals, but this—this isn't what I wanted to see. I was trying to locate my sister in the palace. I think my magic messed up." Just like his coat had.

She scanned the shadows. "This is the night your sister disappeared, isn't it?"

Fetch nodded.

"Why would your magic bring you back here?" Suddenly, Esme froze, tilted her head, and whispered, "Listen."

Fetch heard the footsteps before he saw her.

With a thundering heart he turned just as Violet rounded the corner. Unlike that night, now he paid close attention. He studied her willful eyes, her determined jaw, and the clover birthmark right beneath her chin that she thought made her lucky.

He watched as she tugged on his coat. "There are no books on dragons here, Fetch."

He wanted to scream. To force this version of himself to pay attention to Violet. But just like that night, his other self uttered, "Mm-hmm. Try a book on the lost unicorn horn."

"But dragons are my favorite," she said with a huff.

Other Fetch nodded absently. "I'll be done in five minutes."

No! His heart twisted painfully. He knew what came next.

Violet whispered, "The shadows are loud tonight."

Then she wandered off. Fetch went to follow, but his feet were like two cement blocks.

"Wait!" he hollered, but of course she didn't hear him. With sinking despair, he watched her vanish behind the bookshelf.

He spun toward Esme. "What do I do?"

"You're the cleverest fox I know. You'll figure out what to do."

"I don't feel very clever."

Then, in a hushed voice, she said, "We aren't alone. Do you feel it?" She began to fade.

"Esme!"

"Oh, drat! One petal just isn't enough." And then she was gone.

Fetch whirled back to his dream self. "Look! Don't let Violet go!" How different he had been then, so distracted, so caught up in adventures inked in the pages of books. So very sure of his legacy of magic.

But his other self just kept reading, and when he finally did look up five minutes later and saw that he was alone, that Violet was nowhere to be found, he began searching for her, thinking she was playing hide-and-seek.

"I know you're here," he teased, slipping around bookcases, ready to pounce on his hiding sister. But she was nowhere to be found.

And in the space between now and then, Fetch felt the presence of something else, a sliver of magic that pulsated in the darkness. As if it had followed him into this world.

He ran. Through the grand hall, down the shadowy steps, and into the street.

"Violet!" he shouted, his voice swallowed by the thickening fog.

But Violet was gone. The only sign of her was the heart-stitched handkerchief dropped on the snowy cobblestone road. A cold wind tumbled toward him as he snatched it up.

Then Violet's voice, low and urgent, whispered through the mist. "Fetch."

"Violet?" His chest tightened. "Are you really here?"

"Stay away."

A knife of panic pierced his heart. "What . . . why?"

"Please." Her voice faltered. The distance between them growing as her handkerchief warmed in his paw. He looked down.

A single stitch vanished before his eyes.

Chapter Six

"Fetch!" a voice called. "Fetch, wake up!"

Blearily, the fox opened his eyes. Garzo's round face loomed over him, his silvery hair standing at attention.

The fairy gulped in a giant breath. "I thought you were dead! Do you hear me? DEAD! How could you put me through such a dreadful experience?!"

Rubbing his head, Fetch sat up. "I—I was trying to locate Violet, but I fell into—" What? A dream? A vision? A horrible memory? Fetch had no idea, but it had all felt so real—and so painful.

He stared at the handkerchief. It hadn't been a mistake. A stitch had vanished, leaving only eleven.

What could it mean? As a Zindero, he understood the power

of weaving with enchanted threads. But Violet had been only five when she'd stitched this. She hadn't yet come into her full power. Was she somehow communicating through the threads? But how? And why now? Could it have something to do with her birthday?

"Locate her?" Garzo looked confused. "But you already know she's in Sterling."

"I need the precise location where she is in the palace."

"I thought you were kidding. Or I hoped so." Garzo's face went pale. "You don't really think you can march into Sterling and abscond with your sister?"

Fetch felt a swell of courage, the kind that made his teeth feel sharper, his claws longer, and his heart fiercer. "Garzo, while I was in that weird dream state, she talked to me. I think she's communicating through these threads." He held up the handkerchief as proof.

"What did she say?"

"Well, it was really just a whisper. . . ."

Garzo tapped his small foot impatiently. "A whisper that said what?"

Suddenly Fetch wished he'd said nothing at all. "To stay away from the palace," he admitted.

"Exactly! There are all sorts of dangers there, even more than those undead soldiers. Things like wicked crows that eat flesh! And did you ever hear of the seven black swans that steal your vision? Let's not forget the dark spell protecting the grounds!"

"Spells that won't be in place because of the festival. Don't you see? This is my chance to get in there unnoticed. It's the perfect distraction—and before you argue, I don't care what Violet says or doesn't say, I'm going!"

"Yes, well, you're stubborn like that. But it's the getting *out* that will be the problem. I'm a magnificent spy. I know these things."

Fetch looked down and counted the stitches again, hoping he'd made an error. But no—still eleven. "There is no way the queen will send me an invitation," he said, his mind turning so fast he felt woozy. For all Fetch knew, the queen had sensed his location spell, his betrayal of her orders to never search for Violet, and was sending her army here even now.

"Don't look at me," Garzo groaned. "If I do get an invitation, I'm using it. I'm certainly not going to waste it on a dreadful escapade that's sure to result in dismemberment."

Fairies were so dramatic.

"Why are you here anyway?" Fetch asked. "Why did you come back? Were you worried about me?"

Garzo's face burned red. "Fairies do not worry! Well, unless it's about ourselves—which is precisely why I am here. I would like a refund for this poorly constructed vest. Especially since I can only use it during daylight hours and this right pocket is smaller than the left."

Fetch studied the vest's fine stitching: the flawless hem,

the extraordinary buttons. "The vest looks perfect to me, but if you want, maybe I can—"

"It might *look* perfect, but it didn't work," Garzo growled.

"How so?" Fetch worried his semi-broken magic had mucked things up for the fairy too.

Garzo paced briskly. His iridescent wings opened and closed. Then with a grunt and another dramatic shake of his head, he said, "I followed those zombie soldiers. I overheard things."

"You what?!"

"Yes, I know, I am quite brave indeed. But that is not the point. The point is that the vest did *not* give me extraordinary strength. Though it did allow me to fly quite fast, I will grant you that."

"Garzo, you could have been killed! Why would you do something so foolish?"

"I am Spy the Magnificent! It is in my nature." He thrust out his little arm as if brandishing a sword.

"What did you hear?"

"You will most certainly not like it, although you will be singing my praises, thanking me for my goodness. And if I am put to death for treason or some other unjust crime, then I hope you will at least create the finest death garments for me that the world has ever seen. And make them lavender—to match my eyes."

"Garzo." Fetch's whiskers twitched. He had no idea what

the fairy had heard, but whatever it was, it could never be enough to stop Fetch from trying to rescue Violet. "There's nothing you can say to change my mind."

Garzo floated in midair, folding his arms defiantly across his chest. Then with a glower he said, "The winter queen is setting a trap!"

Chapter Seven

"Trap?" Fetch repeated. "What kind of trap?"

"How should I know?"

"Well, maybe you misheard or—"

"How dare you insult my splendid ears!"

Fetch said, "I'm sorry. Please go on."

With a harrumph, Garzo drew out his notepad. "To be more exact, I heard the following." He looked down at the page, cleared his throat, and pushed his shoulders back like he was about to deliver an important speech. "'The festival is a trap they won't see coming.' Blah. Blah. Blah." His gaze met Fetch's. "The *blah*s are the parts I didn't hear."

Fetch's heart twisted.

"'The prisoners,'" Garzo went on, "'will be chained with—'"

"With what?"

"'The most powerful soul-bending magic.'"

Fetch took a deep breath, trying to calm his nerves, which felt like they were on fire. Violet was a prisoner. Was she in danger of being chained with soul-bending magic?

"What else did you hear?" Fetch asked.

"Isn't that enough? We've got a duplicitous monarch on our hands who's setting a trap for we don't know who. Oh, stars. It could be for any of us."

"So that's why Queen Celeste is throwing the festival," Fetch guessed. "It's a decoy for something more sinister—but what?"

"I don't know, but now I hope I *don't* get a wretched invitation."

"Garzo, we need to find out." He hadn't been able to save Violet five years ago, and now that he knew the queen's plans, there was no way he could let another innocent creature fall into her clutches. "We have to warn whoever it is the queen plans to ensnare."

"*We?* I think not. Whoever is walking into the queen's web will just have to learn the hard way."

"But you're a spy. Isn't this what spies do? Find things out?"

With a groan, Garzo said, "I already risked my life for this information. And you can never tell a soul that you heard it from me. I would very much like to live."

Fetch pressed his paws together. Did this trap have to do with the new law limiting magic to daylight hours? And what, or who, was the queen after? Fetch shook his head. The questions were sidetracking him from what mattered most: Violet.

He got to his feet. "You've been a good friend, Garzo," he said, and he meant it. "But right now, I need to make a plan to get in and out of Sterling."

"Well, I'm certainly not going to do anything to help you," Garzo huffed. "But if I *were*, I'd start with a map."

"There are no maps of Sterling," Fetch reminded the fairy. All the maps had been destroyed long ago to prevent outsiders from getting inside. "For security measures, remember?"

Garzo rolled his eyes. "Obviously you need an ancient one that was created eons ago before all that security nonsense, one that shows you the hidden passages."

The fairy's words triggered a memory. "Garzo! You're a genius."

"That's what I've been trying to tell you."

There was only one mapmaker who might have the kind of map Garzo mentioned. Fetch had never met her. The tree spirit was his grandfather's friend. Or maybe *friend* was too generous. More like a collaborator. She lived in Scarred Hollow, the deepest, darkest forest in Ocho Manos—but that didn't matter. Fetch would endure any danger to bring his sister home.

He looked up to the ceiling, considering his options. His head grew fuzzy and light, as if it was filled with dust. "I'll need help if I'm to succeed."

Garzo threw his hands up. "Don't look at me."

"I'm not asking you to go with me, Garzo. Don't worry." Still, Fetch couldn't do this alone. He began to pace. "I need someone cunning. Someone intelligent. Someone brave." His whiskers twitched. "I need a warrior!"

Garzo frowned. "Do you have enough coin to hire such a person?"

"No."

"Then where do you plan to find this warrior?"

"Maybe I can't find one, but . . ." His mind churned. "I might be able to create one." He hurried into his sewing room.

Garzo was right behind him, wings flapping as he landed atop the worktable. "You think you can *sew* your way out of this?"

Fetch blew out a long breath. He'd never actually made a creature from thread, but he knew it was possible. He'd once seen his grandfather create a walking, talking hedgehog, and a five-winged butterfly that made music with the flutter of its wings.

Besides, Fetch was no beginner at creating things from his threads. He'd made explosives, magical concealment coats, even a mind-reading hat once . . . though that had only worked for thirty-five seconds.

He surveyed row after row of magical thread, his adrenaline and his hopes soaring.

"What kind of warrior?" Fetch wondered aloud. "A giant?"

"Too unpredictable," Garzo said. "And they sleep way too much."

Fetch twisted his furry mouth. "How about a mighty dragon?" He could use their fire and fierceness, plus a warrior that could fly would certainly make traveling long distances much easier.

Garzo began to laugh, a deep throaty sound that annoyed Fetch. "You don't think I can do it?" the fox asked.

"Maybe a doll, but not a real live dragon."

"My grandfather made living creatures." *If only Lorenzo the León were here now.*

That had been Fetch's grandfather's nickname. Given for his fierceness and majesty, and also for the head of thick red hair that had framed his angular face.

"Your grandfather was the mightiest Zindero in history," Garzo argued. "He didn't even need threads, Fetch."

It was true. Lorenzo had been so powerful he didn't require the enchanted spools to weave magic. *His* magic flowed from his fingertips. And when Fetch had asked how he could grow to be that powerful too, his grandfather had smiled and offered four useless words: *time and unconditional love.*

Fetch quickly gathered three spools of thread: scarlet for ferociousness, silver for the strength of storms, and finally, gold for life. At the last moment, he also snatched a dark blue spool for intelligence, because what good was a warrior who couldn't think properly?

He hesitated. Or was olive-green thread the one for intelligence?

Don't overthink!

With trembling hands, he set the spools on the table.

Garzo said, "I'd like to state for the record that this is an abysmal idea and one sure to end in failure."

"Do you have a better one?"

Garzo buttoned and unbuttoned his vest. "I already gave you my best idea, which is to stay far, far away from the palace. But since you are a stubborn ninny, I suppose I can offer you something to help. But only because I do not want you to die."

Fetch was taken aback by the fairy's generosity. "That's really nice of you."

"I'm not doing it for you." Garzo sniffed, averting his gaze. "I have many more garments I would like made and if you're dearly departed, I will be cursed to wear the same old fashions forever. And wouldn't that be a travesty for someone as striking as I am?"

Fetch smiled, happy to have the fairy's assistance. "Yes, a travesty. So how can you help?"

Garzo sighed, then reached behind his back and tugged a long, silky strand from his left wing. "Here," he said, pushing his little hand forward. "This will help with the dragon wings."

Fetch's heart expanded as he stared at the silk in his paw. "Wow . . . thank you."

"Just don't mess it up, because I'm not giving you any more of my beloved silk—and let's be clear that I am now owed seven new garments."

"Deal," Fetch said. He clutched the strand from Garzo's wing and took a deep breath.

With great precision he began to dance his paws in the air, slowly at first, then zipping left and right, up and down like a conductor.

There was a rhythm to magic, to hitting just the right notes at just the right speed with just the right intention.

The process usually happened naturally, in the same way that no one tells their brain to breathe or to move their arms or legs. It was simply an intuitive response. That's how easy it had always been for Fetch to connect to his magic. Now, though, his arms grew heavy. His eyes narrowed, searching the air for the familiar pull, the familiar hum. It should've been there, a constant companion, but now it felt . . . distant.

It had all started when he came back from the Otherworld. Did it have something to do with traveling between dimensions? Or had the beastly insect sting messed with his powers somehow?

Fetch took a deep breath. He'd already mucked up the location spell. And then there was the issue of his malfunctioning coat. . . . No. He could *not* let this spell fail.

He ignored the heat spreading through him, the ache that cut through his chest, his muscles, his bones. Clenching his jaw, he redoubled his efforts. The air whirled with flecks of sparkling light like glitter.

Straightaway, each thread unspooled, twisting up and up,

shimmering in great bursts of gold, red, blue, and silver. The air crackled with tiny bolts of lightning.

With a wince and a groan, Fetch continued weaving his magic. His arms felt like lead, making the effort even more exhausting. At one point he nearly doubled over but, somehow, he forced himself upright and kept imagining his dragon warrior—its vast wingspan, its sharp fangs, its cunning mind. The fire it would breathe!

Fetch's ears pricked and his bushy tail whipped back and forth nervously. And then the magic fell silent.

The room went still.

With a *poof*, a cloud of smoke appeared.

Coughing, Fetch waved his paws to clear the air.

Garzo gasped.

And Fetch? Well, he stared into the eyes of a teeny, tiny bone dragon.

Chapter Eight

Fetch couldn't breathe. It was as if his lungs were filled with glue.

"What is that thing?" Garzo bellowed. "It is certainly no progeny of my precious wings!"

"Greetings, wolf," the little beast said in a small and not at all ferocious voice. "Greetings, goblin."

Fetch scowled. "I'm not a wolf!"

"And how dare you call me a goblin!" Garzo looked as if he was half a breath from a tirade.

The dragon, no bigger than Fetch's paw, wobbled on his tiny feet. A creature that on second glance wasn't *exactly* a bone dragon. Or at least not like any Fetch had ever seen. This one had some similarities, with its skeletal wings, and a shimmering green and gold and blue tail half the size of his body. But unlike a bone dragon, this little guy had floppy ears, deep brown eyes, and dark purple fur all over his head and body, almost as if he was part mouse.

A purple mouse with a tail of shimmering scales. *Not* a warrior dragon.

"Are you my keeper?" the creature asked.

Garzo groaned. "How does this thing know so many words?" he asked Fetch. "Or how to talk at all, for that matter? Tell me you didn't do this on purpose."

Fetch scratched the side of his head. "I wanted a warrior who understood my mind and heart," he admitted. "Someone who wouldn't need me to explain too much. You know, to cut down on teaching time."

"Well, you should have focused more on the warrior part! The threatening, fire-breathing dragon part."

Maybe Garzo had a point, but while Fetch was performing his magic, his heart had been missing Violet, and maybe more than anything he had wanted someone who reminded him of her. Maybe he'd let his heart get carried away. Or maybe his magic really was malfunctioning.

"What are you?" Fetch asked the creature. "Are you a mouse or a dragon or . . ."

The creature stared down at his tiny, clawed feet before returning his gaze to Fetch. "Aren't you the one who created me?"

Fetch dragged a paw down his face. "I was trying to make a warrior—not . . . not . . ."

"Not a tiny mouselet with bone wings!" Garzo growled.

The creature puffed up his puny chest, widening his already-enormous brown eyes. "I *am* a warrior!" He stretched out his itty-bitty wings. Then, gazing at Fetch, he lowered his voice and asked, "What's a warrior?"

"So much for intelligence," Garzo muttered.

Fetch plopped into his chair and dropped his head onto the table. This was all his fault. He shouldn't have tried to do something so advanced.

But he couldn't waste time wallowing. He had to think of Violet. Forcing himself upright, he explained, "A warrior is a very brave fighter who will die for a cause or person that means everything to them."

"Die?" The creature's eyes grew wider. "I just got here."

Fetch wondered what Esme would say about this mouse dragon. She'd probably put him in her pocket and feed him sunflower seeds.

"But I am very brave," the creature announced. "Do you want to see?" He threw his tiny legs up in a series of karate kicks.

"Yes, that's a good start," Fetch managed as Garzo snorted on repeat.

At this the mouse dragon smiled. As expected, his teeth were *not* sharp fangs.

"Tell me," Garzo said to the creature. "Do you possess any magic? Any skills of value? Surely you must, if I sacrificed some of my silk wing for you."

"Oh," the creature said. "Your wings are magnificent. Shiny too."

Garzo lifted his chin proudly. "And quite magical. Better than most fairies, but I use a first-rate conditioner."

The creature looked around, his eyes landing on Violet's handkerchief. "What's that?"

"Don't touch it," Fetch said.

But the mouse dragon was already peering at it closely. "It's missing a thread."

"Observant," Garzo muttered.

Fetch said, "It belonged to my sister."

"Belonged?" the creature asked.

"She vanished," Fetch said gloomily, "and I need to find her. So I can give this back."

The mouse dragon hopped closer to the fox. "You're going to find your sister, don't you worry. I am quite excellent at locating things."

"How do you know?" Garzo asked.

"I can feel it. I will prove to be great." The mouse dragon snorted a few times, emitting little clouds of smoke. "So," he said, frowning at the smoke. "What's my name? I'll need one for this quest." He considered a moment, then squealed, "Mighty! Or Brave. Or Daring! Or . . . Smoky!" His wings flattened down his back. "No, those don't feel right." Then, glancing at the fox and the fairy, he asked, "What are your names?"

"Fetch."

"Garzo, also known as Spy the Magnificent." Then to Fetch, "I have done my good deed, and now I must go. Good luck."

"Wait!" Fetch hollered. "Garzo, you can't leave now. What if—"

"Under no circumstances will I go on this futile expedition," Garzo said. "I already told you, I am not a fighter. Good night." And before Fetch could stop him, the fairy was gone.

The fox stared after him with disappointment. Garzo had shown such promise for a moment, yet now he was abandoning Fetch when he needed a friend most.

"It's getting late," Fetch said, thinking of all that lay ahead. "We should get some sleep." With a heavy heart, he headed into his bedroom with the dragon wobble-flying next to his ear.

"You have a very nice home," the creature said.

Fetch pushed a pile of books off a nearby chair and onto the floor, replacing them with a pillow. "You can sleep there."

The mouse dragon hopped onto the makeshift bed and curled into a ball. His iridescent tail wrapped tightly around his body. "Cozy."

Exhausted, Fetch turned off the lamp and collapsed onto his pillow, his thoughts zinging every which way. He couldn't risk trying to make another warrior—but he also couldn't do this alone. The mouse dragon was right about one thing: Fetch needed help.

"Fetch?"

"Yeah?"

"I'm not tired."

A low growl vibrated in the fox's throat. "Count sheep."

Silence.

Then, "What are sheep?"

"How do you know what a wolf or a goblin or a dragon is, but you don't know a fox or sheep or—"

"I know lots of other things."

Fetch got up and turned on the lamp. He grabbed a snow globe off his dresser. It had been a gift from Violet. Holding it out to the mouse dragon, he said, "Do you know what this is?"

The creature shook his head. "It looks very pretty, though."

"It's a snow globe." Fetch shook the thing and watched as the mouse dragon's eyes went big.

"It's snowing in that little world," the creature said. "Oh, and look at the forest! And what are those black creatures?"

"Those are dojees," Fetch said. They had been Violet's favorite beasts. They were large as bears, looked like them too, but were gentle in nature. "They're peaceful, majestic beings who serve as oracles to the four queens. They live in isolation up in the northern caves of Mount Majesty."

"Oracles?" the mouse dragon said, pressing his nose to the globe.

"They see the future."

"I love them," the mouse dragon whispered. "Do the dojees love the queens? Is that why they serve them?"

Excellent question, Fetch thought, and one he didn't have

the answer to. "I think they do it out of honor but also to keep the peace."

"I want to know more."

"Uh, let's see," Fetch said. "They can only be killed by fire."

"So they're quite mighty!"

Fetch grabbed a book and set it before the mouse dragon. "Can you read?"

The little beast's eyes scanned the title. Back and forth, back and forth, for so long Fetch was sure he was going to say no. Then, to the fox's great surprise, the mouse dragon smiled and said, "Oh, yes. I believe I can!"

"Well," Fetch said, "this book is about how the dojees saved the world from an evil sorcerer with an army of killer frogs. It's quite good."

While the mouse dragon read, Fetch fell into a deep, dreamless sleep.

Several hours later, he woke to find the creature perched on his pillow, staring at him with enormous dark eyes.

Fetch bolted upright. "You startled me!"

"I read three books! And I have chosen a name," the mouse dragon said cheerfully. His wings were glowing a pale blue.

"Uh, your wings..."

The creature glanced over his shoulder. "I learned they do that when I am happy or joyful or thrilled. So many words," he muttered to himself as his little tail whipped back and forth. "And that's not all. I am a dreamer, Fetch! I dreamed so many things!"

"Wait a second," the fox said, circling back. "You read three books?"

"Well, not the terrifying ones."

Great. So Fetch had created a wing-glowing speed-reader who was afraid of scary stories. "You said you picked a name?"

"Beckblade!"

Fetch stretched his memory until he remembered where he had heard that name before. "You mean after the lizard with the magical tail?"

"The mighty little lizard who saved the whole kingdom!"

"Right. Okay, well . . . Beckblade."

"Beck for short."

"Beck."

"I like the sound of it," the mouse dragon said. "Rolls right off the tongue. But you're distracting me from the most important matter. I dreamed something you should know. Unless you'd rather not know because it isn't pleasant."

Fetch stood and stretched. Did this mouse dragon ever stop talking? "We really need to go. Maybe you can tell me on the way."

"You went into a dark forest." Beck whispered the last words as if they were a powerful spell. "Scarred Hollow was the name."

Fetch's pulse quickened. How could Beck have known about his plan to visit the mapmaker in Scarred Hollow? He must have read about the dangerous woods. "What did I do there?"

"You didn't come out."

Fetch snorted out a laugh, half expecting Beckblade's solemn expression to morph into a teasing smile. "Look," he said, "dreams can feel very real sometimes. But they're just stories that your mind makes up while you sleep."

"So you aren't a half-cursed fox?"

Fetch stared at the tiny creature. "How—how did you know that?"

"That's what I've been trying to tell you!" Beckblade hopped onto the fox's shoulder. "I'm a dream dragon!"

Chapter Nine

Fetch hadn't intended to make a dream dragon.

He'd never even met one. That type of dragon was found only in the pages of books. Maybe that's where Beck had gotten the idea—but there was no denying that the dragon knew things he couldn't have known otherwise.

Fetch shrugged on his coat. "Can you stop flying in front of my face for a moment and tell me how you can be certain you're a dream dragon? And don't leave out the parts about the curse and Scarred Hollow."

"I told you, I dreamed it all. And I can affirm," Beck said, "that I am a descendant of bone dragons, but also of dragones de sueños. So I guess you could call me half bone, half dream." Then, leaning closer, he whispered, "But I think I'm much more dream, at least on the inside."

"So you—you can dream the future?" Fetch asked, recalling that this rare type of dragon could also dream hidden truths. Like the fact that Fetch was half-cursed.

Beck flapped his wings and whipped his shimmering tail. "Can we eat? I'm quite hungry."

They hurried into the kitchen, where Fetch whipped up some bacon and eggs along with some peppermint tea to relax his nervous stomach. He felt like he might be coming down with a cold. His head throbbed and his muscles ached, and there was also the matter of that odd vibration beneath his skin. Ointment had helped the insect sting, but Fetch couldn't help but feel like there was something in that sting, something that was to blame for these strange symptoms.

Beck stared at the eggs and scowled. "I don't like that squishy yellow thing. It smells awful." Then he began to wolf down a pile of bacon, stabbing each piece with a talon before stuffing it into his mouth.

"Before we leave you should know that this mission is going to be dangerous," Fetch said. He went on to tell the little dragon about Violet's disappearance and the queen's mysterious trap. "If you're scared, you don't have to come."

"Who does she want to trap?"

"I wish I knew so I could warn them."

"I will be the best warrior you've ever met." Little streams of smoke floated from his nose. "And I will be a good and loyal companion." He folded his wings around his mouselike body and bowed his head. His ears flopped forward. "I pledge my wings and claws and heart to you."

Oh. Fetch hadn't been expecting that. "Well, uh . . ."

Beckblade beamed and as his wings glowed cheerfully, the fox felt a weight on his chest. He'd have to find a way to keep the dragon safe. A special garment, perhaps?

Fetch cleared his throat, getting back to the task at hand. "So we'll need a map of the palace—an old one that will show us any hidden passages and secret rooms that aren't guarded."

Beck's little tail lashed back and forth as he gobbled up more bacon, making a game of tossing it into the air to catch in his wide jaws. "Where do we get one of those?"

"From the mapmaker. She's a tree spirit and she, uh . . ." Fetch might as well tell the dragon now. "Well, she lives in Scarred Hollow."

"The forest from my dream? The one you don't come out of?" Beck let out a small burp. "That sounds like a not-so-good plan."

The dragon was right. No one dared venture into the Hollow during the winter months. Not when the beastlings' senses were sharpest during their hibernation. They were nasty little four-legged monsters with tusks and razor-like claws that sucked the blood out of their prey until their victims were bone dry. Thankfully, they never ventured outside the Hollow.

Fetch glanced down at his pocket watch. "It'll be light in about thirty minutes." He explained to the dragon about the new rules of limited magic that would be put into place that day. The morning light would appear soon, and once it did, it would last only a few hours.

"But my magic stirs when I sleep," Beck said. "What if it stirs when it's dark out?"

Yes, that was going to be a problem. "Maybe because your magic isn't in the real world, only in your dreams, no one will be able to detect it?"

At this Beck brightened.

"Come on." Fetch's heart thumped dizzyingly fast as he and the dream dragon made their way to the door. "Beck, you should ride in one of my pockets."

"Why?"

"Just to be safe."

To the fox's surprise, Beck agreed, stowing himself inside Fetch's chest pocket. "Cozy," the dragon said.

Fetch pulled his collar higher, took a deep breath, and climbed into the wintry world above.

Malvada

The Malvada stirred, longing for the space to stretch properly. Longing to strike. If only it were strong enough. But the fox's magic could never keep the darkness satisfied. It needed more strength. More power.

For a moment, the Malvada allowed itself to remember what true power felt like. Born of a god's hatred and vengeance, it once had been a small, weak creature locked away to die in the Cave of Mist and Gloom. Until an old witch appeared. She fed the creature shadows, shaped its form into that of a boy, who learned the witch's magical ways and grew into a formidable sorcerer. But one night, when the witch was gathering herbs in the woods, she was killed by witch hunters—and at the exact moment that her soul fled her body, the sorcerer vanished into a thread of shadow, realizing too late that he had never existed in true physical form at all; he had only ever been a spell created by the witch. Small and weak once more, the shadowy darkness writhed in fury and grief, vowing to find a vessel to grow its power so that it would never be powerless again.

The Malvada shook away the unpleasant memory. Thanks to the fox's pathetic scheming, the Malvada now knew exactly where it needed to go: the palace. In this the Malvada and the fox were aligned. But while the fox wanted to avoid the queen, the Malvada wanted nothing more than to find her. To possess her—and her winter magic.

Could it be done? *It* must *be done*, the Malvada thought. But if it continued to feed on the fox's magic, the creature would grow weak. For this to work, the Malvada needed to lie in wait until just the right moment and it needed the fox to be strong enough to carry it on this journey.

A journey that would take the darkness straight to the winter queen.

Chapter Ten

Bits of snow shivered from the steely sky.

If it had been an ordinary day, Fetch might have caught the snowflakes on his tongue. There had been a time when winter was his favorite season. He had once loved the crisp air, the sweet scent of simmering apples, the white, glistening world that tickled his ears like a whisper.

But now he saw that beneath all the shimmer was something dark and awful.

Just like the terrible secret he was carrying about the festival being a trap. Who was the queen trying to capture?

Stay away.

Violet's warning rang in his ears. It had to have been his own fear talking. How else could she have communicated with him?

"Are we there yet?" Beck asked from inside Fetch's coat.

The fox grumbled as he headed north, relieved to see that the roads weren't very populated yet. Easier to navigate, he thought as he slipped past a few hooded pedestrians and across the river that flowed beneath the promenade.

A cold wind whooshed down the snowy lane as Fetch passed drab cottages and thatch-roofed storefronts. Shadows stirred behind the first-floor windows.

Fetch cut down alleyways and narrow roads lined with skeletal trees until he reached a snowy pasture at the edge of town. He ignored his fears and Beck's constant "Are we there yet?" questioning, keeping one foot in front of the other, crunching over the snow as the sky grew lighter and his heart grew heavier.

As they drew closer to the Hollow, Fetch summoned a gray spool of thread.

He unraveled several lengths around his wrist and then paused. The vibration of magic was barely there, faint like a dying pulse.

It has to be enough, he thought.

"What are you doing?" Beck asked.

"I need to try something." *To protect you.*

With hopeful determination, Fetch began to weave his paws through the air, slowly at first and then with gusto. Up and down, forward and back. Zigging and zagging.

Gray light swirled.

Distantly, Fetch heard Beck ooh and aah. Then came a

chorus of incomprehensible whispers, blowing like a winter wind.

In the next breath, a hush fell over the landscape. Fetch glanced down.

There on the snowy ground was not a scarf to protect the dragon as Fetch had intended. No, the only proof of his attempted magic was a heap of tangled thread.

"Oh," Beck said, drawing closer. "What is it?"

Deflated, Fetch stomped on the thing and said, "It's nothing," then continued plodding through the snow.

Several paces later, Beck said, "This world is quite nice. Like the dojee snow globe."

"Yes, well, looks can be deceiving."

"So it isn't nice?"

"Parts of it are, I guess."

"Like us," Beck announced, popping out of the coat and onto Fetch's shoulder.

"Like us?" Fetch leaped over a short wooden fence.

"Parts are good and parts not so good."

The dream dragon wasn't wrong, Fetch reflected as he turned down a path engulfed by gnarled black bushes. He thought of Violet, of how she was an ocean of questions, just like Beck.

Sharp branches stabbed at Fetch like hungry claws, closing in with each step.

His fur prickled. The dríada *had* to help him. He had no backup plan, no other way to get into Sterling without a map to show him the hidden entrances. No way to navigate the palace. Or even to find his way out.

Remembering Beck's dream, Fetch asked the dragon, "Did you see exactly what happened to me . . . in Scarred Hollow?" He didn't really like the idea of being dragged into a hole in the ground to be fed upon by beastlings.

"I did not, but I promise to get better at reading my dreams."

"Then maybe you're wrong," Fetch declared with optimism. "Maybe I do walk out of the forest. Did you happen to see the tree spirit or the map in your dream?"

Beck shook his head and sighed.

Fetch recalled only two things about the dríada from his grandfather's stories: First, she had only one eye. Second, and most important, she owed Lorenzo a favor, but he had up and taken his last breath before he'd had a chance to collect, so that meant she now owed his grandson a favor. Or at least that's how Fetch saw it.

Beck took flight, staying close to Fetch. "Do you think I will grow into a large dragon someday, or did you create me to stay small?"

Fetch wasn't sure how to answer. "I guess time will tell. Would you like to grow big?"

Beck thought for a moment before he said, "Doesn't every dragon want to be mighty?"

"I guess you're right." Fetch hoped Beck got his wish someday. Although it was hard to imagine.

"Did you know if you take one *r* away from *scarred* it becomes *scared*?" Beck asked.

"Maybe you should stay inside my coat," Fetch said as they drew closer to the Hollow. "It's warmer there." And safer.

Beck snorted out a small laugh. "And miss all this shimmer and quiet and—"

The dragon spoke too soon, for another gust of wind barreled down the weed-choked lane, twirling Beckblade like a sock. Beck righted himself, landed on Fetch's shoulder, and dug his little talons into the fox's coat. "That was unexpected. Like the time the original Beckblade fought the windstorm to get to the enchanted cave. Must have been quite difficult for a small lizard." He spread his little wings. "I suppose it might have been easier if he'd been large and fierce."

He said the words with a longing that tore at Fetch's heart. "Small things can be fierce too," he said.

He plodded around an icy bend, then stopped. They stood at the dark edge of Scarred Hollow, a forest marked by endlessly tall fir trees. Their black trunks scarred from too many lost battles, for they had once been the summer queen's soldiers before they were cursed by the fall queen to become trees, to stand guard over the beastlings and make sure they never left the Hollow.

"This is it," Beck whispered. "Just like my dream."

With an absent nod, Fetch stood there for a moment staring into the expansive darkness. His ears pricked, listening to the faint rustling sounds. The scent of old magic hung in the air.

It smelled of mildew and wet fur.

Fetch's tail swished impatiently. Anxiously.

"Listen," he said, trying to calm his thudding heart. "We must be quiet in there. No talking. Barely breathing." He quickly told Beck about the beastlings.

"I read a bit about them," the dragon said with a shiver. "Small but nasty things. There was a drawing of one—it looked like a very scary porcupine with tusks, don't you think?"

Fetch had never thought of the monsters that way, but Beck did have a point. If the drawings were to be believed, then yes, they did look like very scary porcupines with tusks.

"Didn't you say the beastlings are hibernating?" Beck asked.

"Yes."

"That means deep sleep," the dragon said. "So how can they hurt us?"

"Their senses are heightened when they hibernate," Fetch explained.

"That's odd."

"A lot of magic is," Fetch said. "And if we wake one . . . well, let's just say it makes them very, very angry."

Beck blew out a breath. Then, lifting his chin, he whispered, "I'll go first . . . to scout the woods before you go inside."

"No way," Fetch insisted. "We go together."

"But I'm your warrior."

Fetch felt a sudden wave of nausea. A terrible cold rippled through him. He clutched his stomach and bent over.

"Fetch! Are you all right?" Beck asked.

The fox caught his breath, willing away the dizziness and discomfort. "Just give me a second," he managed. Regaining his composure, he stood and looked at Beck. "There's something I need to tell you."

The dragon hovered before the fox.

"I haven't been feeling like myself," Fetch began. "Something isn't right, and it hasn't been since . . ." *Since I came back to Ocho Manos*, he thought. Since that wicked insect sting. Maybe some kind of venom really did get into his bloodstream and was messing with his magic.

"Anyway," he went on, "I'm not sure why but I don't feel as strong as usual, which means that you're in more danger than you know. I—I couldn't let you go in there without telling you the truth."

Beck's large eyes softened, his gaze calm but pointed. Then, with a smile, he spread his bony wings wide. "That's why I'm here! A mighty dragon to help you and protect you. Rawr!"

Fetch didn't have the heart to tell Beck that as powerful as words could be, saying them didn't make them true. So instead he replied, "I appreciate your bravery."

Fetch stood there, staring into the Hollow, with its blackened deep-grooved trees, with horrid-smelling streams of mist rising from the earth. He felt a stab of fear, not about dying but about dying *here*. "You said I don't make it out."

Beck sighed, folding his wings in. "Maybe my heart didn't interpret the dream right."

Fetch was counting on that *maybe*.

"So," Beck said, "how do you know how to find this mapmaker dríada? Does she have a sign? An address?"

Shaking his head, Fetch muttered, "Hers is the only tree that isn't scarred."

"Why would she want to live here?" Beck asked with a curious frown. "With the porcupine monsters and that awful smell."

"My grandfather said it was to protect her magic. No one dares bother her here."

"Except for you."

Fetch snorted. He steeled his nerves, and with his tiny warrior, he stepped into the dark woods.

Chapter Eleven

Fetch slipped through the shadows on light feet, for the beastlings were known to hibernate underground. Lucky for him, he was nimble and rather skinny.

Scarred Hollow wrapped itself around the fox and the dragon like a shroud left in the cold for too long. The only light was a scattering of faint rays that had managed to slither through the thick, twisted trees.

Icicles hung from the branches like knives.

With each step he hoped and prayed that the dríada wasn't far. That maybe her home was only a few yards away, not buried deep in these perilous woods.

Frigid winds whistled through the dark forest. Fetch desperately wanted to use a discovery spool to speed things along, but that sort of magic would only awaken the beastlings, who would sense it the moment he snapped the thread. Some said they could even hear the threading of a needle miles away.

No. He couldn't risk it.

Each trunk wore dozens of deep gashes. Fetch wondered who the trees had once been. Fathers? Mothers? Sons? Sisters? Some had the faces of who they once were intricately carved into their trunks. A creepy reminder of a life that was gone.

"I think that tree blinked at me," Beck said, pointing.

Fetch glanced over. The trunk wore the face of an old man with a deep furrowed brow and wide-spaced eyes. Fetch's ears twitched and he froze mid-step, his hackles rising. "I—I think his mouth is moving," he whispered.

The tree creaked and groaned, then, in a deep, resonant voice, it said, "Get out!"

Fetch stumbled back. Beck pinwheeled through the air.

More voices rose up—an entire chorus. *Get out. Get out. Get out.*

In the distance came a shrill noise—like a shriek, hiss, and growl all in one.

Folding his wings around his body, Beck ducked his head under Fetch's coat collar with a tiny tremble, peering out as he scanned the woods.

"My dream," he said. "I remember . . . this is the part where—"

A murderous growl erupted behind them. As the sound ricocheted across the forest, Beck thrust himself into the air, bony wings spread, and shouted, "You cannot have Fetch!"

No! Fetch leaped, grasping for the stupidly brave little dragon.

But as he spun, as his magical coat twisted around his body and the cold air whistled around him, he found that he was all alone in the Hollow.

Beckblade was gone.

The trees went eerily silent.

Fetch searched up, down, and across the thick, shadowy grove. His heart pounded like a giant fist. There was no sign of Beck. Had a beastling stolen him? But what would a beastling want with a mouse-sized dragon?

Regret settled into the fox's bones—the same terrible weight he'd felt the night Violet was taken. He shut his eyes tight, willing the memory away.

I should have watched her more closely.

I should have protected Beck better.

So many *should have*s.

For a flicker of a moment, he thought he might cry—but he wouldn't allow himself to lose focus. He wouldn't fail. Not this time.

He lifted his head and sniffed, long and deep. Searching.

There.

He caught the scent of something—no, *someone*.

Fetch reached into one of his many coat pockets and retrieved a pea-green thread that, once snapped, would act as a grenade and create enough burning gas to flush out an enemy.

Then, just as he was about to break the thread, he felt a

sudden rush of air, followed by a blade pressing into his back. He went stone-still.

"Paws in the air, Fox."

A girl's voice. Here? In Scarred Hollow?

"Who are you?" he asked.

"No magic," she warned, "and I won't gut you. Do we have a deal?"

He nodded slowly. Was this the part of Beck's dream where Fetch didn't make it out alive?

"Say it," she insisted.

"It's a deal," he said.

The blade retreated, and he turned to meet his assailant. A girl dressed in a tawny fur cape glared at him with wild green eyes. Her black hair was a shrub of tangles that fell around her petite face. Absolutely *not* a beastling.

She was smaller than Fetch, yet terribly fierce by the look of her murderous gaze.

"Where's my dragon?" Fetch held out the noxious spool of thread like a threat.

"I don't have him."

"You're lying!"

She inched closer, narrowing her green eyes. They were dull like a swamp. A darkness pulsed behind them, sparking a curious anxiety in Fetch.

"You come into my hollow and accuse me of lying?"

"*Your* hollow?" Fetch tried to put the pieces together. As far as he was concerned, all this noise should have awakened every beastling in a ten-mile radius. "Are you—are you the dríada?" Except this girl had two eyes.

"Do I look like a tree spirit, you empty-headed menace?"

"Well, you don't look like a beastling either."

The girl stood frozen like a block of ice. Her steely gaze studied Fetch, but not in a curious way. It was more like she was trying to figure out where to stab him first.

Fetch curled back his lips to expose his sharp teeth, hoping to appear intimidating. *"Give me my dream dragon."*

"He vanished," the girl said. "Into thin air. I had nothing to do with it. Wait—did you say dream dragon?"

"Why does that matter?"

"They're prone to narcolepsy, fall asleep involuntarily."

"Even if that were true," Fetch said, "he wouldn't have just vanished."

"Obviously you don't know—"

Beck reappeared at their feet, his skinny tail glowing blue.

Though his eyes were closed, he was smiling—clearly having a happy dream.

How nice for him, Fetch thought scornfully as he scooped up the sleeping dragon, shielding him from the girl's reach.

"You need to come with me," she said.

"That's not going to happen." Fetch was rather intuitive when it came to danger, and something told him this girl was made of it, probably ate it for dinner every night. After all, Beck had predicted that Fetch wouldn't leave these woods. Maybe the girl was a scout for the beastlings and was about to lead Fetch to his death. Except that he'd never heard of beastlings having scouts, and she'd had the chance to run that blade through him and hadn't.

With a shrug, she made like she was going to walk away. "I'll let the dríada know."

"Wait!" Fetch said. "You know the dríada?"

With a smirk the girl said, "Who do you think sent me?"

"Why?" And, more important, how did the dríada know Fetch was here? Ah . . . the trees. They must have warned her with all their shouting.

"I didn't want the job, believe me," the girl said. "So you can either follow me or try to find your own way out of the Hollow without getting devoured. Your choice."

"Speaking of devouring," Fetch said. "Why didn't all this ruckus wake the beastlings?"

"That's a secret you don't need to know."

Beck stirred. He stretched with a mighty *oomph*, sat up, and opened his enormous eyes. "That was a cozy sleep," he said to Fetch, "and a remarkable dream."

"You vanished into thin air," Fetch said. "I thought she abducted you."

"I *told* you I didn't steal him!" she retorted.

Beck turned to the girl and smiled. Then with a little bow, he said, "I'm Beckblade the Second, pleased to make your acquaintance."

"There's two of you?" the girl asked.

"Certainly!" the dragon beamed. "Beckblade the First is

a mighty lizard from a story I read at Fetch's house. A very noble creature, and brave too. That's why I chose the name."

Fetch was growing antsier by the moment. He did not want to be standing in Scarred Hollow conversing with a feral-looking stranger while the beastlings were underfoot, probably waking at this very moment.

"How did you just vanish like that?" Fetch asked Beck. "She said you might have narcolepsy, and that you traveled to the dream realm."

Beck shifted from foot to foot. "Narco-what?"

"It's when you fall asleep without meaning to," the girl put in.

"That's not very convenient," Beck said, his face falling.

"It's a superpower," the girl said.

"How?" Beck asked.

"Your dreams are calling you to tell you something important."

"Oh!" Beck grinned from ear to ear. "That's why I had that dream about you."

The girl frowned. "Me?"

Beck nodded. "Your name's Hawthorn and—"

With a whoosh, claws erupted from the girl's hand. "How do you know my name?" she asked.

Excellent question, Fetch thought as Beck floated into the air. "I told you . . ."

"Why would you dream about *me*?" she growled.

"I don't know how my magic works," Beck said with a small shrug.

"What did you dream?" Fetch asked. "Does she murder us in these woods, or feed us to the beastlings?"

"She's not a beastling," Beck said. "Though she could be any number of other creatures with claws."

Hawthorn didn't move or make a sound. She simply stared at Fetch and Beck as if she wasn't sure who she wanted to skewer first. "You know nothing!" she grumbled as her claws retracted into her fingertips.

"Actually, Fetch knows many things," Beck said.

"We're wasting time," Hawthorn said. "And Sabía doesn't like to be kept waiting." She turned on her heel, fur dragging across the snowy earth.

Fetch and Beck followed.

With a keen eye, the fox studied Hawthorn's movements as she strode ahead, leading them deeper and deeper into the dark hollow.

Fetch slowed his pace, allowing Hawthorn to venture farther ahead so he could talk to Beck in private.

"What do you know?" he whispered to the dragon perched on his shoulder.

"I can hear you," Hawthorn sang. Her voice echoed through the trees.

Beck leaned closer to Fetch's ear and whispered, "There *are* no beastlings."

Chapter Twelve

"What?!" Fetch froze.

Surely the dragon was mistaken. Everyone knew Scarred Hollow was filled with the monsters.

"All the beastlings are dead," Beck said.

"Your comments are unoriginal and dull," Hawthorn called out.

"She has excellent hearing," Beck whispered.

Fetch shot the little dragon a side glare.

The deeper they ventured into the woods, the colder the air became, and the stronger the stench of fur and mildew and even death. Fetch studied the trees—their gnarled limbs, their scarred trunks. They looked somewhat sickly, as if something was sucking them dry.

I know how you feel, he thought.

"We're here," Hawthorn announced. She looked back at Fetch impatiently. "By all means take your time, Fox."

A moment later Fetch came to stand before a grand fir tree, so tall it seemed to reach beyond the sky. The dark trunk had no scars. No carved face. But it did have a door covered from top to bottom with tiny bronze hands hammered into the slick mossy wood. Charms to keep away unwanted visitors.

Hawthorn turned to Fetch and Beck, a creepy smile tugging at her mouth. "Once you enter that door," she whispered dramatically, "you will never be the same. You will never return to the life you knew. And if Sabía is not moved by your request, well." She shrugged. "Let's just say she has a rather large oven."

"Eep," Beck squeaked. "I'm far too small to eat. Mostly bones, so I bet I don't taste very good."

"How do you know we have a request?" Fetch asked.

"Because no one in their right mind would venture into this hollow unless they were in desperate need of something."

Was that why Fetch's grandfather had come here? Had he been desperate too? And what could Lorenzo have possibly given the tree spirit that was so big that she was indebted to him?

The fox's blood roared in his ears. Not because he was afraid of Sabía, but because this was his one chance to call in his grandfather's favor and get his hands on a map of Sterling.

His one shot to rescue Violet.

Maybe he needed to practice his pitch. Get the words just right, make his facial expressions sad but not pathetic, his demeanor confident but not . . .

Hawthorn opened the door with a creak.

They all stepped over the threshold into a small room. It was a bit dusty and smelled of cherry blossoms. A fire crackled in the corner fireplace, casting flickering shadows across a green velvet sofa, a tall brass lamp, a stack of baskets, and a tree stump made into a makeshift table.

Thick branches twisted up walls so high Fetch couldn't see where they ended. Only that there were hundreds and hundreds of bookcases built into the branches.

To the left was a circular wooden staircase that led from the first floor to a series of rope bridges that zigzagged up into the shadows.

"Look at all those books!" Beck exclaimed, taking flight to check them out more closely.

"Do *not* touch those," Hawthorn warned the dragon, but Beck was already tracing his bony wings across the spines. The girl rushed up the steps so fast, she looked more like a blur of light than—

"If it isn't the fetchling."

The fox whirled to find a small, stout woman standing behind him. Her short brown hair was slicked back, emphasizing her round, wrinkled face and golden skin. She wore a dark green patch over her left eye. Her right eye was a brilliant violet.

Fetch spun around. Where had she come from? And where was the door they had just walked through?

"You must be Sabía," Fetch managed. "I— I'm pleased to meet you."

"Are you?"

Was this a trick question? As Fetch was searching for an answer, Hawthorn growled somewhere on the second floor, but he didn't dare look away from the tree spirit.

"I've been expecting you," Sabía said, drifting closer.

"You have?" How was that possible?

Sabía smiled a not-unpleasant smile. "We dríadas see and hear everything. You must know that trees make for a wonderful network of spies."

No, Fetch hadn't known that.

"Come, let us get on with things," she said, crossing the room. Her silky pants dragged along the split oak floor.

Fetch followed her to the green sofa. She sat on one end, he on the other.

"Oh, Fetch," Beck shouted. "You must see this grand book of heroic tales! And this one, and—I think these bridges go on forever!"

Hawthorn, having given up the dragon chase, swept back down and plunged herself onto a deep chair opposite Fetch. "He's an unruly beast, that dragon of yours."

"He loves books," Fetch said as Sabía turned to him.

"I imagine you're here to collect on a favor," she said.

An excellent start, Fetch thought, nodding, but not too enthusiastically. "Yes, and—"

"A favor that was not promised to you."

The fox's heart began to sink. He could already hear the no in her voice before he'd even asked the question.

"You are in dire straits," Sabía went on, inspecting her nails. "That much is obvious, and now you believe I am the only one who can help you." She scowled. "Drat. Another hangnail."

"Well," Fetch began. "You sort of are the only one who can help me."

"I no longer create destiny maps," the tree spirit said, ripping the hangnail free with a wince.

Fetch had heard of such maps, though he'd never seen one, and he wasn't so sure he'd want to know his destiny and see his life journey unfold before him anyway. Where would be the surprise in that?

"I . . . I don't need that." *Best to get it over with*, Fetch decided, before plunging ahead. "I need an old map of Sterling."

Sabía threw her head back and laughed, a boisterous guffaw that sounded part delighted, part ominous.

"Dimwit fox," Hawthorn muttered.

Fetch tugged a spool of thread from his pocket. "I can make a trade."

"I don't want your enchantments," Sabía said, "nor are they of any use to me."

"It's not for me," he said. "It's for my sister, Violet. She was stolen and now she's locked up in Sterling and . . ." Fetch tried to stop himself right there, but his mouth kept prattling on endlessly. "Her heart's stitches are vanishing. Well, the ones on the handkerchief she sewed with magical thread and—"

"What's that about stitches and hearts?" Sabía asked, clearly alarmed. Fetch showed the hankie to the tree spirit and quickly told her what Violet had said about her heart and safekeeping.

Tracing her stubby fingers over the stitches, Sabía murmured, "And the thread vanished before your eyes?"

Fetch thought he heard Hawthorn gasp, but he was too focused on the tree spirit to be sure. He asked Sabía, "Do you know what it means?"

"I can feel deep magic in this thread." The woman pressed her thin lips together. "You said when you used the spell to try to locate your sister, you had a vision of the past instead?"

Fetch nodded and was about to spill the truth about Violet urging him to stay away, but what if it only dissuaded the tree spirit from helping him?

"I see," Sabía said with a long exhale.

"Is something wrong?" he asked. A terrible question, because if he had to ask it, the answer was likely yes.

"It seems that this spell you used also put the thread's magic into motion."

Fetch's throat constricted. "What do you mean 'put the magic into motion'? My sister was only five when she stitched that. She hadn't even come into her powers yet."

"Ah, but love can spark magic faster than a match ignites a flame," she said. "Unfortunately, the stitches will vanish, one each day, and when the last stitch is gone, your sister's heart will be lost forever unless you free her first."

"You mean . . . will it stop beating?" Fetch felt sick.

"It is important to remember that a heart is more than a vessel that pumps blood," Sabía said. "It is also where memories are stored. Where love is born. It's where hope grows. To lose it means to lose yourself, your history."

Fetch felt as if a vise was tightening around his chest. "How do you know?" he asked. "How can you be sure?" Oh, how he wanted the woman to be wrong. It was bad enough he'd lost Violet, but now he'd put her in even greater danger by trying to find her!

Hawthorn snorted as though insulted by his question.

Sabía said, "We tree spirits are highly intuitive. We can sense spells, intentions, all forms of magic. It might take a beat or two, but the truth will always make itself known to us."

"Are you saying I only have eleven days to rescue her?" How could he have messed everything up so badly when his intentions had been so good? At least the festival was nine days away, so he still had time.

Sabía handed the handkerchief back to Fetch. He felt woozy, as if he might float away. "Please. I need that map!"

"You're asking me to commit treason!"

"Then why did you let me in?" Fetch said, his anger stirring. "If it was only to tell me no. Why did you send Hawthorn to bring us here?"

Hawthorn threw off her cape. Beneath it she wore a white fur vest, dark leggings, and lace-up boots.

Sabía said, "As I mentioned, the trees are my eyes and ears; they communicate through their roots. And the moment you stepped into the Hollow, I knew who you were, so I sent Hawthorn to bring you to me. I am, after all, fair enough to hear the request, especially since I was so close to Lorenzo."

Fetch had so many questions, but time was ticking away. He glanced at his pocket watch.

"Am I boring you?" Sabía asked.

"No! It's just the daylight is fading and—"

"Ah, yes, the new rules limiting magic," Sabía said. "The trees informed me. They also told me that the Legión Inmortal is passing along the outskirts of the Hollow as we speak, so you might as well settle in for the next hour."

Fetch's skull vibrated with dread. Why were they here? If Fetch's spell to locate Violet was enough to awaken the magic in her stitches, was it also enough to alert the queen that he was planning a rescue mission? But years had passed since Violet had been taken. Maybe the queen was no longer paying attention. Maybe—

Terror took hold of Fetch, knocking the confidence out of him.

"You don't seem worried," he said to Sabía.

Hawthorn snorted quietly while, two floors above, Beck whistled, oblivious to the fact that Fetch's world was slowly caving in.

"Why would I be worried?" Sabía asked. "I am protected in my woods. In this ancient tree." She lifted her gaze. "No one can sense my magic here and no one would dare come inside Scarred Hollow unless they were delusional or—"

"Desperate," Hawthorn put in quietly. And for the first time her expression was one of half concern. Like maybe she really did have a heart.

No one would dare come inside.

"But the undead aren't afraid of any creatures, not even beastlings," Fetch said.

"Ah, but they are afraid of the spirits that possess the trees," Sabía said, "the fallen soldiers from other kingdoms."

The ones who had shouted for Fetch and Beck to get out.

"Makes excellent sense," Beck said, swooping in. "Speaking of the beastlings, there *are* none. Right?"

Sabía and Hawthorn shared an uneasy glance that made Fetch's fur stand on end.

"But if there aren't any monsters," Fetch said, "Scarred Hollow isn't dangerous, so why—"

"Come on, Fox," Hawthorn said. "Isn't it obvious?"

Fetch frowned. The only thing that was obvious was that this girl was rude and impatient and quite unlikable.

No other beastlings. No one dared come into the Hollow.

And then the fox understood. "It's a myth," he breathed. "A story to scare people away."

"Stories are quite powerful, especially when believed," Sabía said, looking pleased. "The stories we tell ourselves, the stories we tell others to manipulate them. The stories we create," she added, "to protect ourselves and those we love."

Just like magic and power. To protect those Fetch loved.

"I couldn't agree more," Beck said, flying once more to the bookcases above.

Fetch knew the tree spirit was right, yet he'd never considered that Scarred Hollow might be built on lies. He'd so easily believed the myth, which made him wonder how many more lies existed in Ocho Manos.

"Now we have to kill you," Hawthorn said casually, "since you know our secret."

Sabía sighed. "Hopeless."

Ignoring the girl's threat, Fetch said, "I came here to collect on Lorenzo's favor. And even if you won't give me the map—" He stopped himself from making any threats. After all, that was no way to earn the tree spirit's favor.

Sabía stood and tossed more logs onto the fire. The flames hissed and sparked. Leaning against the stone mantel with her back to Fetch, she said, "Your grandfather was a good man. He spoke often of you and your sister."

Fetch felt something loosen in his chest.

"I was very sorry to hear of his death," Sabía added softly.

Hawthorn's shoulders sagged and she turned away, her

dark hair falling across her face, making her expression unreadable.

It suddenly hit Fetch that he hadn't asked the most important question. "Why did you owe my grandfather a favor?" he asked Sabía.

But it was Hawthorn who turned to the fox and said, "Because he saved my life."

Chapter Thirteen

Fetch's fur prickled. "How? When? Why?" The words rushed out in a storm of confusion. "What did he do? Tell me everything."

"That's a lot of questions." Hawthorn looked suddenly flustered. "Sabía, you tell him."

"It is your story," the tree spirit said gently. "And this will be good practice."

Hawthorn groaned. "I'd rather not."

Sabía narrowed her gaze.

"Fine," Hawthorn said. "Then it's going to be very short."

"Perhaps tea will help this go down more smoothly," Sabía suggested. Straightaway, the branches growing up the walls shifted, then parted, revealing another room.

"Do you have any bacon?" Beck called as he winged down and followed the woman through the opening.

Fetch stood and began to pace in front of the crackling fire. His tail whipped furiously. He stared at the girl expectantly, but all she did was scowl. "Well?" he asked.

"Lorenzo found me as a baby in these woods," she said, clenching and unclenching her jaw. "He took me to Sabía and she raised me. The end."

Fetch wasn't sure which question to ask first: *Why were you here? Who are your parents? What was Lorenzo doing in the Hollow in the first place?*

Sabía returned carrying a silver tray with pink cups, a plate of bread, tiny jars of jam, and a floral-painted teapot. Beck landed on the mantel, a piece of toast sticking out of his mouth. "I do love boysenbark jam," he managed, gobbling it up. "Have you ever had it, Fetch? It is quite delicious. Indescribable, really. Sweet but also salty."

"He is quite astonishing," Sabía said, watching the dragon.

Beck wiped a smear of jam from his grinning mouth. "Fetch made me that way. And I can read too. I've already read two books since we arrived here! One about pirates and magical pigs, and another about Atotolin, the great king birds, now extinct."

"Not extinct," Sabía said. "They dwell in the Land of the Dead."

"They're bigger than dragons!" Beck said. "And their wings are made of fire. And they can devour anything and everything in their path!"

The tree spirit chuckled.

"Pirates and pigs and king birds!" Beck sang. "Now, that would make for a good story."

"Speaking of stories," Sabía said. "Did Hawthorn tell you how your grandfather saved her?"

"In two sentences," the fox replied.

Hawthorn said, "Three."

Sabía set the tray on the table. "This is thistle tea. It will relax the nerves." She poured a round, then turned to Hawthorn. "Three sentences do not make a story."

"Well, technically they could," Beck offered.

"Look," Fetch said, "we're wasting time, and it's going to be dark soon." And if those wicked soldiers were still patrolling the area, he'd find a way to slip past them.

Hawthorn poured herself some tea, then slumped into the chair and flung a leg over the arm. "I've already told him enough," she groaned.

The tree spirit tossed another log onto the fire. "You asked why I owed Lorenzo a favor, Fetch. I have lived alone in these woods for more than a hundred years, contentedly, happily. All that changed one stormy night." She took a nip of tea and began to tell an extraordinary tale.

"A terrible squall blew across Ocho Manos, the likes of which we'd never seen. Rain flooded the Hollow. The whole world felt as though it was being wrung out, twisted, turned upside down. That was the night all the beastlings drowned. I was swallowed by grief, for they had been like family to me. But all was not lost, because the storm had also blown Lorenzo into the Hollow. A new friend—well, that took some time, as most cherished friendships do. The poor man was soaked to the bone, cradling a baby, desperately seeking help. How could I turn him away? He didn't know how Hawthorn had survived, only that she did. And as the years passed, Hawthorn grew stronger, faster, and more powerful, never knowing what or who she truly was."

Sabía collected herself for a moment before continuing. "I told Lorenzo I was not fit to raise a child. And do you know what he said?" Here she paused and took a shaky breath. "He told me that no one is ever prepared for that kind of love. So, you see, I owe him a favor because he gave me a daughter."

Hawthorn shifted in in her chair. "This is making me very uncomfortable."

The story was beginning to click into place. Fetch said to the tree spirit, "You didn't tell anyone that the beastlings died."

"No reason to invite people into my hollow," Sabía said.

With a faint smile Sabía added, "Lorenzo and I became friends, and soon we began weaving the most glorious maps using my magic and his enchanted thread. Maps powerful enough to reveal hidden places. Although I'm afraid I cannot give you the map you seek."

"Why not?" Fetch asked.

"The only one in existence was lost in a flood."

"We don't need directions!" Beck announced. "I am a mighty warrior and you, Fetch, you are a great Zindero."

"Lorenzo knew the palace," Hawthorn chimed in, "and all its secret passages."

Fetch frowned. "He did?"

Hawthorn glanced around the room at everyone's eyes now glued to her. "Why are you all looking at me like that?"

"What else did he tell you?" Sabía asked.

"When he was younger, he went to a winter festival there," Hawthorn said matter-of-factly. "He got lost."

"And?" Fetch's pulse raced. Why had his grandfather never told him this story?

Hawthorn said, "From one of the gardens, he stumbled into a maze of hidden tunnels beneath the palace."

Fetch had been right! The tunnels did exist.

"Did he give you any details?" Fetch asked. "A clue that might help?"

Hawthorn plucked a twig from her tangled hair. "Only that the palace was bigger than he had expected, and the passages were ghost infested, and darker than any place he'd ever been. He said it took days to find his way out. Nothing more."

Even more reason they needed an old map of the place. Fetch couldn't afford to get lost. Or trapped.

"If only he was here to ask," Beck said.

Sabía paced, thinking.

"What is it?" Fetch asked.

She stopped and shook her head. "It's far too dangerous."

"I'll do anything to save Violet," Fetch insisted.

Sabía's sharp gaze was dark and penetrating, and for a moment Fetch was sure she was going to tell him to be on his way. Then she said in a low voice, "Lorenzo spoke of an ancient artifact called the Silver Drum. He'd learned about it during his travels across the island. Some called it a myth, but he said the threads had whispered the truth to him. If you find it, you can speak to your grandfather. He can direct you through the palace. *He* can be your map."

It took Fetch a moment to process what the woman was telling him. Talk to Lorenzo? It sounded too good to be true. "How could a drum do that?" he asked.

Sabía inched closer. "Because it awakens the dead."

"What if they want to stay dead?" Beck whispered.

"The dead must grant your request," Sabía said. Her expression tensed. "I can give you a map to show you the way to the drum, but even if you find it, it's not just a matter of thumping it. There is more to waking the dead than that."

"Of course," Hawthorn muttered.

"But first, you must find the drum. It will be a challenging journey. Such an object will be heavily guarded," Sabía went on. "Then you must secure it, and finally you must be worthy enough to play it."

Fetch swallowed. "Worthy?"

"Only a bold and worthy heart with the purest intentions can use its magic," Sabía said.

But he didn't feel worthy at all. He felt like a speck of sand blowing on a sharp wind, directionless, powerless. And entirely unconfident.

Hawthorn sipped her tea casually, watching and listening, but mostly glaring.

"So you'll give me the map to the drum?" the fox asked. After all, Sabía still owed Lorenzo a favor for bringing her a daughter—a grouchy daughter, but still. At least Fetch would be rid of the girl and her claws and bad temper soon.

Sabía opened her mouth, but it was Hawthorn who rushed in with, "She'll give you the map to the drum on one condition."

"What's gotten into you, child?" Sabía asked. "You cannot dictate conditions."

Ignoring the woman, Hawthorn squared her shoulders and said to Fetch, "I'm coming with you."

Chapter Fourteen

"Impossible!" Sabía shouted. "You're only thirteen! You've rarely stepped out of this hollow! Why would you want to go with them? The world outside is perilous!"

All excellent points, Fetch thought, nodding emphatically (desperately) as Hawthorn said to the tree spirit, "I was born in the winter. You told me that every birth is magically chronicled and housed in the palace vaults."

Sabía straightened her eye patch, which had gone askew. "So?"

"So this is my chance."

"You want to go with us to the palace so you can see your birth record?" Fetch asked, trying to follow.

Beck tucked his wings at his sides, hopping from foot to foot like an antsy pigeon. "I vote yes." Then to Hawthorn: "You'll be bringing that fur cape, the cozy one, right?"

"It's not a good idea," Fetch said. He didn't want to be responsible for anyone else. Plus, there was the matter of Hawthorn's foul temper.

"I didn't ask your opinion," the girl replied. "You said you'd do anything to find your sister."

"I will—I mean . . ." Fetch took a deep breath. "Why is it so important to see your birth record?"

A look of understanding crossed Sabía's face. She slumped into the chair. "Birth records detail parentage," she said.

Oh. *Oh.* Fetch looked at Hawthorn. "You want to know who your birth parents are."

Hawthorn nodded.

"I will not permit this!" Sabía bellowed.

"Don't you think I deserve to know about my past?" Hawthorn pleaded. "Would you rather I sneak off alone with no help at all?"

"You wouldn't dare." Sabía fanned herself as she slumped further.

Hawthorn didn't have to reply. It was clear she absolutely would.

Sabía stood with an *umph*. She frowned and paced, worrying her knotty hands.

"How about a little tune while you decide?" Beck suggested before he began to whistle. Little puffs of smoke trailed from his mouth.

"Not now, Beck," Fetch whispered. *Of all the bad luck in the world*, he thought. *Hawthorn can't come with us. She's a liability, with an ill temper and no manners!* Then before he could stop himself, he blurted, "It's too dangerous. The queen is setting a trap!"

All eyes turned to him, waiting for him to explain.

He told what little he knew, never once giving a clue as to where he'd heard the dreadful news, only that it was from a very trusted and reliable source. He even threw in the part about the prisoners being chained with powerful soul-bending magic.

Sabía sighed in a resigned way that told Fetch she already knew.

"The trees have heard murmurings" was all she said.

"Do you know who the trap is for?" he asked.

Sabía shook her head. "But now that you have told me about these chains of powerful magic, I have to believe that the trap must be for someone mighty."

So not Violet, Fetch thought with a wave of hope.

"I have sent a warning through the root system," Sabía went on, "and made some careful inquiries, but nothing has come back. Which is even more reason for you not to go, Hawthorn. Something is amiss, and there are far too many dangers out there."

Fetch was pleased the tree spirit saw his logic.

Hawthorn's pleading eyes looked to him as if he might help convince the woman. He didn't blame her for wanting to know the truth of who she was. Which reminded him of something Sabía had said. "You said you can sense spells and all forms of magic, so does that mean you know what magical classification Hawthorn belongs to?"

Sabía said, "Of course I know this, as does she."

"Oh." Beck turned his eyes to Hawthorn. "What are you, then?"

Hawthorn deadpanned, "If I wanted you to know, I would have told you."

"Maybe you can show us," Beck said brightly.

"No one can hide their magic," Fetch put in. "It'll appear eventually."

"Oh yeah?" Hawthorn challenged. "Watch me."

"She was spelled when she came to me," Sabía said dryly. "Someone wanted to protect her identity."

Now Fetch understood. How could he blame the girl for wanting to know the truth about her past, and why someone had spelled her?

Sabía looked at her daughter, her eyes soft and sad. "I always knew this day would come," she said. "I just . . . if only I could come with you."

Fetch was about to ask why Sabía couldn't come when Hawthorn went to the tree spirit and took the woman's hands in her own. "I'll be back," she reassured her. "I promise." And then she began to whisper in a language Fetch had never heard. The walls' branches writhed and twisted. The bridges swayed gently. Several large, star-shaped leaves floated down from somewhere above. Whatever language Hawthorn was speaking, the tree understood.

"All right," the woman replied. There was a quick nod and a tear before she walked over to the far wall. The branches parted like a curtain, and she reached her arm inside all the way to her shoulder, closed her eyes, and uttered something Fetch couldn't hear. Then she took a few breaths and slowly drew her arm back out.

In her grasp was a paper scroll.

"Oh!" Beck squealed. "That was marvelous!"

"This is the map that will lead you to the Silver Drum," Sabía said. Fetch made a move to reach for it, but she handed the scroll to her daughter. "Hawthorn is a skilled map reader. She will guide you. After you get what you need from the drum, you will help her retrieve her birth record. Deal?"

This quest was getting muddier by the minute, but what choice did Fetch have? If he wanted to slip into the palace undetected—if he wanted to get to Violet—he had to have that map. Which meant he had to help Hawthorn.

The world is filled with terrible choices, Lorenzo used to say. No kidding!

Then, remembering the new rules of magic, Fetch said, "We won't be able to travel much if we can only use the map during daylight."

Sabía chuckled. "Hardly. This was created in the past, long before the rules were executed. It's a *recording* of magic, if you will."

"Like a loophole," Beck said.

A loophole Fetch hoped wouldn't land their necks under the boot of an undead soldier.

Beck swooped onto the woman's shoulder. "Fear not. I am a mighty warrior. I shall protect Hawthorn."

The girl threw a scowl in the dragon's direction. "I don't need protection!"

"You will all need to protect one another," the tree spirit said. Then she asked Hawthorn and Beckblade to pack some food and water, an obvious ploy to be alone with Fetch.

Fetch was sure Hawthorn would protest, but surprisingly she swept out of the room with Beck.

Turning to Fetch, Sabía said, "Beckblade is quite unique."

"I know."

"There are many who would do terrible things to procure his magic."

"I'll—I'll make sure he's safe." A promise Fetch was scared he couldn't keep.

"Tell no one he is from the dreamworld."

Fetch nodded.

"Before you go, you should also know something about Hawthorn. Her claws can be poisonous or healing according to her wishes. They can cause a slow or swift death, or a deep sleep. Once I saw her create a tiny sliver in a wounded bird to release its pain and heal it."

"Why are you telling me this?" Fetch asked.

"Most will see her claws and think weapons. They don't

know they can also heal." Sabía's smile tightened. "I suppose I wanted you to know she is gentle too."

"Okay," he said somewhat skeptically.

"And one more thing. Your grandfather and I . . . we created a destiny map for Hawthorn once. It was incomplete and messy and . . ." Tears pooled in the woman's eyes.

"And what?" Fetch asked.

"I knew she would leave, and I knew . . ." Here she paused and studied Fetch intently. "I knew you'd come for her."

Fetch's fur bristled. "What are you talking about?"

"You are a part of her destiny."

"Wait—I . . ." His skin buzzed. "What else did you see?"

"Nothing."

Just then, Hawthorn and Beck returned with a burlap sack filled with supplies.

"We packed some food," Beck announced. "No bacon, but we do have drinks, and biscuits with my favorite jam."

"The trees have informed me that all is clear now," Sabía said, waving the fox away. "No soldiers for miles. Get on with it, then. I am not one for drawn-out goodbyes."

The door that had vanished after their arrival reappeared, but this time it was red and split down the middle.

Sabía hugged her daughter fiercely. Fetch felt a dull ache in his chest, missing his own family—his grandfather, his sister. The idea of talking to Lorenzo again, even for a brief time, thrilled him, but why hadn't his grandfather ever told him about Hawthorn if he'd known her destiny included Fetch?

A mix of frustration and anger flooded his chest.

Sabía said, "You are so much like Lorenzo. But bravery can be foolish, Fox."

"I'm not trying to be brave," Fetch said. "I just want Violet back." *I want to make right all I've done wrong.*

The tree spirit nodded. "May I see the handkerchief once more?"

Fetch handed it over.

Sabía traced her fingers over the threads. She closed her eyes and took several deep breaths, then she opened them again and with a frown handed the handkerchief back. "It's as I feared."

"What is?"

"The stitches Violet used to protect her heart," she paused, gazing at Fetch with an intensity that scared him. "They have bound the two of you together."

"What—what do you mean?"

"She tied her heart to yours. If you do not find her, your heart will also be lost, I'm afraid."

The words were a blow to the chest. "Why would she—"

"Because she loves you, and because she likely thought she was protecting your heart too."

Fetch felt the terrible urge to close his eyes, to sink into a darkness where he didn't have to face any of this. "If I lose my heart that means all hope is lost, all love, and even—even my memories. And without those, Zindero magic will—" He could barely get the words out. "It will die forever."

All the color drained from her face. "I wish I was wrong, Fetch."

Yeah. Me too. Strengthening his resolve, Fetch managed, "Thank you. I won't forget this."

And he stepped across the threshold.

Chapter Fifteen

Fetch, Beckblade, and Hawthorn stood in a nighttime meadow.

There were pockets of trees to their left and right, illuminated by the scythe-shaped moon curving into the black sky.

Fetch stood there, his nose wet and cold. His fur prickled and, once again, he felt a wave of nausea.

"Where are we?" he asked, hiding his discomfort from his friends.

"On the north side of the Hollow," Hawthorn said, taking the lead, pack in hand. Her fur cape swept across the frosty earth.

"How do you know?" Beck asked innocently, soaring above. "Sabía said you've rarely ventured out."

Hawthorn shot the dragon a glare. "I've traveled enough."

"How many times equals *enough*?" Beck asked.

"Five."

Fetch dragged a paw over his face. "Oh, stars."

Hawthorn gave the fox a stormy look. "You don't trust me to be your guide?"

"I do!" Beck sang.

Hawthorn flared her nostrils. "I'll have you know I am an excellent navigator, and I've been educated in art, science, poetry, logic, magic, politics, history, *and* geography."

None of that proved she could get them to the Silver Drum. Fetch was placing his fate, and his sister's fate, in the hands of a stranger.

A stranger Lorenzo had thought was worth saving.

The fox tipped his head to one side and studied the girl. Her dark hair fell in tangles down her back. Her nose leaned a bit to the left, her chin was pointed, and she had three freckles on her right cheek that he hadn't noticed until now.

"How do you know we're headed in the right direction?" Fetch asked.

"I just do," she said.

"Okay, but *how*?"

Beck hovered in front of Hawthorn. "Can we talk more about everything you studied and learned, Thorn? Or maybe you could teach me some poems!"

Hawthorn froze mid-step. "*Do not* call me that," she snarled.

Fetch pressed his lips together to avoid smiling or, worse, laughing. She absolutely looked like a Thorn.

"But it suits you," Beck said. "And nicknames are interesting and offer variety. For example, Beckblade is rather formal but—"

"Beck." Fetch gave the dragon a little shake of his head.

Hawthorn stalked ahead, and Beck and Fetch hurried to catch up. The fox did his best not to show how winded he was feeling, how unwell. Chilled, almost as if a fever was coming on.

The dream dragon's tail shimmered in the moonlight, silver and gold and green and pink. So bright, in fact, it was enough to illuminate the path before them.

Too bright, Fetch thought miserably. This would not do. He would have to stitch a sock for Beck's tail, something to hide all that dream magic.

A few moments later, they stopped at a crumbling stone wall. Hawthorn glanced over her shoulder, then squatted and unrolled the map. Fetch had expected a diagram but instead a glowing 3D image, no bigger than a book, floated up.

Beck flapped around the image gleefully. "It's a town!"

The place was made up of colossal buildings made of purple sand with shell roofs, so tall they reached the clouds.

"Mammoth," Hawthorn uttered.

"Where's that?" Beck scratched at his nose.

"Where giants dwell." Her voice came out a whisper.

"Oh my." Beck peered closer, blinking his wide eyes. "I would very much like to meet a giant. Did you know that their teeth can grow so big, you could make a house out of two or three?"

"Why would I want a tooth house?" she asked, then turned to the fox. "Have you ever been to Mammoth?"

"Never. It's very far from where I live." Plus, he wasn't a big fan of giants. They had horrendous breath and were bigger tricksters than duendes and fairies combined. Their magic was legendary, mined from the great caves near Mammoth. Many could fly, see as far as a hundred miles away, and even create giant bubbles of protection that no magic could break through.

And then there were the tales about things like a witch getting crosswise with a giant, who tossed her into his shoe and trapped her there for so long the giant forgot—and then *splat*.

"How far is it?" Beck asked.

Hawthorn waved a hand through the image. Instantly, the map darkened, then sparked back to life, illuminating a single path: a long road that ran through Corvino. Beyond the little town was a dark blue mountain range that led to Mammoth.

At the beginning of the path were three figures.

"Hey!" Fetch peered closer. "That's us!"

"It's to show us our starting point," Hawthorn explained. "We can make it to Corvino by tonight. We'll camp on the outskirts and get some rest before crossing at dawn."

"I love sleep," Beck said. "Well, mostly I love to dream." He yawned a giant yawn. "Can I curl up in your cape again, Hawthorn?"

Studying the dream dragon, she said, "Do you really dream the future?"

"I do." Beck puffed up his chest. "But it's not very clear and I don't control what I dream, so you can't ask me a question about your future or anything."

"Did you know dream dragons can also dream the past?" she asked Beck.

"Indeed, but sometimes it's hard to tell the past from the future," Beck said, "and I read things wrong."

Hawthorn opened her cape. "Magic isn't always easy, but you'll get better at it with time."

Beck nestled into the thick fabric, where he fell asleep.

Fetch and Hawthorn trekked down a winding road.

The moon's wintry light was a warm buttery color, bright enough to see the details of the landscape.

On each side of them were very tall, very bare knotted trees. The trees were so close to each other that their branches had become entwined, making it hard to tell where one began and the other ended.

Like a tangle of thread, Fetch thought woozily.

"Hey, you okay?" Hawthorn asked.

The world tilted. He swayed but stayed on his feet. "Fine."

"You don't look fine."

"I-I've, uh, been having these spells."

"Spells."

"I feel weak sometimes."

"From what?"

"No idea."

"Stress?" she said. "It's a killer."

Fetch didn't want to focus on how weak he felt. He'd hoped it would get better on its own, but it hadn't, and now he felt like a spool of thread slowly unraveling.

He tugged Violet's handkerchief out of his pocket. Still eleven stitches. He felt a pinch of optimism, even though he knew that when morning came, there would only be ten, and that his sister's heart as well as his own would be that much closer to being lost.

What had Violet been thinking? How could an act of love lead to so much misery? He tried not to consider the consequences of failure, but they clung to him with every step. Every breath.

If I don't find Violet, Zindero magic will die forever. Such magic couldn't live without hope or love or memory. And maybe what he was feeling was the beginning of all that.

For over an hour he and Hawthorn walked in silence across rocky terrain. Everything was gloomy and cold. It felt hardly alive, as if Hawthorn and Fetch were all alone in the world.

"What exactly are your powers?" Fetch asked.

"That's a secret."

"Don't you think we should know about each other so we can work together more efficiently?"

"Not really."

Swallowing his annoyance, Fetch plowed ahead. "So far I know that you have claws, and Sabía said that they can be poisonous or healing according to your wishes. Also that you speak tree. Oh, and you're fast as lightning."

Hawthorn kept her gaze on the road ahead as a frigid breeze swept down the lane, swaying the skeletal trees. The branches brushed against each other with an eerie *creakkshh*.

"Are you always this talkative?" she asked.

"Listen," he said, "we have to work as a team if you want to see your birth records and—"

Hawthorn halted. Her green eyes fixed on the fox with a sharpness that felt like it could slice him open. "I don't care about my birth records, you knothead. That was a scheme so Sabía would let me out of the Hollow."

"What? Why did you want to come with us then?"

Hawthorn looked away.

A low growl escaped the fox's throat. He had foolishly decided to trust her and now it turned out she was a liar. "Why would you risk your life to go to Sterling?"

She turned to him now, frowning. "I'll tell you, but can you not make it a big deal? At least not until we get to the palace."

Fetch's fur stiffened. "I do have a truth-telling thread. I can *make* you tell me."

One by one, Hawthorn's claws emerged.

"You have a foul temper, you know that?" Fetch said,

realizing he'd have to wait for her truth. He hoped it was worth the lie.

"Compared to what?" Hawthorn marched ahead, flinging her tangled hair over her shoulder.

With a grunt, Fetch followed, wishing he could figure this girl out. He'd seen how gentle she had been with the tree spirit. There had to be a tender heart in there somewhere.

Several minutes later, Hawthorn pulled her hood up and turned to him. The cape's tawny fur shifted around her pale face. "You know, Lorenzo told me about you."

Fetch hadn't expected that. "What did he say?"

For an instant, Hawthorn's deep green eyes looked lighter. As if the darkest flecks had been touched by moonlight. "He told me we'd meet someday."

Fetch's heart quickened, then a wave of anger crashed over him. Why would his grandfather have told her and not him?

She nodded, pressing her lips into a thin line as though she was trying to keep something in.

"What else did he tell you?" he asked.

Color rose in her cheeks. Her eyes darted to the ground, avoiding his.

Fetch said, "It can't be that bad." Well, it could, but no reason to emphasize that.

"If I tell you I can never *un*tell you, do you understand?"

Yes, Fetch understood. He knew whatever words she was about to speak wouldn't be round and soft and gentle like those she'd spoken to the tree spirit. The fox nodded, bracing himself.

"He said that on the day we met," Hawthorn said, "the two of us would begin a journey."

"What kind of journey?" he asked. To the Silver Drum? To the palace?

Hawthorn lifted her gaze. "A dark march toward death."

Malvada

The Malvada unfolded like an evening shadow. It tasted the fox's fear, heard his doubts, felt his emptiness. But it felt something else too—the weakness in him, growing like a poison. An ill-fated consequence of the Malvada consuming bits of his magic.

It couldn't afford to drain the fox entirely. No. It was time for a bolder tactic.

I must find a way to speak to him.

Chapter Sixteen

The words rolled out of Hawthorn's mouth so fast that Fetch had to repeat them in his mind. *On the day we met, the two of us would begin a journey. A dark march toward death.*

Hawthorn flapped a hand in front of his face. "You're not going to faint, are you?"

"If that were true, my grandfather would have told me!" he shouted. Lorenzo wouldn't have told some random girl he'd found in the Hollow. Fetch's resentment blazed.

"Stop shouting," Hawthorn insisted.

"Sabía said that she and Lorenzo saw me on your destiny map."

"Yeah, well, destinies change all the time. Free will and all that," Hawthorn said. "He really didn't tell you?"

Fetch shook his head, parsing the words, trying to rearrange them into something less bleak but failing miserably. "What did he mean, 'a dark march toward death'?"

Hawthorn shrugged. "No idea."

"That's all he said, and you didn't think to ask for more information?"

"Of course I asked. He said he wished he could share more, but that was all he knew. And he wasn't wrong. We *are* marching toward death," Hawthorn added. "The drum to wake the dead?" Her tone teetered on the verge of *Isn't it obvious?*

"And also the palace," Fetch added, knowing he was grasping at straws.

Hawthorn twisted her mouth to the side, considering. "But he also could have meant our own deaths."

"That doesn't feel right." Lorenzo had been a man of many words and endless tales. "He was always precise with language, even the way he deliberately enunciated words. And besides," Fetch went on, "if he had seen my death, he'd have warned me."

A cold mist began to rise from the earth, swirls of ghostly white fingers reaching for them. Hawthorn came to a sudden halt, then pressed a finger to her lips and rushed toward a gnarled tree. Fetch followed, watching as she closed her eyes and pressed her forehead against the trunk.

Fetch's body went stiff. She wasn't using magic, was she? Had she forgotten about the queen's rule about no magic during the hours of darkness? Maybe she just needed a little rest, or—

A white light, like a stream of liquid lightning, coursed the length of the trunk, illuminating every groove, every deep furrow.

"You can't use magic!" he snarled.

"I am not using magic! I'm using *language*."

With a shiver, he glanced down the long, misty road, imagining the undead army materializing, stomping their undead feet, searching with their undead eyes. But all he saw was a colorless world of gloom and shadows.

Fetch had never felt more lost.

It was as if something was loosening inside him, like the threads on Violet's handkerchief.

The stitches will vanish, one each day, and when the last stitch is gone, your sister's heart will be lost forever.

Maybe the tree spirit was wrong, and no hearts would be lost. But deep down Fetch knew better. That thread was magically connected to Violet, and he had been the foolish one to put the spell in motion.

The tree's light pulsed once, twice, then vanished. Hawthorn opened her eyes. "Change of plans, Fox." She began to haul Fetch into the thicket.

"What? Wh-why?"

"Because there's a band of witches coming down that road in thirty seconds. And they're in the market for fur."

Fetch and Hawthorn slipped through the trees like stealthy thieves.

In the distance, warbly voices sang, "Winter's cold and so we go *brr brr* as we hunt for fur."

He and Hawthorn drove deeper into the forest.

Thick branches began to fold around them.

"What the . . ." Fetch ducked and weaved, but there was no getting away.

"They'll protect us," Hawthorn whispered, grabbing hold of his arm. "Could you stop moving?"

Fetch stopped and took a few deep breaths while the branches stretched out, taking shape, shielding them in a protective hut.

There they huddled, hidden, listening to the sound of clomping and that terrible song.

Brr brr *as we hunt for fur.*

Specks of snow began to tumble from the sky. The air grew icier.

"Our footsteps," Fetch grumbled. They'd made tracks, and the snow wasn't falling nearly fast enough to cover them.

Hawthorn cursed under her breath, then whispered something in her tree language. Instantly, the trees outside the hut lowered their branches and swept the path.

Handy.

In the darkness, Fetch made out three figures coming closer. Shadowy, wrong shapes that—

"Those aren't witches," Fetch whispered. "They're *goats*."

"Technically they're gwitches," Hawthorn said.

The gwitches had black fur, with long, wiry hair that hung from their bellies, dragging along the ground. With each touch, the earth turned to ash.

"We're safe in here," Hawthorn said, her breathing unsteady and not at all confident.

The goats paused about twenty feet away. They sniffed the air. Their ears pricked. The tallest of the three stepped closer. "Come out, come out, wherever you are."

Fetch and Hawthorn didn't so much as flinch.

"I smell fur," one of the goats said.

"Fox," another purred.

"Foxtail! That'll catch a good lot," the tallest said. Her head began to rotate around and around, a full 360 degrees, until she caught them in her gaze. "All caged up, just the way I like."

"I don't want to scare you," Hawthorn said. "But gwitches are carnivorous and, um . . . sort of bloodsuckers too."

Now all the goats turned their attention toward them, grinning.

"They don't have teeth!" Fetch said.

"I *told* you they were toothless," Hawthorn said.

"You said *ruthless*, and how can they be carnivores if they have no teeth?"

"Do you really want to know?"

No, Fetch did not want to know.

The goats came to the edge of the hut, stopping short as if there was an invisible barrier they couldn't cross. Fetch wanted to shrink back but Hawthorn just sat there, daring the goat witch with her glare.

"You can't stay in there forever," the tallest goat said.

Another said, "We promise to skin you gently, Fox. And that lovely tail of yours will only require one quick whack. It won't hurt too much."

The other goats laughed, stomping the earth with their rotting hooves. They formed a circle and began to dance on two legs as they sang,

"We have a fox, such a treat, his fur is prized, but so's his meat. He will cry, might even wail, when we slice that precious tail!"

Fetch went cold. If only he could use a magical thread to obliterate the gwitches, which were rather unsightly and also giving him a terrible stomachache.

"They're pretty skinny," Hawthorn whispered as the trio celebrated Fetch's doom. "And their hooves are decayed. We can absolutely take them."

Fetch shot her a side glance. "You want to fight the bloodsucking gwitches?"

"Do you have a better idea?"

Not exactly, Fetch thought. He might not be able to use magic at this hour, but he *was* a cunning fox with sharp teeth and sharper claws. And he was fast. Maybe not as fast as Hawthorn was, but . . .

"You're right," he said. "I'll take the taller one and—"

He didn't even finish his sentence before Beck burst out of Hawthorn's cape, zooming toward the witchy beasts, claws extended, howling as though he was part wolf.

"NO!" Fetch tried to punch through the branches, but they were like steel.

"Open it!" he shouted at Hawthorn.

"I'm trying!" She touched the twigs, throwing commands in her tree language, but nothing happened.

"BECK!" Fetch watched in horror as Beck zoomed around the goats' heads. They leaped and swatted at him as though he were a fly.

"Get that dragon!" a gwitch hollered.

Beck blew a tiny puff of fire from his mouth. The gwitches laughed, hopping with glee, getting closer and closer to snatching up the little dragon.

The night air buzzed with forbidden magic, surging and swelling like a violent wind.

Fetch couldn't just sit there. So he did the unthinkable. He reached for his magic—a spool that acted as an explosive.

Wait, a voice within him warned. The voice wasn't his, but it was very real. Deep and commanding.

"Wait for what?" Fetch whispered.

"Who are you talking to?" Hawthorn asked.

Suddenly, the tangle of branches beyond them parted and a moonbeam bathed the scene in light just as Fetch launched the thread at the hut's vines, blowing them wide open.

Hawthorn burst out of the hut in a stunning streak of light.

Fetch sprang free, lunging at a gwitch. He wrapped his arms around its neck, dragging it to the ground. But then—

He lost his hold.

There in the flood of moonlight, the gwitches exploded in a screaming blaze, transforming into figures with horrifically long limbs. Their mouths foamed. Their chests heaved.

Spear-like broomsticks with razor-sharp points materialized in each of their grasps.

The gwitches cackled with delight as Fetch charged again. His legs buckled and a familiar weakness rippled through him. He collapsed onto the icy earth.

A spear zipped through the air toward a fast-moving light. Toward Hawthorn.

No!

Get up, that mysterious voice growled from inside the fox. *Now!*

He struggled to his feet, tripping on his coat.

"Fetch?" Hawthorn's voice came to him from some faraway place.

He looked up. Bits of snow fluttered and danced around her. She was on her knees, cradling Beck in her hands protectively. Tears rolled down her face as she looked down at her chest.

At the broomstick driven through her heart.

Chapter Seventeen

In moments of great agony, or terror, when all hope is lost, time slows to a crawl.

At least it can feel that way.

And in this very moment, when Fetch's heart was failing and the light in Hawthorn's eyes was dimming, and the moon was beaming, and the gwitches were dancing, something *else* was happening. Something that sped time back up.

Out of nowhere shot a fairy in a magical vest.

In one mighty swoop, Garzo thrust out his hands. Lightning poured from them like water, zapping the ambushed gwitches with such ferocity that their eyes popped right out of their now-burning heads.

Then, *zzzzapppp . . . poooofffff*! The gwitches were obliterated into nothing more than a trail of black smoke that drifted into the sky, along with the smell of burning fur and echoes of nightmarish shrieks.

In a panicky haze, Fetch staggered toward Hawthorn.

Beck wiggled out of her grasp, wings flapping furiously. "Thorn!"

"A thank-you would be in order," Garzo barked, landing next to the fallen girl.

Fetch dropped to his knees in front of Hawthorn. He waved a paw through the smoky air to get a better look at her, at the spear driven through her heart.

Hawthorn's hair fell in tangled heaps around her pale face as she looked up with a pained expression. "Fetch."

"I'm here," he said, wishing he knew something about broomstick spears and their magic. He glanced at the blood seeping through Hawthorn's vest, staining the white fur. "We have to get this out of you."

"Don't die!" Beck whimpered.

Garzo sat on a nearby log, polishing his wings with a small cloth. "I'd rather not witness any more blood today."

Fetch's head swam with the memory of the fairy's lightning hands. When had Garzo learned that magic? How had he even found them—and why was he here? And how come the undead army hadn't arrived after that display of magic?

Fetch stared into Hawthorn's eyes. *The color of spring leaves*, he thought. "This might hurt a little."

She clenched her jaw. "Do it!"

Shakily, he took hold of the weapon, praying that this small mercy didn't kill her. With a tug, he yanked it free. Hawthorn crumpled to the ground.

White and gold sparks forced Fetch to shield his eyes. When they subsided, he looked back.

Shock waves rolled through him. Somewhere in the distance, echoes rang out. Garzo and Beck were shouting, but all Fetch could do was stare at the creature before him.

A black bear with green eyes.

"Hawthorn?" he whispered.

She was now on her feet, standing at least eight feet tall.

A soft arc of light glowed around her and then, just as quickly, she shifted back into her regular self.

"Great crows!" Garzo shouted.

Hawthorn gasped, clutching her chest. "Well, that was miserable."

"Thorn!" Beck cried.

With a wince, she managed, "I feel funny."

Fetch caught Hawthorn by the arm. She waved him away, saying, "I'm fine. I don't need your help," before leaning on him.

Fetch said, "You're—you're not bleeding anymore."

Hawthorn took a few breaths, steadying herself.

Beck hopped onto her shoulder and tried to wrap his tiny wings around her neck. She frowned, looking as though she might flick him away, but then she patted his head gently.

Fetch felt as though he might collapse again, this time from relief. Total and utter relief that Beck was okay, that Hawthorn was alive. That the gwitches hadn't pulverized them.

"Hawthorn," he said softly, "you're ali—"

"I know, Fox. But how—"

"Are you not dead?" Fetch asked.

"She's a dojee!" Beck sang.

"A creature that can only be killed by fire," Garzo said, "which is why that broomstick didn't kill her."

Hawthorn's frown grew deeper. "I'm only *part* dojee," she insisted.

Fetch's head was swimming. "What—how—have you shifted into a dojee before?"

"The protection spell prevented it," Hawthorn said.

Beck flapped his wings furiously. "What did it feel like?"

Hawthorn's expression shifted faster than a stormy sky. One second she looked angry, the next confused, and the next sad. "It was like a surge of power, and then I was looking through a prism and I could see things so far away and—"

"So the broomstick broke the spell?" Beck asked.

"But why would anyone want to spell your dojee magic in the first place?" Fetch asked.

Garzo said, "By royal decree, dojees are never to mingle with any creatures other than other dojees, which means someone broke the rules and was trying to hide their crime."

Hawthorn's gaze hardened. "You think I'm the result of a crime?"

"That's not what he meant," Fetch argued, though the fairy had a point. That's probably why Hawthorn had been abandoned, found by his grandfather. Someone had been trying to hide the truth. Trying to protect her.

Beck tucked his wings against his small body. "You are remarkable, Thorn. Don't you see that? I know all about the dojees, how intelligent they are, how powerful but also how peaceful."

Garzo barked out a laugh.

Hawthorn looked as if she might lunge at the fairy, so Fetch stepped between them, paws up. "It must be a shock to transform like that," he said to the girl. "Believe me, I know. When I was changed into a fox it took a lot of getting used to. Try threading a needle with paws! And I was never given the choice to shift back and forth, but you clearly can and that's amazing. And pretty soon we'll be at the palace, and you can look up your birth record and—"

"Stop!" Hawthorn said. "I don't want to talk about it another second. I want to forget about it, do you hear me? You must all swear you'll never tell anyone." She was staring at the fairy when she said this.

Garzo huffed. "I am a vault. Do you know nothing about fairy secret keeping?"

"I swear," Fetch said.

"Me too," Beck put in.

"*But*," Garzo threw in, "if anyone did find out, the dojees would be in grave danger. They would be brought before the queens' council to identify who the guilty party is and then—"

He ran his little finger across his throat and made a *ssshhkk* sound.

Fetch shook his head. "But the queens need the dojees for their oracle powers, so why would they kill one?"

"They don't need all of them," Garzo said, "and according to gossip, there are a mere half dozen left anyway, which means the queen could kill off one or two as a warning to others."

"Why aren't they allowed to mix with other creatures?" Beck asked. "That doesn't seem very fair."

Garzo fluttered his wings and sighed. "Too much power, young dragon. Better to keep their numbers to a minimum, force them to live in isolation. Lure them with promises of peace, because that is the highest calling of every dojee, and they'll do anything to protect it even if it means harm to themselves."

"It's sick," Hawthorn ground out. "My highest calling for sure isn't peace and I'm only half dojee. So you're wrong."

"So no oracle powers?" Garzo asked, though he didn't wait for an answer. It was as if he already knew what she was going to say because he was shaking his head. "You would most definitely be one of the first to die if you can't even be of service to the queens."

"Never!" Hawthorn spit.

"Well, you should keep your shifting to a minimum. Or better yet," Garzo said, "no shifting at all."

"Why not?" Fetch asked.

"The dojees will sense her powers every time she transforms, and the longer she's in dojee form the stronger the call. She'll be like a beacon, a regular lighthouse drawing them closer."

"Well, I don't plan on being impaled again," she said grouchily.

Fetch stared at the girl, realizing just how much danger she was in. No wonder she lived in Scarred Hollow. If anyone found out the truth about her, she'd likely be put to immediate death.

After a few moments of awkward silence, Garzo said, "Let us focus on what matters most, and that's me and my heroism. I saved you all, and what thanks do I get for my troubles but a few words that won't feed me or honor me?"

"Actually," Fetch said, thinking he'd had his fill of surprises for one day, but he had to know, "why don't you tell me where you learned to summon lightning? And how you—*we* broke the rules. We used magic, so why aren't any undead soldiers attacking us?"

"All in good time." Garzo pointed at the spear lying on the ground at their feet. "Do you know what this is?"

"A really painful stick." Hawthorn rubbed her chest. "This blood better not stain my cape!"

"Such incompetence," Garzo muttered. "Really, Fetch. You couldn't do better than this ragtag team of—"

Hawthorn grinned. "How about I stab you with the spear and you can see how it feels for yourself."

Garzo unbuttoned his power vest and stretched his neck.

"Such an ill temper. It's rather unseemly for a dojee, who are well known for being gracious and polite."

"Say *dojee* again and I'll claw you in half," Hawthorn threatened.

"No one is clawing anyone," Fetch said.

Beck hopped around the silver broomstick. "So shiny."

"To be more precise"—Garzo eyed the spike greedily—"this is Enero's spear."

Fetch's whiskers twitched. "Enero?"

Garzo explained that only three spears like it had ever existed—now only one, since he had destroyed the other two when he defeated the gwitches. "Oops," he said with a wicked little chuckle. "Each one was forged from a sorceress's tears. Tears that came when she lost a great battle and died.

"This spear has tremendous power. First," he continued, holding up a stubby finger, "it will cut through any element. Second"—here he held up another finger—"whoever possesses it will never miss their mark, no matter how far. And if you're stabbed by one and live? Well, that means"—he glowered at Hawthorn—"you wield its powers, and it will bend to your will. Which seems rather dangerous given your foul temper."

Hawthorn stared at the weapon with disdain. "I don't want that wretched thing."

"No choice," Garzo said smugly. "It's indestructible, and even if you tried to bury it, it would find you and will remain with you until you die, which could certainly be sooner rather than later."

"What happened to the bushy broomstick part?" Beck asked, inspecting the thing.

"That part likely vanished with the gwitch who possessed it," Garzo said.

"How far can it travel to hit its mark?" the dragon asked. "A mile? A hundred miles?"

Good questions, Fetch thought, but there was something he was even more interested in. "Does she only have to think of whatever—whoever she wants to spear?"

"I'm not impaling anyone!" Hawthorn glared at Garzo. A slow smile spread across her mouth. "Well . . ."

"No, no," the fairy grumbled. "They must be in her line of sight."

"How far can you see, Thorn?" Beck asked. "Do you have super vision or anything like that? Didn't you say you could see far when you were in, uh, you know, that big bear form?"

Garzo stared at the dragon. "How on earth is it possible that we're connected?"

"Connected?" Fetch asked.

"It's why I'm here," the fairy said to Fetch. "It appears that when I gave you a silk thread from my wings to produce this creature, I inadvertently bound him to me in the most torturous of ways. In my sleep!" Garzo bellowed. "And now he haunts my dreams. I can hear his annoying little voice right in my ear like a tiny buzzing insect, and there is no escaping!"

"You heard me?" With a triumphant leap, Beck snickered. "I dreamed of the gwitches before I actually met them, and I'm very sorry, Fetch, but I was swept up too soon to tell you—in my dream, I was screaming for help."

Garzo scowled. "Did you have to scream so loud? I was in the middle of a rather pleasant dream."

A small laugh bubbled out of Hawthorn. "So you have Beck in your head forever?"

Garzo shot her a glare. "Did you not see the lightning in my fingertips?"

"Speaking of . . ." Fetch said.

"Yes, yes, the lightning," the fairy grumbled, tugging on his vest. "To be sure, it is a not-unpleasant side effect of this vest you made for me, so . . ." He cleared his throat twice. "Erm . . . thanks. However, my magnificent powers and quick thinking saved you, so you should be thanking *me* for the rest of your life."

Fetch hadn't intended for the vest to give Garzo such powers, just like he hadn't intended to create a dream dragon. Maybe when he set Violet's spell in motion, it had also affected his magic in some way. Was that why he was having bouts of weakness? And why he'd heard that voice speaking to him back in the woods during the battle with the gwitches? Who did it belong to and why had it warned him to wait?

"What I want to know, Garzo," Fetch said, "is how any of us used magic just now without the army of the undead coming here and slaughtering us."

"Hmph. Yes." The fairy smoothed his wispy hair back.

"An important matter indeed. That is why I'm here. To tell you about the loophole in this no-magic madness."

"What is it?" Beck and Fetch asked simultaneously.

The fairy glanced at his fingernails, then looked up and flashed a devilish grin.

But before he could say another word, the spear began to shimmer green. Hawthorn jumped back as if it were a poisonous snake. "What's it doing?"

Enero's spear floated up and up until it was level with her gaze. The light burned with such intensity Hawthorn's eyes looked like two emeralds. Leaves began to sprout from the shaft, growing and twisting into a thick vine.

"I think it wants you to hold it," Beck said.

Hawthorn recoiled. "What if it bites?"

Garzo sighed. "Such a waste of magnificent magic."

"I've never heard of a biting spear," Fetch said.

Hawthorn blinked, then seized the leafy spear and exhaled.

"See?" Beck said, smiling as Hawthorn inspected the weapon. "Why did it grow all these leaves?" she asked.

Garzo sighed. "The spear belongs to you now and will take on the appearance of your magic. Perhaps it has leaves because the dojees love and honor all nature."

Hawthorn frowned.

"She *does* speak tree," Fetch said.

"Do you feel different?" Beck asked the girl. "Now that you possess Enero's spear?"

She rolled her eyes. "Other than having something else to carry around?"

Instantly, the spear vanished in a spark of light.

"Ow!" Hawthorn cried, looking down at her wrist.

"Did it bite you?" Fetch asked.

Hawthorn shook her head and held up her wrist.

A small leaf tattoo was inked there.

Chapter Eighteen

Fetch craned his neck to see. "Amazing."

"Stupendous," Beck sang.

"What a tragic waste," Garzo muttered.

Hawthorn flicked her wrist, and the spear briefly reappeared in her grasp before she vanished it again. "Handy."

Fetch nodded. Clearly, she was the right person to carry a weapon like that. Hours ago, he might have thought differently, but not now, after witnessing her bravery and the way she'd rushed to save Beck. Though there was still the matter of her being part dojee—even if she didn't want to talk about it, she was going to have to face it eventually. And maybe she could learn to harness that power and shift at will, especially now that the spell had been lifted.

"Thanks, Hawthorn," he said to her. She gave the tiniest

of nods as if to say she understood and he didn't need to utter another word.

"How about *my* thanks!" Garzo boomed.

"Yes, thanks to you too," Fetch said. Then, realizing that his appreciation needed to be grander to feed the little fairy's ego, he added, "You're very brave and noble."

Garzo grinned. "I am, aren't I?"

"You said there's a loophole in the queen's new law," Hawthorn reminded him.

The fairy opened and closed his wings, raising a finger to emphasize whatever point he was about to make. "Indeed, for I, Garzo, Spy the Magnificent, have unraveled the mystery. Let us turn to the facts of my brilliant discovery." Garzo paced with his small hands clasped behind his back. "Fetch, do you recall when the capitán said that we cannot use magic in the hours of darkness?"

The fox nodded.

"And what time is it?"

"Who cares?" Hawthorn smirked.

Fetch looked at his watch. "It's four thirty p.m."

"Still technically daytime, right?" Garzo raised a single eyebrow. "Do you see?"

Fetch thought back to the capitán's cold voice, his icy sneer, and remembered his words: *magic is now prohibited during the hours of darkness.* "It's not *actually* the hours of darkness yet," the fox said.

"Bingo!" Garzo sang.

Beck scratched his head. "But it's still dark. So . . ."

"Correct." Garzo nodded. "But, technically, at this time of day it *should* be light, right?"

"Are you saying, even though it is dark where we are, we can use magic if the time is right?" Hawthorn asked.

"That would be preposterous," Garzo said.

"Then how is this a loophole?" Fetch asked.

"We only need light from a natural source, and voilà—our magic is ours to command."

Hawthorn froze. Her eyes went wide with understanding. "That's why the branches didn't let us out. They knew! They waited, and then they parted for the moonlight so we wouldn't use magic before it was safe."

"Couldn't they have told you that?" Fetch asked, remembering how the voice had told him to wait.

"Well, to be fair," Hawthorn said, "we *were* in a moment of panic, and I probably wasn't listening."

"Shocker," Garzo said just as Beck's tail shimmered, making the fairy's lavender eyes look even brighter. "Ohhhh." Garzo offered a knowing smile. "Well, that's advantageous."

Beckblade swung his tail, grinning from ear to ear. "I'm like a torch!"

Catching on, Fetch growled, "Never."

"Why not?" Garzo asked.

Fetch ignored the fairy and began to march out of the grove, shaking his head. "Stop shining that tail!" he demanded. "It's like advertising to the world that you're a dream dragon."

The dragon flew over to him. "This is my purpose," Beck insisted. "I see it now. This is why you created me. Not just for my prophetic dreams but to use my light."

There are many who would do terrible things to procure his magic.

"I didn't create you for that," Fetch said.

"Didn't you?" Garzo put in.

Hawthorn offered Beck a sympathetic glance.

Fetch stopped and turned to the fairy hovering next to him. "Why would you say something so wicked?"

"Because you created Beck after Ernesh's announcement," Garzo reminded him. "And perhaps somewhere in that fox heart of yours you *intended* to make the dragon this way. Even if you weren't aware, your magic was."

Lorenzo had always told Fetch that the first rule of Zindero magic was intent, and that he must envision what he desired most in the moment. But Fetch hadn't intended to do this to Beckblade. He'd never planned to create a tiny dream dragon with narcolepsy.

"Beck," he said gently, "I'd never do that to you. I promise."

"It's okay, Fetch," the dragon said in a small voice. "My light is yours. I took a vow. And even if I didn't, you're my friend."

"Enough!" Fetch barked. "We aren't using your light. If anyone saw your tail, they'd know you're of the dreamworld. They'd use you, Beck." He inhaled sharply, trying to regain some composure. Flakes tumbled from the sky, thicker and heavier.

Garzo shivered. "Couldn't you have made this vest a bit warmer?"

"We'd better find shelter," Hawthorn said.

Fetch nodded. "Which way?"

She rummaged around in her pocket, then switched to the other one. "Uh . . ."

"Sounds ominous," Garzo said with a yawn.

"Where's the map?" Fetch asked.

Garzo scowled. "Map?"

Looking up, Hawthorn said, "It's—it's gone."

"What do you mean gone?" Fetch's fur spiked and his pulse raced.

"I don't know!" she hollered. "I probably lost it in that blasted fight with the treacherous goat witch monsters."

Fetch bolted back toward the battle scene. The wind roared through the branches above him. The snow grew thicker, fiercer. Falling so fast now that there was no path to follow.

Hawthorn appeared next to him in a flash. "Fetch, it's too late," she shouted.

"No!" The fox dropped to his knees and began to dig furiously. His paws grew numb, and his heart grew cold. He needed that map. How would they ever find the Silver Drum without it? How would he rescue Violet? How could he save their hearts and their magic too?

Hawthorn knelt next to him and tugged on his sleeve. "It's gone, Fetch."

But Fetch wouldn't stop searching.

"The storm is getting worse," she warned. "We have to find shelter."

Fetch was tired of feeling weak. He was tired of carrying the weight of his worthlessness. And this only made him feel a terrible desperation, the kind that makes you do reckless things.

He reached into his coat, probing for a locator spool.

"Fetch, no!"

If he had been in a better state of mind, he would have listened to the girl, would have noticed that there wasn't enough moonlight to shield his magic from the queen's undead soldiers.

He closed his eyes, willing the right spool to emerge just as he had always done.

"Fetch!"

The fox ignored her pleas, more fixated on the fact that no spool was coming forward. Like before, there was no stirring deep inside, no tingling in his limbs. No magic to be found.

No! It wasn't possible. He needed to focus. To try harder.

Tears burned his eyes. *I'm not worthless. I'm not powerless!*

Just then, a whisper rose inside him. *I can help you.*

Fetch felt a shiver work its way through his body, a thread of power that instantly soothed him. *How?* he asked silently.

Not now. But soon.

Hawthorn dragged Fetch up by his elbow. "Do you want to die out here? What good will that do Violet!"

Fetch could barely make out Hawthorn's face through the

driving snow as she hauled him to his feet. He followed, knowing (and hating) that she was right.

The night grew darker, and the wind began to howl and shriek.

Hawthorn gripped Fetch's arm tight. "When we get out of this, Fox, I'm going to—"

Her threat was swallowed by a bitter gust.

With his head down, Fetch placed one foot in front of the other, sinking deeper and deeper into the snow. Every lash of wind was like a dagger of ice, stabbing his face, his neck.

The voice's words echoed across Fetch's mind.

I can help you.

Then help me now, Fetch thought.

"It's too dark!" Hawthorn shouted as Fetch struggled against the storm, against the darkness pressing in on them.

Then, a flicker.

Fetch blinked away the snowflakes clinging to his eyelashes. He stared, hoping he wasn't imagining it.

He wasn't.

For there in the distance, a familiar gold-and-green light shone through the storm.

Chapter Nineteen

Beck never faltered.

His light was so bright, in fact, that the snow seemed to melt around it as they trudged back.

Just as they stepped out of the thicket, the blizzard waned, easing up before it took its fury farther south, leaving only an icy chill in its wake.

Garzo shook his head. Frost clung to his thick eyebrows. "Of all the foolish, heedless moves!" he said. "I could have frozen to death waiting here for you!"

"You could have used your lightning fingers to help us," Hawthorn growled.

"Do I look ready to die?" the fairy tsked. "Besides, my light isn't natural."

"Natural?" Fetch asked.

"I wasn't born with it," Garzo added begrudgingly. "Not like Beck's tail."

Beck landed on the fairy's shoulder. "You have many other gifts, Spy the Magnificent."

This seemed to cheer the fairy.

"Beck," Fetch said. "You're very brave, and I—I know you took a vow to protect me, but what if you hadn't found us, or you died, or—" The options were many and terrible.

"I would have come no matter what," Beck said. "Just like you would for me."

With a grateful nod, Fetch glanced down the road in both directions. "We needed that map to get to the giants and . . ."

Garzo's eyes bugged out. "Did you say giants?"

"We're going to see them so we can get the Silver Drum," Beck announced cheerily.

Fetch quickly explained their plan.

"Preposterous," Garzo shouted. "What do you plan to do, Fetch, march into Mammoth and tell some of the most fearsome, angry creatures in the land to let you borrow their ancient drum?"

"Not borrow."

"Steal," Hawthorn put in.

"You cannot be serious," Garzo said.

Hawthorn turned to Fetch. "We need to keep moving."

"Even if we find Mammoth," Fetch said, "how will we find the drum without the map?"

"Oh, I know," Garzo said brightly. "We can ask for directions along the way. Surely, someone knows how to find something as common as a mighty magical drum that raises the dead, and I'm certain they will give the information to us freely."

"You're very negative," Hawthorn said to the fairy.

"I'm a realist!"

"Hawthorn's right," Fetch said. "We need to stay positive."

"I have an idea," Beck chimed in, but the rest of the group had already erupted in an argument, talking over each other.

The dragon floated in the center of the quarreling trio. With a mighty inhale, he released his best roar, then spit out an itty-bitty stream of fire.

"Watch where you point that fire, you little toad," Garzo growled.

"I've been trying to tell you," Beck said, panting. "I can take us to Mammoth, to the drum. We don't need the map!"

Fetch's ears stood up. "Beck, what are you talking about?"

"I remember everything I read. Down to the smallest details." He tapped a wing to his head. "And I've got that map right here, all snuggly safe."

"Like a photographic memory?" Hawthorn asked.

"That's incredible," Fetch said as Beck smiled and pointed to the right.

"Surely he inherited this trait from me." Garzo puffed up his chest. "Fairies have marvelous memories."

"We go in that direction for five point two miles," the little dragon said. "Then we hook a right at a large stone column that looks like three fingers, or maybe the end of a pitchfork."

"Three-pronged stone," Fetch repeated. "Got it."

"From there," Beck said, "we travel quite a distance to Corvino."

Hawthorn frowned. "The bird town?"

"It was built by *magnificent* birds of all varieties," Garzo argued, "ancient creatures with incredible magic—and, furthermore, the town was blessed by the Atotolin."

"The king birds," Fetch put in.

"Amazing!" Beck flapped his wings excitedly. "I'd love to meet a king bird someday."

"Impossible," Garzo said. "They dwell in the Land of the Dead."

"And they eat souls for breakfast," Hawthorn put in.

Beck's eyes went wide. "Eep."

"But not dragon souls," Fetch said.

"Phew," Beck said, swiping a wing over his forehead.

"Where to after Corvino?" Fetch asked the dragon.

"At the southern tip of the town we should be able to see the road that leads to the blue mountain just east of—"

The dragon vanished in a spark of light.

"Unfortunate," Garzo muttered. "How long will he be gone?"

"For as long as the dream takes." Fetch sighed.

"How far do you think Corvino is?" Hawthorn asked.

Garzo said, "At least two days' walk, but of course I could fly there much faster."

"We need to find a quicker way than on foot," Fetch said.

"Use your handy-dandy coat," Garzo said.

"Coat?" Hawthorn asked, looking perplexed.

"His coat is enchanted," Garzo said. "It allows him to fly."

Hawthorn turned her gaze to Fetch. "And you didn't tell me this before because . . . ?"

"I can't exactly fly," Fetch said. "But the coat allows me to soar." *When it's not blowing me off course.*

"What's the difference?" she asked.

"Flying requires skill," Garzo harrumphed. "A straight line to a destination. Soaring, well—" He cleared his throat. "You might as well be a balloon."

"It's not quite that bad," Fetch argued.

"How far can you *soar*?" Hawthorn asked.

"Far enough, but the coat's been acting up." Fetch then told his friends how the garment had taken him off course when he returned to Ocho Manos.

"Perfect," Hawthorn said. "So we could end up a hundred miles from Corvino."

"Or you could fall to your death," Garzo said.

"Let's get to the main road," Fetch suggested. "Someone is bound to pass. Maybe we can hitch a ride."

Garzo's lavender eyes bulged. "Fairies do not hitch!"

An icy feeling crept over Fetch as they journeyed on, and he had the eerie sense he was being watched. But not from the outside. It was more like a stirring deep within, an uncoiling.

Like a snake waking from its hibernation.

Chapter Twenty

For the next hour they trudged across snowy meadows, up rocky hills, and through dead woodlands. Fetch was damp and cold and exhausted. His eyes flicked up to the night sky, to the thousands of sparkling stars above, and he wondered about the voice inside him. The one that sounded so very different from his own—rough and impatient. Who did it belong to—and why were they trying to help him?

Hello? he said silently. *Are you here?* But there was no answer.

The trio came to a muddy road. A thin layer of mist hovered beneath a half-moon.

Hawthorn looked in both directions. "Look at all the carriage tracks. I bet someone will come by soon."

"Did you know this road runs parallel to parts of Queens' Road?" Garzo asked. "Separated by a dense forest, miles apart."

"Really?" Fetch asked. Although he knew Queens' Road was spelled to simultaneously run not just north and south but also east and west, leading to whatever palace was in season.

Hawthorn adjusted her hood over her head. "You mean the heavily guarded road that no one but the queens is allowed to use."

Fetch was growing impatient. "We should keep walking until someone comes."

"Or you could try to use your coat," Hawthorn suggested.

"It would save time," Garzo agreed, "and humiliation."

Fetch sighed. His friends were right. What harm would it do to try? He walked a few paces ahead. Using his coat was as natural as blinking. He didn't even have to think about it. But today, he found himself focusing, willing the garment to do *something*.

The garment billowed, lifting Fetch several feet off the ground; then, as if it had changed its mind, it dropped him with a *thud*.

"Oh," Hawthorn breathed.

"Just give me a minute," Fetch said. His next attempt was no better, made even worse when the coat collar tightened, pressing against the fox's windpipe.

"Perhaps this is not the time to try after all," Garzo said.

Fetch struggled with the coat's grip, loosening it enough to catch his breath. He growled stubbornly. He'd created this coat and he most certainly wasn't going to let it best him. He tried again. He lifted into the air—five feet, fifteen. His heart quickened.

Hawthorn cheered.

Fetch soared higher. The air grew colder, but he didn't care. He loved being airborne, this feeling of weightlessness, as if he could fly all the way to the stars.

But then . . .

The coat twisted around him and, instantly, he was zipping toward a massive tree. He attempted to redirect but the magic had spun out of control. Again.

"Fetch!" Hawthorn shouted.

Fetch wrestled with the coat. He needed to get the thing off.

He was going to slam into that tree in three . . . two . . .

Hawthorn shouted something in her tree language, and just before the fox made impact, the tree reached out its branches and caught him.

He dangled there uselessly, feeling like the world's biggest fool.

In a streak of light, Garzo appeared. "You really are a burden." Then, holding the hem of Fetch's not-so-magical coat, he guided the fox safely back to the earth.

Fetch's paws touched the ground in defeat. "Okay, so no coat," he said. His ears pricked. "Do you hear that?"

Hawthorn went still, listening. "Sounds like carriages. Four, to be exact. Two minutes away."

"This is our chance," Fetch said.

"What if they're not friendly?" Hawthorn asked.

Fetch stared down the path. "We can't risk it. When they come around the bend, we hide and then we stow away. Garzo, can you provide a distraction? Get them to slow down?"

Garzo wrinkled his brow. "Like what? Would you like me to lie down in the road and play dead?"

"Not a bad idea," Hawthorn said as Fetch pulled her behind a bush, where they crouched and waited.

Slisssshhhh. Slisssshhh.

A caravan, Fetch realized as a sleigh cruised into view, followed by another and another, each being pulled by massive white horses with thick fluffy manes that shimmered in the moonlight.

The first zoomed past, and then the next.

"Garzo!" Fetch growled. "The last one is coming. Hurry!"

With a grunt, the fairy flew to the middle of the road, where he hovered and waved his little arms. "Hello, good sir."

The driver, a burly man with stringy black hair, didn't slow the wagon. Garzo shouted louder. "Just one moment of your time. Perhaps you could slow down."

The horse snorted, and the tarp-covered wagon continued sliding down the path like a star streaking across the sky. It drew closer and closer, but at this speed it would be impossible to jump inside.

"Maybe we should just ask the driver to do us this favor," Hawthorn whispered.

"Too big a risk." Plus, the man looked like he was in a hurry. Fetch's muscles twitched with anticipation.

"Out of the way, you little gnat, or I'll drive right over you," the man shouted at Garzo.

"Excuse me, I am no gnat! I'm a fairy with tremendous powers!"

The man guffawed. "No magic in the dark, gnat."

Garzo's face reddened. The carriage plowed straight for him. This was it—in five seconds the cart would be in the perfect position for Fetch and Hawthorn to leap inside. Garzo just had to get the thing to slow down.

"Oh, to stars with this nonsense," the fairy grumbled, then zoomed toward the horse in a brilliant flash of light. The magnificent creature whinnied mightily and reared, nearly toppling the carriage.

Fetch sprang into the wagon beneath the tarp. Hawthorn was right behind him, cursing under her breath as she lay next to him. "It smells like chocolate in here," she whispered.

"I'm on the queen's errand," the man growled. "An important delivery to the palace for the festival, and *you* are disrupting royal business!"

Fetch heard Garzo snort. "Oops. I thought you were someone else," the fairy sang. "Toodle-oo."

And with that, the carriage zoomed on its way.

As they slid along the road, Fetch tried to stretch his legs, but there was no room with all the boxes. "You think they're *all* filled with chocolate?" he asked Hawthorn.

"Only one way to find out." And before he knew it she'd opened a box and pulled out a small chocolate crown dusted with silver. "It's almost too pretty to eat," she said, then with a shrug she popped it into her mouth. "Delicious."

"Do you know what the penalty is for stealing from the queen?" Fetch teased.

Hawthorn licked her fingers. "It's so good it's worth it. Want one?" She reached into the box and came out with a handful of more crowns.

Fetch took one, remembering how much Lorenzo loved sweets. Pies, cakes, jelly beans—he used to say that sugar was "one of the delectable delights of life." Fetch placed the candy in his mouth—the velvety smoothness set his tongue tingling. He smiled. "You're right. Delicious."

"Want to know a secret?" Hawthorn turned to Fetch, a smear of chocolate on her lower lip. "When I was little, I wanted to be a chocolatier."

Fetch had a hard time imagining the fierceness of Hawthorn buzzing about a candy shop. "Seriously?"

She nodded. "My grand plan was to spell each piece—I wanted to make mermaids that gave someone a beautiful singing voice, or little unicorns that only delivered sweet dreams."

Fetch popped another crown into his mouth as Hawthorn sighed, then said with a smirk, "And then I would make others to poison my enemies."

Fetch chuckled. There was the Hawthorn he had come to know and even like. "What about you?" she asked. "Did you have any dreams as a kid?"

The wagon rattled along, bumping over dips in the road.

Fetch wasn't sure why she was telling him all this and asking about his own dreams. Maybe it was their near-death experience with the gwitches, or the fact that they were headed toward a town blessed by king birds who ate souls for breakfast.

"Well," Fetch began, not sure he wanted to tell her since his dream wasn't nearly as fun as being a chocolatier. "I . . . uh . . ."

"Oh, come on, I told you mine."

A bit of canvas blew back, giving Fetch a view of the stars clustered above. "I wanted to be a scientist."

Hawthorn clucked her tongue. "In a world of magic, you wanted to study *science*?"

"Science is predictable," Fetch explained. "Magic is just so . . . so—"

"*Un*predictable."

"Exactly," Fetch said. "And science is logical."

"And what were you going to do with this science?" Hawthorn asked.

Fetch thought a moment, then with a wry smile, he turned to her and said, "Probably make poisons for your chocolate."

The two laughed, the rolling sort that once it gets started it's hard to stop, and soon tears were rolling down Fetch's face and Hawthorn was clutching her stomach, and he realized there was nothing funny enough to justify their outburst, but maybe they just needed to blow off steam.

For just a moment they needed to pretend that there was

no mysterious trap, no imprisoned sister, no undead armies, and no wickedness in this world of theirs.

It took two hours to reach the outskirts of Corvino. The moment the sleigh slowed around a bend, Fetch and Hawthorn leaped out unnoticed.

Fetch stretched and stared into an icy stone tunnel. A carved sign hung above the arch: CORVINO. A TOWN BUILT ON WINGS.

Garzo appeared out of the shadows. "That was humiliating, do you hear me? Throwing myself in the middle of the road, risking my life! Good thing I'm fast. That sleigh flew like the wind."

"Thanks, Garzo." Fetch handed his friend a chocolate crown.

"I'm allergic to chocolate. Do you know nothing?"

Hawthorn said, "Hey, Garzo. I have a question."

"I'd rather not answer."

"When you were a kid, what did you want to be when you grew up?" she asked.

The fairy snorted, then lifted his chin haughtily. "Why, a king of course."

Hawthorn narrowed her eyes. "I don't believe you. Fetch, tie him up with that truth-telling thread of yours."

Fetch snickered as Garzo balked. "How dare you."

"Fetch and I told each other," Hawthorn said. "We'd tell you too if—"

"I wanted to be a scientist," Fetch told Garzo, who was flapping about awkwardly.

Garzo's lavender eyes flitted to Hawthorn. "Let me guess—you wanted to be an assassin."

Maybe the chocolate had warmed Hawthorn's heart, for she uncharacteristically skated right over the insult and said, "A chocolatier." Then with a smirk, "But poison wouldn't be out of the question."

Garzo grumbled and Fetch thought he might vanish into the night with a huff, but surprisingly, the little fairy shook his head and said, "I wanted to be a florist. To create beautiful, dazzling gardens."

Fetch said, "You still could."

Garzo worked his jaw back and forth. "No gardener ever made history," he said gruffly. "Now, enough talk of useless dreams."

Fetch didn't think any dreams were useless, or at least he hoped they weren't, but now wasn't the time to argue with the fairy.

"What do you think is taking Beck so long?" Fetch asked. "He's been gone for hours."

"Maybe he found himself a nice dream that was far better than this place," Garzo said.

"Or maybe you scared him off with all your soul-eating talk," Hawthorn argued. The fairy harrumphed and flew ahead.

A minute later, they'd made their way through the ice tunnel and emerged at the top of a snowy hill. Below was a walled town whose streets were lined with elegant stone buildings. The flat roofs were dusted with snow. Ice coated the windows. A cold breeze blew across the landscape, scattering small clouds of mist through town.

"Oh," Hawthorn said. "It looks so peaceful. Like a painting."

Like the kind of place where nothing bad could happen, Fetch thought.

"Come on," Garzo said, "we need to find lodging and a nice hearty soup and a very hot cup of tea and perhaps a warm fire to thaw my beautiful wings."

The town was bustling with people, all dressed rather formally in fine wool coats, bright scarves, and decorative feathered hats. The sidewalk cafés were crowded, and laughter and woodsmoke drifted up into the winter night. There were countless shops selling all sorts of goods: books, leather, pipes, and tea.

"Why is everyone dressed so nice?" Hawthorn whispered, fidgeting with her cape.

"The citizens here are quite refined," Garzo said, "both in taste and mannerisms."

The trio drifted through the stylish crowd, trying to blend in. Fetch caught wisps of conversation as he passed:

"My dress for the festival will be magnificent."

"I'm taking the queen a most marvelous gift."

Keeping his head down, Fetch blew past the chatter and into a pub called the Nest.

The place was small, only six tables, half of them full. A steady fire burned in the stone fireplace and the air smelled of salty meats and fresh-baked bread.

A boy no older than Fetch came over. "Table for three?" he asked. He was taller and lankier than Fetch, and his face was part bird—he had a beak, beady eyes, and black feathers poked out of his neck and head.

Fetch stared at him a moment, thinking the boy looked far too tall for a birdling, as he led them to a table in the back corner where they sat.

That's when Fetch saw it.

A wanted poster. With his face on it.

Chapter Twenty-One

Fetch sank lower in his seat, trying to hide in a pocket of shadow. Hawthorn's eyes drifted to the poster. Garzo gasped.

Beneath Fetch's mug shot were these words:

Wanted by the winter queen for treason.

A bitter cold twisted up from the wood planks as he read on.

The cursed fox is dangerous.
A reward of Queen Celeste's immense favor
if brought to the palace alive.

Fetch couldn't believe she'd put out notices asking for his capture—and yet hadn't the queen promised to hunt him down if he ever looked for Violet? What had tipped her off? Had it been the location spell, or was it something else? Either way, she clearly knew of his plans and had likely already hidden Violet deep in the palace, somewhere Fetch couldn't reach.

He needed Lorenzo and he needed that map now!

"This is dreadful." Garzo's face flushed.

"Look," Hawthorn said with a tremble in her voice that put Fetch on edge, "we just have to stick to the shadows and not—not get caught."

"Did you not see that the queen herself is hunting him?" Garzo squeaked out.

"I have to get to the Silver Drum," Fetch insisted, "and fast."

But it was too late—the bird boy was whispering into another bird boy's ear, their beady gazes cold and hollow as they studied Fetch with a greed that turned his stomach.

They began to walk over. Their arms were long, swinging at their sides. The taller bird boy said, "No sudden moves, eh?"

The other smiled at Fetch. His teeth were pointed and quite yellow. "You don't look so dangerous to me."

"It would be in your best interest," Hawthorn said, "to back away and let us go."

The taller bird boy sneered. "Why would we do that when we could collect on the queen's reward?"

"Look," Fetch said. "We don't want any trouble, and that

wanted poster is all lies." He would much rather reason with these boys than fight them, and then there was the matter of escape. They were seated in the back corner, far from the exit.

Enero materialized in Hawthorn's hand and she tapped the glowing green spear across her palm. "We're going to get up now and walk out of here." Her words held a threat that didn't seem to bother the boys.

Dark wings sprouted from their backs, their edges burning with flickering embers.

Fetch's paws clenched. His chest ached with a familiar feeling of fear, of powerlessness. It was too late in the day to use magic, but he was desperate.

Besides, he was already wanted. What was one more crime?

"Boys!" Garzo sang, taking to the air. "Did you not read the part about this fox being cursed? He's got poison in his veins, and if it spills out, well, you'll be dead before you can even blink."

Fetch felt a dark cold spread through him. He reached for his magic. There—just at the edge of his grasp. So close. *PLEASE work*, he thought.

Yes, the voice whispered. *I can help you find your power.*

For a flicker of a moment, the room slipped out of focus. A low growl rose from deep in his chest.

Magic sparked and curled in Fetch's toes. It coursed through his body, pulsing with urgency. He could feel the spool rising. His Zindero power buzzed in his skull.

There was an explosion of light and then—

Hundreds of bees—an entire horde—swarmed the boys. The pub swelled with panic.

"Run!" Fetch hollered.

He and his friends bolted into the picturesque town, into the laughter and the light.

A roar charged up behind them. Fetch didn't slow down to look at who was chasing them, but he was pretty sure he'd never heard a bird roar.

Hawthorn streaked past in a rush of light. Her hand grabbed Fetch's paw, and before he knew it, she was whisking him along. His feet didn't even skim the snowy earth.

The town passed in a blur, soon giving way to a thick black forest up ahead.

As the wind howled and snow battered down, a purring sort of chuckle spun through the air.

Just as they rushed over the threshold into the dark woods, Fetch summoned a mud-colored thread.

Every step felt like it could be his last, yet there was no turning back now. He launched the thread over his shoulder.

The entrance to the forest closed with a *swish*.

They didn't stop running until the thread had stitched the forest completely closed and the storm that was the queen was far behind them, locked out of the dark woods.

But it wouldn't be long before her undead army found a way inside.

"How did you carry me like that?" Fetch asked Hawthorn, trying to catch his breath.

"Yes, that would have come in quite handy," Garzo put in, "when I was throwing myself in the middle of the road."

"I—I didn't know I could do that," Hawthorn said, looking pale. "It was all panic and instinct and, I don't know, maybe it's a dojee thing."

They trudged along until they came to a sloping mountain, scattered with tall pines that in the moonlight looked more blue than green.

A trick of the light? No. There was definitely a strange blue glow to the forest, made even eerier by the silence. An uneasy stillness that made it feel as though time had stopped.

Near the tree line, a half-burned cabin stood in the moonlit shadows, its windows broken and blackened.

"Looks like an old farm," Garzo said. "See the ruined wall over there with all those hooks spread out?"

"What kind of farm?" Fetch asked.

"Tree worms," Garzo said.

"The worms are large," Hawthorn explained, "like fat cats, and they hang from the branches in the spring. Their mucus can be poisonous."

"Slime is more accurate," Garzo said. "It grows on their skin and possesses magical qualities that can also be used for spells, ointments, and brews. It's quite a delicacy, though a bit salty for my taste. Of course, the wrong dosage will make you so deranged you claw out your own eyes."

Fetch took a deep breath. He suddenly felt exhausted. "We can build a shelter from that hay over there," he said.

While he and Hawthorn built a small enclosure, Garzo watched, shaking his head, telling them in no uncertain terms that no fairy would ever sleep in such a hovel.

"After you, Garzo," Fetch said, gesturing to the tiny entrance.

The fairy sniffed. "Have you heard nothing I said? You cannot expect me, Spy the Magnificent, to lay my head in such a—such a barnyard manner."

Hawthorn shrugged. "More room for me." And she crawled inside.

"Come on, Garzo," Fetch said, patting his friend's shoulder.

"Give me one good reason."

"You'll freeze to death out here."

"That might be better."

"And your beautiful wings might disintegrate."

With a snort, Garzo zipped into the shelter.

Fetch ducked inside and took an empty space near the entrance.

"Will Beck be able to find us here?" Hawthorn asked.

Fetch nodded while Garzo grumbled, "He'll always be able to find Fetch because the fox created him. And it's likely he can also find *me*. A travesty, I tell you."

Fetch hoped that Beck being gone for the last few hours didn't mean anything bad. But what if Garzo was right and the dragon really did like the dreamworld better and had decided to stay? Fetch pushed the fear aside. Beck was too loyal to leave him, of that he was certain. And, truth be told, he missed his dragon friend.

The fairy rolled from side to side. "This is so bumpy and prickly. I am accustomed to fine linens. A fire, some rose tea."

"Just pretend," Hawthorn suggested, wrapping her fur cape tighter around herself. "I've heard fairies have vivid imaginations."

"Not *that* vivid!"

Within minutes, Fetch's friends were snoring. As exhausted as he was, though, he couldn't sleep. The best remedy for sleeplessness had always been stitching, and Fetch's paws itched to create something with his magic.

Lorenzo had once told him, "The most powerful magic comes from love. Remember that."

Not wanting to wake the others, Fetch silently slipped out of the shelter. The air was cold, biting even, as he stood beneath a half-moon and hundreds of twinkling stars. Again, he wondered what was keeping Beck. The dragon had never been gone this long. Which reminded him.

He'd promised to make something to protect Beck.

By the light of the moon, Fetch shook out his furry arms, then reached into his coat pocket. As he did, he imagined Beck's big, round eyes, his wide smile, his floppy ears, the way he had so quickly and selflessly vowed to protect the fox. The way he had offered up his light without a second thought.

Fetch's skin tingled. His paws hummed. His tail swished across the snow.

A tug in his heart, like a string pulling tight.

Hope bloomed in his chest, radiating down his arms.

He kept going, too afraid to stop the blossoming magic.

So different from the power he'd felt back at the pub. There, his magic had expanded with a rush of cold darkness he'd never experienced before. Had it been panic? Fear? Or maybe his Zindero magic was weakening as Violet's stitches vanished.

He retrieved her hankie. Still eleven stitches. The tightness in his chest loosened a little.

He closed his eyes and brought Beck's face into view again. His magic was still rising gently, unhurriedly. His paws trembled, but he couldn't get impatient. He needed to stay focused.

A moment later, a spool of white thread floated out of Fetch's coat. A tiny orb of light.

Fetch reached again, calling up a shadow thread. A spool of black appeared in his paw. He tossed it into the air, dancing his arms up and down, back and forth, weaving the white thread with the dark.

Moments later, the orb's light blinked out, and before him on the snow was a black sock, one so thick, no one would be able to see those shimmering scales on Beck's tail.

With a wave of relief, he scooped it up. He felt a pull in his chest. An unease crept into his thoughts. Could he really protect Beck? Would his magic be enough?

He took a few breaths to clear his head, then he whispered silently, *Are you there?*

He expected the voice to ignore him like last time, but a dry sound like the rustling of leaves scraped across Fetch's bones.
Yes.
Who are you? he asked. *Why are you helping me?*
Do you want the truth?
The fur on the back of Fetch's neck stood on end. *Yes.*
Sleep, and I will show you.

Chapter Twenty-Two

Fetch crawled back into the shelter and curled up near the entrance, shivering with the memory of the voice: *Do you want the truth?* Fetch did, but in that moment, as he settled in to sleep, he wasn't so sure.

He closed his eyes. His heart pounded in his chest. *Thrumthrumthrum.*

After several fitful moments, he began to sink, deeper and deeper, until finally he was in a dream.

He stood at the edge of a snowy forest. A group of swallows descended onto a ruined half wall shrouded in mist. The sun was a cold white sphere.

Fetch felt peculiar. Smaller.

He glanced down to find that he was standing on four furry legs just as a growl sounded from the dark woods behind him.

Startled, he took off running, across the snowy mounds, between the tightly woven trees. He leaped over boulders, darting through the shadows.

The rush of the cold air, the speed and agility of this fox form, made him feel wild and free.

He sprang over a fallen branch, soaring up, up, through the air—

In the next breath he was inside his workroom.

A candle burned in the corner, where he saw himself at his sewing table, bent over working on something, but from this vantage point he couldn't see what.

The walls shimmered, shifted, and rolled, and for a blink, Fetch thought he saw a flickering ghostly image—bars. No, a cage.

The mirage vanished as that same voice came to him, deep and resounding. *The road is long and perilous.*

"Who are you?" Fetch asked again as he crept over to the worktable to get a better look.

You cannot succeed without me.

Fetch watched as his dream self pulled a needle through Violet's handkerchief, mending the crooked heart. But with each thread he stitched, another one vanished.

"Who are you?" Fetch asked again.

You know who I am.

"All I know is that you helped me back in the forest," Fetch said. "You told me to wait for the moonlight."

You have kept me alive, the being said. *For that I am grateful.*

"I have?"

Unite with me. I can make you strong again.

"Like at the pub?" Fetch remembered the way cold power had coursed through him, how easily he had stitched the forest closed.

He exhaled slowly, feeling the tension coil tighter in his chest. "What do you want in return?" he asked.

When the time comes—when I command it—you must release me.

Fetch's pulse quickened at the words. Release? Did that mean this being was some kind of prisoner? "You said I know who you are," Fetch said. "But I don't."

A dreadful silence fell over the room.

I am the Malvada.

Terror struck Fetch. How could the Malvada, that wicked creature, be inside him? "But Esme killed you!"

She only weakened me. I followed you to your world, to be given a chance. To live.

"I'd never help you!" Fetch growled.

Even if it meant saving Violet?

Fetch went cold all over.

Instantly, a great gust of wind swept through the room. Sticky threads flew out of the wall, twisting and coiling. Fetch jumped back just as a massive black widow appeared out of nowhere.

The spider drew herself up, glaring down at Fetch with yellow-slitted eyes. The red hourglass mark on her shiny black abdomen pulsed like a beating heart. This no longer felt like a dream.

"I am your queen," she seethed. "How dare you not bow before me?"

Queen? Fetch's pulse flared as a dreadful buzzing began under his skin, tugging, pulling. His knees began to bend involuntarily. He buckled to the floor as the edges of his vision blurred.

The winter queen began to weave a web around the fox, thick and putrid-smelling. "If you do not end this futile search, your sister will pay the price."

Decide, the Malvada said again. *Before it's too late.*

An image materialized, of a grimy dark dungeon. Violet was hunched with her face in the corner, shivering. Her red hair was knotted, spilling down her back. "Fetch," she whispered.

"Violet?" He wanted to run to her, to sweep her up and keep her safe.

"Do you see?" the queen said. "*You* did this to her."

"No!" Fetch screamed.

He struggled against the sticky threads as they wrapped around him tighter and tighter, squeezing his chest, gripping his throat.

She took everything from you, the Malvada whispered. *She took your sister.*

"I'm going to rescue her!" Fetch shouted.

The queen said, "Come and try. Let us see how this game is played, Fox."

A wicked hunger twisted Fetch's heart as unspent rage made his blood run hot.

His magic surged.

Fetch sprang to his feet, bursting through the web. Then, with razor-sharp claws, he slashed the spider's belly, drawing blood. The queen shrieked, recoiling. Her red, throbbing hourglass withered.

Do you see how powerful you can be? You need only say yes, the Malvada whispered. *And we will defeat the winter queen and save your sister together.*

Fetch couldn't think, he couldn't reason, not with that hot liquid anger boiling inside his veins. "You'll make me more powerful?" he asked.

Even the queen will not be able to defeat you.

"But if I release you, you'll hurt people." Fetch remembered the last time the Malvada had been free—the havoc it had wreaked, the witch it had possessed. He could never agree to that kind of violence.

The Malvada spoke softly. *I have no intention of hurting anyone. I merely want to taste freedom and in exchange I will deliver you your precious sister. You have my word.*

Desperation and dread filled Fetch's heart. He'd vowed to do anything, risk everything to save his sister. But this, this was . . .

The black widow shrieked.

You need only say yes, the Malvada said gently. *But this is your last chance. I will not make this offer again.*

The spider charged.

"Yes," Fetch whispered.

The spider queen broke herself against Fetch like a wave against rocks.

And just as she vanished, he felt a swell of unimaginable power.

Malvada

How easy it was to deceive the fox. He believed my lies about only wanting to be free. And to think all I had to do was impersonate the queen to motivate him.

But his sister—how had she forced herself into the dream? How had she called out to her brother?

The memory of it shook the Malvada, but only for a moment.

It matters not, for soon enough, the fox will give me full control.

And when I command him to let me go, he will fulfill his promise to me, I will take the queen, body and soul, and my power will have no end.

Chapter Twenty-Three

Fetch floated in that place between dreams and reality. Tendrils of cold wrapped around his body, an oddly comforting feeling that confused him. He leaned into the chill, feeling stronger, more alive.

Even the queen will not be able to defeat you.

Fetch woke up in the snow, a good twenty feet from the shelter. Beck was perched on his chest, fanning him with his tiny wings.

Glazed sunlight slipped through the thin pale clouds.

Hawthorn stood over the fox while Garzo flitted about, looking frazzled.

"Why are you out here?" she asked with a scowl.

Beck took to the air, looking more frantic by the second.

"You could have frozen to death! I tried to wrap my tail around you but it's not very warm."

Fetch stood and rubbed his throbbing head. "I . . . I must have been sleepwalking." The image of Violet shivering in that horrid dungeon played across his memory. He'd done the unthinkable. He'd joined forces with the Malvada. But what choice had he had? The queen was on the hunt, she would strike Violet down to punish Fetch—but now he had a secret weapon. The Malvada had promised to help him rescue his sister. That's all that mattered now.

"Uh, Fetch?" Beck said, his gaze locked on Fetch's paws.

Fetch glanced down and gasped.

Hawthorn drew closer. "Why are your paws black?"

Swiftly, Fetch rolled up his coat sleeve to reveal that the fur on his arms was thankfully still golden red. "I don't know!" he replied, but that was a lie. The black fur had to have something to do with his dream, but he couldn't bring himself to tell them about it. About the choice he'd made.

"Maybe it's an allergy." Beck flew in front of the fox's face, examining him. His tail whipped wildly. But all Fetch could focus on was the Malvada's words.

When the time comes—when I command it—you must release me.

But doubt niggled at Fetch. What would happen when he released the Malvada? He didn't even want to think about what the Malvada's plans were. He'd use the strength given to him to rescue Violet and then, when the time came, he'd deal with the monster.

"This is a terrible omen," Garzo cried. "Worse than terrible. Dreadful!"

"What kind of omen?" Fetch asked Garzo, hoping this was just another one of the fairy's dramatic outbursts.

"How should I know?" Garzo huffed. "Do I look like a fortune teller?"

Hawthorn folded her arms across her chest. "Then why did you say it?"

"Oh, I don't know." Garzo's tone was mocking. "Maybe because blackened limbs can't be a sign of anything good." He went over to a wood pile and—*zap*. Lightning flew from his fingertips, igniting the wood. "Yes, much better," he said, adjusting his power vest. "Now go ahead, Beck. Tell Fetch the awful truth."

Hawthorn shot the fairy a murderous glare as Beck flew onto her shoulder and folded his wings against his small body.

"What is it?" Fetch asked. "Did you dream something important? Was that why you were gone for so long?"

Beck took a shaky breath. "Violet was in a dark, cold place. She looked frail, and I felt like I needed to stay with her, and . . ."

Fetch went cold all over. He'd seen the same horrible thing. "And what?" he asked.

"The stitches in Violet's handkerchief," Beck said, "they

were looping back and forth, disappearing one, two at a time."

Fetch fumbled in his pocket, removing Violet's hankie. He braced himself to see that another stitch had vanished.

The moment he unfolded the cloth, his heart went stone-cold. With a shaky paw, Fetch held up his sister's handkerchief for the others to see.

One stitch hadn't vanished.

"Four stitches," he breathed in disbelief. "Gone overnight."

Chapter Twenty-Four

Garzo looked from dragon to fox to girl in confusion. "Why do any of you care about missing thread?"

Hawthorn explained to the fairy, beginning with Violet using the enchanted thread to protect her heart. Fetch added what Sabía had told him about how Violet had tied her heart to his, how he had set the spell in motion and now his memories and Zindero magic were also at risk.

Garzo puffed up his cheeks and blew out a long breath. "Oof. That's unlucky indeed."

Fetch regarded his friends and their worn faces. He felt terrible, like the vile deceiver he was. Still, he couldn't bring himself to tell them about his dream, or the agreement he'd made with the Malvada.

"Look," he said, "I know I created Beck to go with me on this journey, but I see now how selfish that was. And it would be even more selfish if I let any of you continue. This is my battle to fight. You shouldn't risk your lives for me."

Hawthorn huffed. "Hardly, Fox. I'm here for my own reasons, remember?"

Fetch studied her. She had risked her life to save Beck's, and as tough as her facade was, Fetch knew there was so much more to her than what she had revealed. Never mind all the secrets she was keeping. Like why she had lied to the tree spirit, and why she wanted to get to the palace so badly if it wasn't to discover the truth about her family.

Beck floated in front of Fetch, flapping his wings. "I'll never leave you. Even if you want me to. I took a vow."

Fetch patted the dragon's head, then with a shiver, said, "We're down to seven stitches."

"And the festival is eight days away," Hawthorn said, "so we have to hope that—"

"Three more don't vanish tonight," Garzo put in.

"You're right," Fetch said, not even wanting to consider the wretched possibility. "There's no rhyme or reason to this, nothing to stop all the stitches from disappearing tomorrow morning. And then Violet's heart—my heart—will be lost forever."

It was a dreadful dilemma—if Fetch continued his search for his sister, he knew the queen would make good on her promises to make Violet suffer, and to kill Fetch. But if he stopped searching, his and Violet's hearts, their memories and

Zindero magic, would be lost.

But he had the Malvada on his side now. He'd use it to his and Violet's advantage.

Hawthorn said, "Beck, tell him the rest of your dream, about what Violet was stitching."

The dragon blinked his big eyes. "It's why I was gone so long. I wanted to be sure I was correctly reading what she stitched."

"Which was?" Fetch asked.

"*Festival* and *dojee*."

Garzo scowled. "Why would she stitch something so nonsensical?"

Fetch felt as if the ground had fallen out beneath his feet. "Violet loves the dojees," he said. "They're her favorite creatures in the entire realm."

"So?" Hawthorn asked.

"So if she was trying to send a message about them," Fetch said, piecing it all together as he spoke, "it must have been really important, and I think—I think she'd only do that if she was trying to protect them."

"From what?" Beck asked.

"The trap," Fetch said. Then his memory landed on the words Violet had stitched, *festival* and *dojee*. He sucked in a sharp breath. "That's it! The trap at the festival—"

"We've established that, thanks to my sleuthing," Garzo grumbled.

"But now we know who it's for!" Fetch said.

All the color drained from Hawthorn's face. "The dojees."

"A wild guess," Garzo said.

No. The one thing Fetch did know was Violet's heart. "This is something she would do," he went on. "Instead of sending a message to save herself, she'd send a message to save the dojees." A sad smile tugged at his mouth.

"Sabía said the trap was for someone mighty," Beck said, "and the dojees are very mighty!"

"Let's say you're right, Fetch," Hawthorn said. "Why would the queen need to trap the dojees when they already serve her?"

"I daresay I agree with the girl, Fetch," Garzo said with a quirked eyebrow. "Your logic seems very flawed."

"What if he's right, though?" Hawthorn asked Garzo. "Then we have to warn them."

"But we're so close to the Silver Drum!" Fetch desperately needed to talk to Lorenzo. He had to stay the course. His tail thrashed wildly beneath his coat as he began to pace.

An idea sparked.

He turned to the fairy. "You're a magnificent spy. Maybe you can find out why the queen would set a trap for already-loyal subjects."

"You want me to commit treason?" Garzo's cheeks reddened. "And risk my beautiful head, my handsome wings?"

Fetch inhaled slowly. "Garzo, there is no one else."

Garzo's face bloomed red. Then he seized his chest. "OW!" He reached into his vest and flung something silver onto the snowy ground.

An envelope with Garzo's name inked across the fine linen paper alongside the queen's seal.

It was an invitation to the Winter Festival.

Chapter Twenty-Five

Fetch scooped up the envelope. "Why didn't you tell me about this before now?"

"Because I was rather busy saving you from the gwitches," Garzo snapped. "And besides, I didn't want this invitation once I learned of the trap. I haven't even opened it, thinking if I ignore it, perhaps it will all go away."

"It's not going away." Fetch broke the seal and opened the envelope. A white moth burst out, chiding, "It's about time. I've been pressed into that envelope for more than a day. What took you so long?"

"You bit me!" Garzo hollered.

The milky-eyed moth flitted about, stretching her powdery wings as the snow continued to fall. "I am a moth messenger," she said, "and you have been summoned to the Winter Festival."

"Summoned?" Garzo squeaked out.

"So not an invitation," Hawthorn muttered.

"An honor and privilege." The moth paused. "What's the next line? Oh, yes. You will feast and dance. Velvet, fur, feathers, and leather are acceptable attire. Absolutely no polyester or cotton. My duty is complete. No questions allowed. Ta-ta."

"Wait!" Fetch said. "There's nothing in here to tell us what time or—"

"I AM THE SUMMONING!" the moth shouted. "Must I repeat the details? No, I shall not."

"You never gave us any details," Beck said, staring inside the envelope.

The moth narrowed her white eyes. "Did you not hear me when I said that you shall arrive at seven p.m. sharp two days hence? If you do not arrive at the appointed time, the queen will have your head."

"Two days?" Garzo snapped. "What happened to eight days?"

"The queen has changed her plans, which is her prerogative because she wears the crown. No more questions." With that, the moth vanished into the snowy air.

"Two days?" Fetch couldn't believe his luck. He nearly leaped into the air. "This is remarkable, the best news!"

"That I have been summoned by the queen into a trap?" Garzo moaned.

"We've been given a gift of time," Fetch explained.

"But the dojees have not," Hawthorn said.

"You'll be hailed a hero," Beck told the fairy. "Imagine if the information you obtain saves the majestic dojees."

Fetch had a feeling it was even bigger than that. All this—the trap, the change of dates, the limited magic—it was all connected, but how?

Garzo huffed. His violet eyes narrowed. "Very well."

"But you need to hurry," Fetch reminded him.

"Spying is precise," Garzo said. "It will take the time it takes."

After a quick breakfast of biscuits, honey, and boysenbark jam, Fetch and his friends ventured into the woodlands.

With each step, the air grew colder, the path steeper, and the forest darker.

Why would the festival date be changed? Fetch wondered. *Could it have something to do with the trap?*

As Hawthorn trudged ahead, Fetch reached into his coat and removed the sock he'd sewn for Beck. "I have something for you."

Quickly, he slipped the sock onto Beck's tail. It was a bit crooked, and tighter than he'd expected. "Did your tail grow?" he asked.

"I'm always growing!" Beck stared at the black covering. "You want to conceal my light?"

"I'm sorry," Fetch said. "But your scales will tell the world you're a dream dragon, and there are evil creatures who would steal them from you."

Beck thought about this a moment, then his face brightened. "They'd have to catch me first, and I'm very fast, as you know." He zipped around Fetch's head to prove his point.

"I know you are." Fetch patted Beck's back. "It's just a precaution."

"But what if you need my light when it gets dark?" Beck asked. "So you can use magic safely?"

Fetch hadn't thought that far. "I guess we can take it off if we need to."

"It's rather itchy," Beck said, waving his tail. It had definitely gotten longer.

Hawthorn stopped up ahead, signaling with a raised fist for everyone to halt. Then, pointing, she asked in a low voice, "What. Is. That?"

Fetch followed her gaze to a transparent, slime-coated cocoon dangling from a branch. Inside was plump white worm shifting and writhing. In the center of its head was a single eyelid. The eyeball behind it roved back and forth.

"It smells like earwax," Beck said, inching closer.

"Let's not wake it," Fetch said.

Beck yawned, then—*poof*—he vanished.

The dreamworld had called the dragon, which meant a message was coming. Which really meant a *warning* was coming. What if Beck learned about the Malvada?

Cold fear expanded in Fetch's chest as he and Hawthorn moved farther into the darkness. With each step he couldn't help thinking about his grandfather's warning to Hawthorn:

on the day you two meet, you will begin a dark march toward death.

Hawthorn glanced over her shoulder at Fetch and whispered, "Why do I have the feeling these worms are not entirely asleep? Like maybe they're watching us?"

A pale gray light pulsed up ahead. There was a hum to it that made Fetch's whiskers twitch. A tightness spread across his shoulders. The trees quaked even in the still, cold air.

Just in case the worms busted out of their sacks, Fetch wanted to be ready. He reached into his coat, calling up the sleeping thread.

His magic pulsed through him, so faintly at first that he thought it might fail him, but then it grew, increasing with a surge of immense power, one he knew came from his union with the Malvada.

Doubt and fear pulsed at his temples, but the deal had already been struck. He couldn't waste time worrying about it now. Especially not when his magic flowed so easily, vibrating in his dark paws as the spool floated up into the fox's grasp.

The path grew steeper as the light ahead glowed eerily, illuminating dozens more cocoons dangling from knobby branches.

Slime dripped slowly into thick, mucusy pools below them. *Shlerp, shlerp.*

"Watch where you step," Fetch said as they hop-skipped their way around the expanding puddles of slime, which glowed sickly gray.

Hawthorn stopped dead. "Fetch."

He followed her gaze to a few human skulls poking out of the snow. The sack above him began to swing as the worm inside squirmed restlessly.

"I think they know we're here," Hawthorn said. "And I really don't want to add to their little bone garden."

Fetch was just nodding his agreement when the worm opened its enormous gray eye.

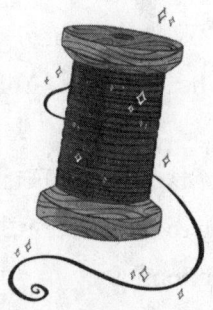

Chapter Twenty-Six

Before Fetch could even blink, the worm's tail whipped out of the sack and coiled around Hawthorn.

Fetch lunged, but he was stopped in his tracks by a pool of sizzling slime that quickly encircled his feet.

"One wrong move, and my slime will swallow you whole," the worm said. Her voice sounded young but threatening. "Just look around at our bone graveyard. Not a pleasant way to perish."

"Release me!" Hawthorn demanded.

"Or what?" the worm asked. "You are no match for my slime. Slowly it will penetrate your skin and scorch your blood until it boils, and eventually your eyes will pop out of your head. Which will be grisly, yet quite entertaining . . . well, for us, at least."

"Let. Her. Go," Fetch growled.

Enero's spear appeared in Hawthorn's grasp. This only made the worm chuckle. "Stab me," she said, "and poison will rain down on you like a great storm."

"Please," Fetch said. "We only want to get through the woods."

The worm blinked her gray eye. "You do not want passage through these woods."

"We need to get to Mammoth," Fetch said.

"Mammoth is the wrong direction," the worm said. "It is always the wrong direction."

Another nearby sack began to glow brighter. The worm inside opened its eye. "Sister," he said, "who disturbs our sleep?"

"These fools want to go to Mammoth."

"That is forbidden," the other said. "No one goes to Mammoth without an invitation, unless they have a death wish."

Heart racing, Fetch held his paws up. "Let us go and—"

"You bear the mark." The worm's gray eye, fixed on Fetch's black paws, widened. Her upper body snaked out of her cocoon, growing longer and longer as she reached him.

The other worm stretched his body, winding through the air like a snake before he stopped next to his sister. "Effie, what are you whispering about?"

Effie gestured to Fetch's paws. "We should slime him now, Archie. Extract him *and* his mark from this world."

"His mark?" Archie's gaze lingered on Fetch's paw. "Is that ink? An allergy? Ew, gross—it's not a weird rash, is it?"

"No, you fool," Effie scolded. "He's been touched by darkness."

"Well, if you're so smart, what *kind* of darkness?"

Effie huffed. "Is there more than one kind? Dark is dark. Evil. You know, something very bad!"

"So you don't know specifically."

"What are you all talking about over there?" Hawthorn asked.

Fetch was in full panic mode. If these worms really did know what the mark was, the last thing he needed was to explain to Hawthorn how he'd made a deal with some kind of dark being.

As the two worms laughed, slime dripping from their mouths, Fetch saw his chance. He reached into his coat and drew up a sleeping thread. His magic's vibration worked through him, twisting at his feet, coursing up his legs and body with an urgency that made his blood sing.

Then he realized Effie was still clinging to Hawthorn. If he used his magic on the worms, it would extend to the girl. Some of his slumbering spells lasted days—time he didn't have to waste.

Fetch threw a glance at Hawthorn, then, in a flash, he hurled a spool. For a blink he wondered if it would work, but then he felt the Malvada twist inside him, as if awakening to help the fox wield a more powerful magic. The thread unraveled in a swirl of light as it entwined around the worms, tying their heads together.

A stone of guilt dropped into Fetch's stomach. He'd enjoyed the darkness's strength. Did that make him evil too?

Instantly, the worms' heads rolled off their bodies and onto the ground with a sickening thud.

The decapitated heads stared up at Fetch, smiling. Their pointy teeth gleamed in the silvery light.

"That's just gross," Hawthorn muttered.

"You think you can defeat us, some of the oldest creatures in Ocho Manos?" Effie bellowed.

"Well, your heads *are* on the ground," Fetch said.

In the next breath, the headless worms stretched and writhed.

"They're growing new heads!" Hawthorn shouted, trying to break free of her captor's thrashing tail.

Archie rolled his new neck. "Much better. Now," he said, "prepare to drown in our slime, writhing in pain as the poison engulfs you."

"Please," Fetch said, hoping to appeal to their reason. "You're brother and sister. I have a sister too. She's trapped in Sterling, and I need to save her."

"We don't care about your sister!" Archie said. "Our duty is to keep you out of Mammoth."

"Your duty?" Hawthorn asked.

"Archie! You loose-lipped ninny!"

"I'm sorry," Archie said. "Words just pop out sometimes. It's this blasted chain, clutching my throat."

"Chain?" Fetch asked, looking closer, though he saw nothing. "You're . . . prisoners?" His mind whirred. He knew he couldn't force the worms to sleep without also dooming his friends to slumber as well, but he did have one more idea up his sleeve.

Careful not to make any sudden movements, and keeping his paws where the worms could see them, Fetch closed his eyes and summoned a truth thread.

"Hey," Archie said. "What are you doing? Did I say you could close your eyes?"

The lavender thread unraveled in Fetch's pocket. His pulse raced as he focused. Not an easy task when standing in a forest of murderous worms.

Then he felt the Malvada stir again. It was pleased—Fetch could feel it.

The lavender strand floated up, invisible as a spider's thread. It drifted unseen across the space and formed a tiny cloud of mist over Effie and Archie.

The worms went very still. They turned their one-eyed gazes to Fetch.

Effie blinked her eye. She looked dazed. "What have you done to us?"

"It's a truth thread," Fetch said, knowing the magic would only last a few minutes.

"Truth?" Hawthorn growled. "Let's get out of here!"

"Go ahead and try," Effie groaned. "It is a mile-long journey through our woods to Mammoth."

Archie snickered. "You'll never make it out before the slime rains down on you."

Fetch turned to the worms. If he could help them in some way, then maybe they'd let him and his friends pass. "Why are you prisoners?" he asked.

Effie struggled against the fox's magic, squirming as her mouth opened and closed. "The giants harvest our slime."

"That's dreadful," Fetch said.

Archie swayed hypnotically, clenching his mouth closed.

"Why do they harvest your slime?" Hawthorn asked.

Archie contorted his face into a pained expression. "You will suffer for this."

"Just answer the question," Hawthorn commanded.

"Our slime," Archie groaned, "provides valuable fuel for their boats, but is also used for its poison."

"Who do the giants want to poison?" Hawthorn asked.

"Their enemies," Effie said. "There is great danger on the horizon. We must be prepared."

"What kind of danger?" Fetch asked.

"We are not privy to such information," Archie said. "But it is danger with a capital *D*. That means very big!"

"The giants have many secrets," Effie offered.

Fetch tried a different tactic. "Why don't you use your slime against them?"

Effie said, "They are unaffected by our poison."

The mist began to evaporate. Fetch didn't have much more time. "Effie and Archie," he said. "What if we could set you free?"

"Why would you do that?" Hawthorn asked Fetch. "You heard them. Their slime will kill us."

"You cannot set us free." Effie grimaced. She glanced up at the vanishing mist. "There are invisible chains that keep us here."

"His magic is loosening," Archie whispered.

"But if we could free you," Fetch said, "would you let us through?"

Catching on, Hawthorn threw in, "I possess Enero's spear. I can cut through the chains."

The last of the mist vanished.

Archie slithered closer, his plump body floating before Fetch. "Prove you can free us."

Gripping the spear, Hawthorn took a deep breath. "The chains are around your throats?"

Effie nodded. "Do you have good aim?"

"The spear does," Hawthorn said.

"I don't trust that one bit," Archie said, "and if you miss, our slime will burn through you."

Fetch pulled Hawthorn to the side out of the worms' earshot. "Are you sure about this?"

"Not even close." She frowned as Beck landed on her shoulder. "I mean, the spear can't miss, but that doesn't mean there won't be some blood."

"Maybe just focus on the chains," Fetch suggested.

"In case you haven't noticed," Hawthorn said, "this spear didn't come with instructions."

"Magic is half instinct." Fetch was barely breathing. If Hawthorn missed by even a millimeter, they were goners.

"You lied!" Archie said. "You don't possess the power to free us. You don't even know how to use that spear."

Slime began to drip from the trees, faster and faster, each drop sizzling as it fell onto the snow, reeking of mold and dead things.

"Now would be a good time to toss that thing," Fetch said to Hawthorn.

Clenching her jaw, Hawthorn took a trembly breath. "Cut the worms' chains," she whispered. She launched the weapon.

It blazed like lightning through the air, and the world tilted around Fetch, blurry and distorted as if time had stopped.

The sound of clanking metal resounded through the woods, making the ground and the trees quiver. Skulls rolled. Branches snapped. Wind gusted.

Fetch thought about his little sister. About how there were so few things worth holding on to in this world, and then there was Violet.

The world sped up again and the next thing he heard was laughter.

He looked up. Effie and Archie were wriggling wildly across a tree branch, singing, "We are free!"

"It worked!" Hawthorn cheered. She had a nice smile, Fetch decided.

The spear continued to blaze through the woods, a great streak of white in search of more chains, slicing through sacks with precision. The slime dried instantly. Joyful cries echoed all around.

Within minutes, the spear had freed hundreds of worms. Every single one swung from their cocoons and burrowed into the snowy earth.

Effie floated over to the trio. "We shall let you pass now. But remember, the giants will devour you for this, so it would be in your best interest to turn back."

"We must find the Silver Drum!" Hawthorn said.

Fetch could tell the worms knew something by the way they glanced at each other. Archie said, "You'll never reach it."

The worms began to wiggle into the ground.

"Wait!" Fetch shouted. "Do you know where the drum is?"

As the dirt and snow covered the worms entirely, Effie's voice echoed back to them. "It is in the belly of Soledad, the loneliest giant."

Chapter Twenty-Seven

Hawthorn frowned. "Did that worm really just say the drum is in the belly of a giant? Why would it be in there?"

"More like *how* did it get in there," Fetch said. "Must be miserable."

Fetch looked up through the trees. The day's light was already fading. Another of Violet's stitches, or more, would vanish along with it. Fetch felt as if he was racing against some invisible clock that kept the wrong time. He could have days or hours before his and Violet's hearts were lost forever. "We have to hurry," he said.

Fetch had read the stories of Mammoth, and of how the giants were experts in cruelty, for they had the longest memories of any creature in Ocho Manos. Those memories were passed down from one generation to the next, making it impossible for them to forget how they had been spurned and tormented for their size.

That sort of thing twists hearts.

Of all the creatures of Ocho Manos, the giants were the most mysterious and the most adaptable. Many could fly, others possessed the magic of witches, and some were chameleon-like, blending into the world so perfectly they were impossible to see.

It reminded him of the giantess who had cut Esme's magical hair. Esme had been so brave, so willing to part with a piece of her magic. What he wouldn't give for her help now.

"Fetch?" Hawthorn's voice pulled him back.

"Yeah?"

"Maybe . . ." But she never finished expressing the doubt or fear she wore plainly on her face. She just marched ahead, and Fetch followed.

Stepping out from the protective shadows of the forest, they crested an icy hill.

The shore below was long and narrow, curving like the soft edge of a shell, and the bright purple sands shimmered even in the dull light. There were fishing boats larger than the biggest houses in Fetch's village, weathered wooden vessels that hugged a huge dock, which vanished around the edge of a craggy bluff.

Iron lampposts stood along the dock. Wind chimes hung

from each, but there wasn't even the slightest of breezes to create any music.

There was no sound, no activity at all.

"It's like a ghost town," Hawthorn whispered. "How will we find Soledad? And even if we do, how can we possibly retrieve the drum from her belly? We can't just slice her open."

"That's step two. First comes step one."

"Which is?" Hawthorn tapped her foot lightly.

"We're going to slip into Mammoth around that cliff."

"There's the itty-bitty problem of being noticed."

"Not if we're invisible."

The girl's mouth turned up ever so slightly.

He summoned a thread of invisibility from his coat.

The clear thread zigzagged across Fetch's paws, creating a delicate web. He danced his arms up and down, left and right, expanding the web wider and wider. The air sizzled with his Zindero magic. With the absolute perfection of it. He hated to admit the joy it brought him, especially because he knew this power came from the dark. And there was nothing joyful about *that*.

But he liked the boost of confidence it gave him.

When the fox had completed his intricate matrix, he floated it over them, pulling the last thread nice and tight to secure the magic. "It will only last an hour or so."

"Define *or so*," Hawthorn said.

"I don't really know how long it will last," Fetch admitted.

"The last time I used this, the magic wore off in fifteen minutes." *But that was before the Malvada.*

With a sigh, she added, "This would have come in handy in that worm netherworld."

"They would have smelled us."

"And the giants," Hawthorn said with a grin, "have terrible senses."

"Exactly."

"Well, just in case, you don't happen to have an invisible, unscented thread, do you?"

"I do not."

Hawthorn pressed her lips together, studying Fetch. "How come I can still see you?"

"Because you're under the web of magic. But don't worry, no one outside can see us."

Hawthorn nodded resolutely. "Let's go find this lonely giant."

The two ventured down the winding cliffside and onto the enormous dock. The wood planks creaked and groaned beneath their feet. The cold water below swelled and splashed.

Hawthorn threw her arm in front of Fetch, stopping him in his tracks. "Do you hear that?"

"What?"

"The march of ghosts," she panted.

Fetch's breath caught. "How do you know it's ghosts?"

"I can tell by the hollow echo of their boots."

Not exactly comforting, Fetch thought. "The Legión Inmortal."

They'd likely been hunting him since he'd stitched the forest closed. "How far are they?" he asked.

Hawthorn tilted her head to the side, listening. "Five miles. The good news is they don't walk very fast."

They raced along the dock.

"These boats are taller than the trees in Scarred Hollow," Hawthorn whispered as they passed.

"Look," Fetch said. "They have names painted on them."

"*Arson?*" Hawthorn wrinkled her nose. "What kind of name is that?"

"This one says *Petulant*," Fetch said, "and that one over there's *Ghoul's Breath*. You're right. Odd names for boats."

"Maybe they're named after the giants. Look for *Soledad*."

But after checking each vessel's peculiar name, there was none marked for the loneliest giant.

Fetch stopped cold. A huge pair of booted feet hung over the edge of a boat up ahead.

"Is he dead?" Hawthorn whispered.

"Or asleep."

A voice echoed, words slurring together as the giant sang a little tune, "Ho ho slippery splassssh, ain't no sssardines in the trassssh."

Hawthorn smirked. "Worst lyrics I've ever heard."

"I think he's drunk."

"Still the worst lyrics."

They slipped past and quickly made their way around the cliff's bend.

Before them lay a town of colossal homes and other structures all built from shimmering purple sand, and the pitched roofs were made of seashell scraps.

"I hate to say it," Hawthorn said, "but it's—"

"Purple?"

"I was going to say pretty."

They hurried down the path, landing at a tall sand archway. A towering tree with pale green leaves and a skinny white trunk stood to the side of the entrance, its crown reaching into the clouds.

The entrance to Mammoth was stamped with the words, GIANT BLOOD ONLY.

Then, in smaller script, OR PERISH.

"Nice welcome sign," Hawthorn said.

"I don't think it's meant to be welcoming."

"Sabía told me that, eons ago, giants used to be the friendliest creatures in the realm," Hawthorn said, "but then there was a great war, and the giants were tricked by one of the queens and imprisoned."

"Yeah, my grandfather said they made some kind of agreement and were set free, but people were afraid of them."

"You mean their power."

Fetch nodded. "I guess all those years of being so mistreated made them untrusting."

For a moment Hawthorn was silent, then she said softly, "Why are people always so afraid of things they don't understand?"

Fetch shrugged. Fear was a trickster, one that fed you lies and dragged you into dark places.

"The undead are getting closer," she said as she walked over to the tree, pressed a hand to it, and closed her eyes.

"What's it saying?" Fetch asked, hoping it was something good, something more welcoming than that sign.

"Shhh." Hawthorn's lips began to move as she spoke her tree language, hard vowels that sounded as if they were stuck in the back of her throat followed by soft phrases on the tip of her tongue.

A minute later, she opened her eyes.

"Well?" Fetch asked.

"The tree said we should leave," Hawthorn said. "And that we should never come back because there are secrets here that it described as . . ." She paused, recollecting. "Oh, right, having sharp teeth and even sharper claws. *Deadly* secrets."

"Well, did you explain that we need to find Soledad?"

Hawthorn rolled her eyes. "Yes, Fetch. Of course I did. The tree said that Soledad is ancient and hasn't been seen in many years."

"Does the tree know where to find her?"

"Didn't you hear the part about her not being seen?" Hawthorn asked. "Soledad obviously doesn't want to be found, but the tree did say it would ask around."

Fetch's ears twitched with frustration. "Ask around?"

"Trees have a very sophisticated root system that allows them to communicate with other trees."

"How long is that going to take?"

She summoned Enero and began to twirl the weapon. "I'm kind of liking this thing."

"Hawthorn."

With a sigh, she vanished the spear. "It shouldn't be long. But I hope it's quick—the ghosts are closing in."

The waiting felt endless. Each second that passed was another step the undead army took toward Fetch.

Hawthorn said, "Maybe Soledad is a prisoner."

Fetch looked across the massive town that went on as far as his eyes could see. He had no idea where to begin. "An ancient giant unseen in many years," he uttered, thinking aloud. He shook his head. "So that probably means Soledad isn't in town."

"Why?"

"She would have been seen by now, right?"

Hawthorn frowned. "Are you saying we came to Mammoth for nothing?"

"I'm saying she won't be anywhere obvious."

Fetch's ears pricked. The sound of hollow footsteps echoed across the land, causing the tree's branches to tremble. A leaf fell to the ground. Hawthorn leaned into the trunk once more. With her head tilted to the side, she listened, then she nodded and spoke a brief sentence before turning back to Fetch. "Apparently, the giants will be asleep for the next fifteen minutes. It's their siesta time."

Fetch's heart pounded like a giant fist. "Did it say anything about Soledad?"

She nodded. "We need to go to the Cave of Always."

"That's where Soledad is?"

"That's where she was last seen."

Fetch's fur bristled and his pulse raced. "Did the tree tell you where to find this cave?"

"You were actually right," Hawthorn said. She started shimmying up the arch like a sea crab. "We need a better view."

Fetch scrambled up behind her. "I was right about what?" he asked.

"The tree said to look beyond beyond beyond. Which means you're right—Soledad isn't in town."

Fetch readjusted the invisibility thread over them. From where he stood, he took in Mammoth: the crowded sand structures, the winding stone roads, and the utter silence, except for a pair of window shutters banging in the breeze. And the echoing footsteps of the undead.

"I hope these giants are heavy sleepers," Hawthorn said as a thick mist curled at the far edge of town, making it impossible to see *beyond*.

Summoning her spear again, she asked, "You think this can cut through that fog?"

"Garzo did say it can cut through any element, so . . ."

She launched Enero. A trail of green light blazed across the town.

At the same moment, Beck tumbled out of his dreamworld and onto Fetch's shoulder. The dragon was panting and clutching his chest. "Oh, thank goodness," he said, collapsing against Fetch's neck. "I got to you in time."

"In time for what?" the fox asked.

"In my dream..." Wheeze. "...you were..." Gasp. "...flying."

Hawthorn twisted her mouth. "That didn't work out so well last time."

That was before the Malvada, Fetch thought.

"Beck," Fetch said, "what else did you read in your dream?"

"You were flying toward the Cave of Always." Beck's expression looked suddenly remorseful. "But you didn't get there."

"Why not?" Fetch asked. "Did an undead soldier get me?"

"No. A giant did."

Fetch's insides twisted. He glanced over his shoulder to find a chilling sight, three undead soldiers marching closer, led by Ernesh. His long white hair fell around his gray face like cobwebs. "We have to go *now*," he said.

"You said we're invisible," Hawthorn argued.

"Can't take any chances," Fetch said.

Hawthorn looked over the rooftops of Mammoth. "Look," she said, pointing at a dimming green light. "The fog—it's parting."

Fetch quickly beckoned a locator thread. The pink spool floated out of his coat and unraveled slowly, looping back and forth. "Where's the Cave of Always?" he asked.

The thread zipped away, whizzing above Mammoth.

Instantly, the ground began to tremble. Thick, stony-looking clouds raced across the sky.

Voices boomed. "Who awakens us?"

The hollow footsteps of the undead pounded.

"Fetch!" Beck cried. "You must go now!"

"You just said we'll get caught," Hawthorn grumbled.

The dream dragon hovered before them, his eyes wide as spoons. "That's the point."

"That makes no sense," Fetch said, his panic growing as more ruckus resounded from the road behind them.

Beck's wings flapped furiously. "The giant who catches you—she has a key to the cave."

A wave of heat rose up Fetch's neck. He began to wrap the girl in his coat when she stepped back and said, "You expect me to trust the coat that nearly slammed you into a tree?"

"Or trust *me*," Fetch said.

"It's okay," Beck told Hawthorn. "In my dream he didn't drop you."

"Oh, well, that's reassuring," she muttered.

"There is one last bit of my dream, but perhaps I shouldn't tell you in this moment of panic . . . and also because the image wasn't entirely clear."

"Tell me!" Fetch insisted.

"There was so much darkness—it was all around you like a shadow, a shadow that breathed though there was no face." Beck's expression sagged. "Please, Fetch. Be careful."

The fox's heart sank deeper than the sea. He gave a firm nod, then, holding on to Hawthorn, he leaped into the air.

His magical coat fluttered in the breeze as he floated up, over the quaking town and the ever-booming giants. Higher and higher they glided, smoothly, easily. Fetch felt a well of satisfaction as they pursued the pink thread that zipped straight ahead beyond the fog and toward the rolling white hills made of rocks.

The air shifted.

Hawthorn shivered as thick snow began to fall, blurring Fetch's vision. He couldn't lose his way now, not when they were so close!

Malvada, are you there?

Keep your eyes on the locator thread!

Fetch blinked furiously.

But then the thread snapped in two, as if something or someone had broken it.

A harsh sound filled the air, like the jangling of keys.

Fetch glanced down.

Just as a giant hand ripped him and Hawthorn from the sky.

Chapter Twenty-Eight

Fetch was instantly consumed by darkness.

Something sharp gripped his waist.

Blood roared in his head.

Hawthorn. Where was she?

Lightning flashed, cutting through the blackness.

The fox caught a glimpse of a tattered dress, of long wild black hair, both blowing in the frigid wind. He blinked, glancing down at the birdlike claws clutching him.

In the next flash of light, he saw Hawthorn dangling like a rag doll in the beast's other claw.

The darkness wrapped around him tighter now. Exhaustion seeped in.

Fetch struggled to keep his eyes open.

The fox was so tired. His limbs were so heavy.

His last thought before he closed his eyes was *I hope Beck's right*.

Fetch dreamed.

Fragmented images, puzzle pieces that didn't connect: a jar of honey, golden in the afternoon light, motes of dust floating onto his bed, his grandfather's worn hands weaving magic, and Violet—her narrow chin, the birthmark right below it in the shape of a four-leaf clover.

The queen's spider face loomed before him, her golden eyes narrowed.

Her red hourglass pulsed. *Thump. Thump. Thump.*

Fetch woke hazily in a small stone chamber. He was upright, his back pressed against a cold wall.

Torch flames flickered. Long shadows crept and curled.

He turned to find a dojee slumped against the wall. A sleeping black bear with glossy fur that shone brighter than starlight.

Hawthorn.

For a blink he was transfixed. She looked so peaceful. Then he remembered what Garzo had said about how her transformation could lead the other dojees right to her. He couldn't let her be found out.

"Hawthorn," he whispered.

She didn't move.

Something cut into his wrists. He glanced down, expecting to see shackles, but there was nothing there. Yet his arms were bound by something—some kind of invisible force.

A terrible cold surged up the fox's throat. "Hawthorn," he said, more forcefully this time.

She stirred. Her green eyes held his with such calm.

"You have to change back!" he said, hoping she could.

His words acted like a spell. In the next breath she blinked, as if coming to her full senses. She glanced down at her dojee form, then back at Fetch. Then, with a long inhale, she closed her eyes and shifted into her regular self. Fetch thought her first words might be a thank-you, but this was Hawthorn after all. "You said I could trust you," she said.

"This was the plan," Fetch whispered, aiming for optimism but hitting all the wrong notes. "Do you know why you shifted?"

"No idea," she said. "But, Fetch, when I was looking at you just now, I—" She shook her head, then tried to move her arms. "What the—"

"I think there's some invisible spell pinning us in place."

She shot him a glare. "Beckblade better be right about this." Then, scanning the gloomy space, she added, "Where are we? How long have we been asleep?"

A ripple of fear snaked down Fetch's spine. He had no idea how much time they'd lost. A hot, sickly feeling gathered in his stomach. Was it already dark? Had more of Violet's stitches vanished? Last count was seven, but what if he was down to four or three or even one?

"Fetch, listen to me."

"Okay." His heart thudded in his ears so loud that Hawthorn's words sounded like they were in a vault a million miles under the ocean.

"Just now, when I was a dojee and I was looking into your eyes, I saw something."

"The future?" Maybe she had oracle powers after all. Oh no! Had she seen the Malvada lurking inside him?

"I saw what you should do," she said. "What the next step should be."

"Yeah, get the Silver Drum. Can you cut through whatever is holding us prisoner?" Fetch asked, suddenly wishing he had asked for more direction from Beck. And speaking of the dragon, where was he? Had the Legión Inmortal caught him?

The thought sent Fetch's heart drumming against his ribs.

Hawthorn tried to move, to access her spear. "It's not working."

"That's because you're bound with magical chains," a woman's voice said.

The wall's flickering shadows began to take shape, long and lean, peeling themselves from the stone until a giantess emerged.

She was at least ten feet tall, gaunt, with paper-thin skin that exposed her thick green and purple veins. Around her waist was a low-slung belt carrying rusted skeleton keys of various sizes.

Fetch remembered Beck's words: *She has a key to the cave.*

Okay, so far so . . . well, not good, but at least according to plan.

The woman looked eerily familiar, but her face was cast in a wedge of shadow so the fox couldn't quite see.

In the next blink, she stepped more fully into the light.

Fetch startled. It was the same giantess who had stolen Esme's hair for its magical flowers back at the gate to Ocho Manos. The white roses, still perfectly preserved, were tied to a thin rope that dangled from the woman's neck.

Fetch couldn't believe his good fortune. "Esme," he whispered under his breath, hoping against hope that somehow there was still a bit of his friend's magic left in those flowers.

One petal just isn't enough, Esme had said in his dream before she'd faded away.

And now here he was, staring down at least twelve of her magical flowers. Twelve!

Thankfully, the giantess hadn't seen him that day, so she'd never make the connection.

"Who are you?" Hawthorn asked. Her voice was like a taut thread, close to snapping.

Hold your temper, Fetch thought. *Please.*

"The better question," the giantess said, "is why were you invading *my* airspace?"

Fetch cleared his throat, never taking his eyes off the keys. Which one opened the Cave of Always? There had to be at least three dozen of various shapes and sizes. "Uh . . . we're looking for Soledad," he said, thinking that honesty was best in a situation like this when you're imprisoned by magic and a giantess with the key (quite literally) to your future is standing a few feet away.

The woman cackled. "The dead have nothing to offer the living."

A wicked cold gripped Fetch.

"Do you know how many have tried to find the Silver Drum?" the giantess asked. "Hundreds. Thousands. And even those who managed to get their hands on it were worthless souls who soon learned that a failed attempt equaled death."

Death? Sabía hadn't said anything about that. Well, other than the journey to the drum being death-defying, hence the worms and the giants. *You must be worthy enough to play it.*

So if Fetch wasn't judged worthy, he'd die? What if the deal with the Malvada somehow influenced his worthiness? What if the drum sensed the darkness pulsing inside him?

Even if he did think his heart was worthy, he was the one who'd let Violet out of his sight. He was the one who put all this in motion when he used that discovery spell. And now his sister's life, her heart, and his were at risk of being lost forever.

"Who decides?" Fetch asked. "I mean, who decides who's worthy?"

"And who does the killing?" Hawthorn threw in matter-of-factly, as if they weren't talking about Fetch's head.

"No idea about the killing," the giantess said. "But I do

know that you cannot use the drum for personal gain, or to hurt someone else, or . . ." She paused, glanced up. "What was the last rule?" the giantess mumbled. "Oh, yes! You must only use the drum in the direst of circumstances and with the purest of hearts."

"Maybe this is the march toward death that Lorenzo meant," Hawthorn whispered to Fetch.

No. Fetch had not come all this way just to have some lonely giant kill him.

"What did you tell him?" the giantess asked.

Hawthorn managed a tight smile. "Oh, nothing, only that we don't want to bother you or the other giants. We just—"

"But you did bother me," the giantess growled, exposing her sharp teeth. "It is *my* job to safeguard the airspace of Mammoth. Imagine what the others will think if I can't manage something as simple as that."

"Well, you've done a marvelous job so far," Fetch said.

"We do not like strangers or trespassers," the giantess went on. "Did you not see the sign that this town is for those of giant blood only?"

Fetch's pulse flared with worry. He needed to free himself and then he needed to swipe the right key. And then. And then. And then. There were so many. Part of him was curious about what Hawthorn had seen when she was in dojee form, but another part didn't want to know, didn't want to be told they were on the wrong path, because he had no backup plan.

"Tell me." The woman narrowed her eyes. "How did you manage to get past the worms in the forest?"

So she didn't know yet that the worms had been freed. Fetch winced, hoping he could escape before she and the other giants found out.

Fetch said, "If you let us go—"

"Hmph. I don't like sentences that begin with *if*." The woman inspected her ragged nails. "They aren't tidy. They break promises and change shape and size and direction, a bit like clouds, storming and then vanishing at will. It's all very unsettling."

Where was Beck? Maybe the dragon couldn't find his way into this well-sealed chamber. Maybe he'd been caught. Maybe Fetch needed to secure the key first.

Hawthorn sat up straighter. "How long have we been here?"

The woman gathered her skirt and drew closer. She walked with a bit of a hobble. Fetch looked down. Her feet were those of a bird, with long, twisted claws that protruded from beneath the dress's hem. "Hours. Days. Who knows? Time is elusive to me."

"Days?" Fetch shouted, wishing he could retrieve Violet's handkerchief from his coat pocket. How many stitches had vanished? One? More? All?

The giantess scowled. "Did I say days? I meant minutes. Or is it hours?"

Fetch grumbled. *This is why giants have such a bad reputation*, he thought.

"Now," the giantess said. "I'm sure you know, Fox, that your face is plastered on posters all over Ocho Manos. The queen is offering a reward too. "

Fetch shot Hawthorn a glance. "Yes, I know," he told the giantess. "But it's—it's not what you think."

"How do you know what I think?" the giantess asked. "I could turn you in right now, call the Legión to my doorstep and watch them carry you away kicking and screaming."

"Then why haven't you?" Hawthorn asked.

Fetch was about to try to smooth things over when the giantess said, "I want something more than the queen's scraps. After all, no one can trust a monarch. I will unlock those shackles and send you on your way in exchange for something of magical value. Do you possess anything like that?"

Fetch felt a glimmer of hope, but then remembered how this giantess had negotiated with Esme, a few inches of the girl's hair in exchange for access to Ocho Manos. The only one who'd kept her end of the bargain was Esme.

"I can give you a magical thread," Fetch blurted.

"Right, right, the posters mentioned something about a Zindero," the giantess said. Fetch couldn't tell if she was snarling or just had a twisted smile. "Do you have any thread that would give me back my real feet?"

A lump grew in Fetch's throat. "Someone . . . did that to you?"

"Are you dull in the head?" the giantess growled. "No other giant possesses such feet. Or walks in such pain. Which is why I prefer to fly."

While Fetch did in fact have a healing thread, it was only useful for minor ailments. Nothing powerful enough to change bird feet back into giant feet. Was that why the giantess had wanted Esme's flowers? Had she thought they'd heal her?

"The flowers around your neck," Fetch said.

"Useless magic," the giant snapped.

So they hadn't helped her. But they *could* help him communicate with Esme. And if there was anyone who could help him figure this all out, it was a powerful chaos witch like his friend. The only problem was convincing the giantess to give them to Fetch.

The woman lifted the necklace to her nose. "But they do smell like a summer garden. Plus, they keep the repulsive stench of bird away."

"Why would someone do something so cruel to you?" Hawthorn asked.

The giantess's expression darkened. "Ocho Manos was built on cruelty."

"Surely with all the magic in Ocho Manos," Hawthorn said, "there is some potion, some spell to help you."

"You think I haven't tried? For years? Consuming all sorts of horrendous things? Things that left boils on my skin and ulcers in my gut." A shadow crossed her gaunt face. "Too many peddlers selling false promises and deceit. But not to worry, they have all been punished."

Fetch's heart grew heavy in his chest. He knew the power of a curse, the way it could shrink your heart and grow your hate. He'd once had an opportunity to break the spell that left him in fox form, but it would have meant giving up his magic, and he hadn't been willing to part with his Zindero heritage. Truth be told, he liked being a fox—it suited him quite nicely.

"I'm sorry," Fetch said softly.

"There has to be a way," Hawthorn said.

The woman sighed. "No one wants to help a giant."

"But then how did you get those failed potions you mentioned?" Fetch asked.

"Messengers. Disguises." She looked like she might say more, but she looked away, her face lost to the shadows. When she turned back, her expression had hardened. "Very well. If you have nothing to offer me, then . . ." Her threat died in her throat, for at that very moment a stone in the wall jiggled back and forth.

Flecks of dust floated to the floor.

With a flourish, Beck popped out of the wall. "*I* have something for you, my dear lady."

Chapter Twenty-Nine

"Who are *you*?" the giantess bellowed.

"I am Beckblade the Second, dream dragon, at your service." Beck gave a tiny bow.

Fetch groaned. Couldn't Beck keep his identity quiet until they got through this quest?

The giantess wrinkled her nose, inching back. "You . . . are quite small, and I do not like small things."

"But I'm growing!" Beck spread his wings and wiggled his tail as if that was proof. Fetch stared in astonishment. Beck's tail had grown another few inches. Maybe more.

"And you're rather bony," the giantess said. "Definitely *not* a dream dragon."

"Ask Fetch."

The giantess snapped her attention to the fox. "Do you know this creature?"

Fetch exhaled. There was no use trying to keep it a secret now. And maybe Beck had seen something in his dream that made him think it was safe to reveal his nature to this strange giant. "I created him," he said.

"Hmph. Well." Then to Beck, the giantess said, "Dream dragons cannot be trusted, so why should I believe you?"

Beck winged into the air. "But I am part bone dragon too, and they are fiercely loyal and highly dependable."

"Can you please stop flapping about?" the giantess groaned. "It's making me dizzy."

Beck swooped back down.

The woman studied the little dragon. "How can such a contradictory little creature possibly help me?" she asked.

"If I tell you," Beck said, "will you free my friends?"

The giantess scoffed. "Do I look like a fool?"

Beck rambled on as if he hadn't heard the giantess's objection. "I'll also need the key to the Cave of Always and, if you're feeling generous, my lady, perhaps you can tell us how to find Soledad as well."

"The key to the cave? But . . ." The giantess tightened her gaze, twisting her mouth to the side. She stared at the dragon for so long that Fetch started to feel nauseous.

"You want three things in exchange for one favor?" the giantess finally asked.

"Indeed," Beck said with a smile.

"That *one* favor to help you with your feet," Hawthorn put in, "is more valuable than letting us go or—"

"Silence!" the giantess shouted. She began to pace, muttering to herself as her keys jingled. Fetch's heart thundered. They were wasting precious time.

"I will not be fooled by hope," the giantess finally said. "I will not be led down a road built on lies again. I could throw you at the feet of the undead army this very moment."

Beck blinked his enormous brown eyes. "But, my lady, your feet are powerful—just like those of the great king birds. The Atotolin. Did you know that they dwell in the Land of the Dead and they have unlimited magic in a single claw? And they eat souls! They're basically invincible."

"I am a giantess!" she roared. "Not a king bird. Nor do I *want* to be a king bird!"

"Of course," Beck said. "Everyone wants to be who they feel they are on the inside, but not to worry, for I have seen your giant feet restored."

The giantess came to a sudden halt. "Then tell me the cure."

"It is not a cure made of words," Beck said remorsefully. "But I can prove that what I say is true."

"Very well." The woman drew herself up to her full height, which was quite impressive and somewhat intimidating. "For every shred of proof you provide that you are indeed a dream dragon, that what you say is true, I will grant you one favor. And to make it more entertaining," the giantess added, "for every falsehood you speak, I will toss a stone onto the floor. If three stones accumulate, I will carve out your heart, Beckblade the Second—and your friends' too. But . . ." she said, raising her eyebrows, "if you speak the truth, that fox friend of yours may choose one key."

"There are dozens!" Fetch groaned.

"Those are terrible odds," Hawthorn put in.

The woman shrugged. "Then I suppose the small dragon had better select wisely."

"I will accept your terms," Beck said to the giantess.

Hawthorn grumbled something under her breath that Fetch didn't catch, though he could guess it was exactly what he was thinking: *This is a terrible idea!*

The giant snapped her fingers and a throne-like chair appeared, fashioned out of purple sand. She sat, sweeping her tattered skirts to the side, exposing her big bird feet. "Proceed."

Beck shot Fetch a sidelong glance as if to say, *I've got this.*

The dragon perched on a twisted vine crawling up out of the floor. Then to the giantess he said, "Your name is Filomena."

The woman snorted. "Hardly proof of anything. My name is no secret!" She tossed a stone onto the floor. "Let us aim for something more substantial, dragon."

"Your bird feet," Beck said, his voice dropping, "weren't a curse."

Filomena tossed another stone.

"Wait!" Beck argued. "I haven't finished my sentence yet."

"I heard a period," she said. "Proof of a declarative sentence."

"A curse is never born of love!" Beck argued. "Your bird feet—they were your choice."

It felt like all the air was sucked out of the room. Fetch's heart stilled. Where was the dragon going with this?

The giantess made no move to throw another stone. In fact, she made no move at all. Her hardened gaze was pinned on Beck, a silent warning to be careful what he said next.

Beck swallowed. "You were trying to save your father from a terrible spell gone wrong. You stepped your feet into the line of magic to save him. You've been looking for an unspelling ever since."

Fetch realized Beck must have dreamed the past.

Tears pooled in Filomena's eyes. A fragile silence filled the chamber.

"That is no proof!" Filomena growled. "You could have learned that—"

"I saw it in my dreams, my lady," Beck insisted.

"I'm bored of this game." Filomena held up the last stone. "Do you have the unspelling or not!"

Beck floated over and hovered before her. "You can unspell yourself."

"Lies!" She launched the last stone. It clickety-clanked across the floor, lodging itself beneath a twisted vine. "And now your hearts are mine."

Beck's tail dropped all the way to the ground. The dragon looked as though he was struggling to stay afloat. He stretched his tail toward the giantess, and the scales began to glow green and blue and gold.

"Oh," the giantess exclaimed.

"Take hold of my tail," Beck said softly. "And you can see for yourself."

She inched back. "This is a trick."

Beck whipped his tail quickly, curling it around her clawed foot.

"Let me go!" she shrieked.

"Please just look," Beck said, and before she could protest, a faint light sparked in her now distant eyes.

And she went perfectly still.

Chapter Thirty

"What's happening, Beck?" Fetch asked.

But the dragon didn't answer. He was entranced, just like the giantess.

Hawthorn exhaled slowly. "Where did he learn *that*?" She nudged her chin toward the giant and the dragon.

Fetch shook his head. He had no idea what Beck's tail was doing.

"Bone dragons," Hawthorn whispered. "Their magic comes from their bones. Maybe his are bespelling her or—"

Just then Filomena blinked, and Beck took flight, floating in the air with his long tail dropping all the way to the ground.

Filomena waved a hand through the air, instantly freeing Fetch and Hawthorn. The fox jumped to his feet and quickly retrieved Violet's handkerchief.

His paws trembled as he frantically scanned it. Two. There were only two stitches left.

NO! His heart shattered into a thousand pieces. How had he lost five stitches in a matter of hours? Unless he'd been here longer than he thought. He couldn't waste another second. The stitches were more than bits of thread—they were Violet's life. He had to get to her before she lost her heart, her memory, her magic forever.

Hawthorn asked Beck and Filomena, "What just happened with you two?"

"The small dragon showed me a truth," Filomena said.

"Amazing, isn't it?" Beck said. "I think it's the bone dragon in me that allows me to show people what I've seen."

"And I do not wish to share it," Filomena said. "Now I will honor my end of the bargain. You are free to go."

"What about the key?" Fetch asked.

The giantess limped over to Fetch, grimacing as if each step caused her pain. "I do not have the key to the Cave of Always."

"What?" Fetch snapped.

"Because one does not exist," Filomena said.

Fetch turned to Beck. "You told me she had the key. We don't have time for this!"

"In my dream," Beck said, "I saw a key and we—we were led to the cave."

Filomena said, "I *do* have a key that will give you access to the drum."

"Great!" Fetch said. "Can we have it?"

"It's always changing, so even I do not know which one it is," Filomena said.

"Your feet, Filomena," Hawthorn uttered. "They're still..."

Filomena glanced down at her claws. "Oh. Indeed. They will not change until I complete an act of selflessness."

"Like she did for her father," Beck said.

"I will take you to the Cave of Always." Filomena's expression softened. "But if it is the drum you seek, you yourself must choose the right key."

"You can do this, Fetch," Beck said softly.

Fetch dragged a paw down his face. The chamber was suddenly hot, and he felt as if he were holding on to a single fraying thread, but he couldn't let go. Not yet.

The fox stared at the row of keys hanging from Filomena's belt. Some were rusted, others bright and shiny. Some were ornate, others plain.

His paw trembled as he reached toward the keys. Maybe he'd feel a tingling, or some other sensation that would tell him which was the right one.

What if he chose wrong?

His pulse raced. He took several deep breaths to try to still his heart.

Then he closed his eyes and brought the image of his grandfather's calloused hands toward his mind's eye. The way they moved when he wove magic. Lorenzo had always made it look easy, effortless, as if the magic was coming from his fingertips and not the threads.

He'd always told Fetch that the first rule of Zindero magic was intent, and that he must envision what he desired most in the moment. But it was the second rule that the fox was fixated on right now.

Zindero magic is not in the threads. The truest form of our magic can only come from an unnameable place within us. A place that can only be reached through unconditional love.

Which was how Violet had tied her heart to Fetch's and how his grandfather could wield magic without the threads.

Eyes still closed, Fetch reached out his paw. Standing this close to Filomena, he caught the fragrance from Esme's roses. He began to float farther and farther into his memory until the day that Esme pledged herself to him shimmered in his mind's eye.

"You pledged yourself to me," Esme said, "and now, well, we don't have anything like a bow in this world, but . . . if you ever need anything—"

Her dark eyes had shone in the afternoon sun so brightly, looking at Fetch expectantly.

Unlike that day, Fetch responded, "How do I choose the right key?"

Think of Violet.

The memory began to fade, and Fetch felt a strange sort of longing in the center of his chest, as though he was missing something he couldn't name.

He focused only on Violet. On the way her blue eyes were both warm and cool, the way she stuck out her tongue when she was concentrating, the way she held a needle in her left hand because her right hand "didn't understand magic yet." And amid all his remembering he felt a pulse of warmth, a spark of magic, a single thread that tied him to his sister—and for that single moment he was at peace.

"You have chosen," Filomena said.

Fetch opened his eyes. Like waking from a long sleep, he had to blink the world back into focus. "Wait. I—I didn't."

But the giantess was already removing a key from her belt. A black, ordinary thing no longer than Fetch's paw.

"You're not listening," Fetch said. "I didn't pick that one!"

Hawthorn inched closer. "You did."

Beck nodded as the giantess handed over the key. Fetch was surprised by the weight of the thing. Had he really chosen this one? Or maybe the Malvada had done so?

"Now let us see if you made the right choice," Filomena said. "Come. It isn't too far to the Cave of Always."

Just as Fetch and the others turned to follow the giantess, a horn blared.

Filomena froze. She might have even gasped. Fetch couldn't be sure because the alarm was earsplitting. "That alarm can only mean one thing," the giantess ground out. "Someone has freed the worms."

Fetch searched for the right words to make his case, but the giantess's neck began to lengthen, stretching longer and longer like taffy. Her face bloomed red. Her scowl deepened.

And then her head hit the ceiling. "You!" she growled. "Do you know what the punishment for such a crime is?"

"Let me guess," Hawthorn said. "Death?"

"A *slow and painful* death," the giantess said, clenching her jaw as if trying to conceal a wince.

Beck flew up toward Filomena, hovering there. "Are you in pain, my lady?"

"It's these feet!" she moaned. "Whenever I lose my temper, my neck grows, and my feet feel even more ghastly than usual." She glanced down at her clawed feet with a sigh. "Selfless," she whispered.

Filomena took a deep breath, and another. Soon her neck shrank to its usual size. She turned toward a wall that was now opening to reveal a long firelit tunnel. "We must make haste before the other giants find you and rip you limb from limb."

"I live for haste," Beck said, flying right next to her.

At the same moment, the chamber walls began to quiver, and indecipherable voices boomed in the distance. Footsteps pounded.

"That doesn't sound promising," Hawthorn said.

"Hurry!" Filomena cried as she rushed into the firelit tunnel.

Fetch was the last to enter and as he did, the wall closed behind him with a *thunk*.

Chapter Thirty-One

Fetch rushed through the dim tunnel, and just before he caught up to his friends, he felt the Malvada stir.

You are wasting time.

"I need the drum, so I can navigate the palace."

This seemed to appease the darkness. In the next instant, Fetch could feel the Malvada settling deeper. *Make haste!* it hissed.

Once he reached Hawthorn, he tugged her back and whispered, "Did I really choose this key?"

"Fetch, I watched your paw with my own eyes."

"But I don't remember it."

"Maybe you were just reacting to the flower petal."

Fetch's breath hitched in his throat. "Petal?"

"It fell from Filomena's necklace," Hawthorn said. "And glittered for a second on the key you chose, before dissolving."

Fetch couldn't believe it. Could Esme's magical flowers have truly helped him? His grandfather always said that magic has a memory. Maybe Esme's flowers remembered him somehow. And if that was true, then the key in his paw had to be the right one.

Or so he hoped.

They journeyed in silence for the next twenty minutes. Fetch fidgeted, glancing over his shoulder every few seconds, half expecting an undead soldier to lurch out of the shadows.

"Do you have a crick in your neck?" Hawthorn asked.

"Just making sure we aren't being followed," he said.

Hawthorn pressed her lips together, tilting her head. "I don't hear anyone coming. Well, the alarm is still blaring, but want to know what else I hear?"

By the scowl on her face Fetch was pretty sure he did *not* want to know.

"Your heart," Hawthorn said. "It's slamming against your rib cage with a terror that has nothing to do with those giants."

"Wow. You can hear that?"

Hawthorn was still scowling. "I need to tell you what I saw in your eyes back in the giant's dungeon—"

"Later," Fetch said. "You can tell me after I talk to Lorenzo." But he didn't really want to know, because he'd seen the way Hawthorn had tilted her chin and steadied her gaze as though she'd seen something she hadn't been expecting. Something she didn't like. What if she'd seen the darkness? Fetch wondered if he could ever make her understand his choice to unite with the Malvada.

Before Hawthorn could argue, the wall before them opened and, to the fox's surprise, they stepped into a circular room, every inch of it glittering with amethyst, which cast a rosy light across the space.

"Oh my!" Beck squeaked with delight. "It's so sparkly. Like my tail!"

Filomena clapped her hands once. The floor jolted, nearly throwing Fetch off balance before the walls began to stretch longer and longer, giving the impression that they were somehow descending.

"What's happening?" Hawthorn asked.

Beck winged about, poking his nose against the shimmering amethyst.

"We are journeying into the depths of the cave," Filomena said.

They came to a hard stop.

The sound of grinding gears filled the space, and the floor began to revolve. Portions of the wall opened into large doors that looked into twelve distinct chambers. Inside each chamber was a massive marble statue, intricately carved in the likeness of a different giant.

"They all look very serious," Hawthorn whispered.

"These are our heroes," Filomena explained. "Great leaders, artists, scientists, astronomers. Did you know giants are the most intelligent creatures in Ocho Manos?"

"Well," Hawthorn began.

"Giants *are* rather brilliant," Beck said. "Quite scholarly, and it's not because of the size of their brains, either. It's because of the size of their curiosity."

Fetch took in the lifelike statues, their stony faces, their distant eyes, their bold stances. Whoever these giants were, they looked fearless.

"What's this?" Beck asked as he pressed a silver knob next to one of the statues.

Filomena barked, "Don't touch—"

A booming voice filled the chamber: "I am Palayo, great astronomer, stargazer, and poet. Oh, the world is filled with such beauty and folly, but—"

Filomena pressed the knob, and the chamber went silent. "We do not have time for history lessons," she said, wiping her brow with the back of her arm as though she was already exhausted by this venture. "Now, would you like to meet Soledad or not?"

"She's here?" Fetch's chest tightened.

Filomena hobbled to the opposite side of the room, stopping before another figure. "*This* is Soledad," she said.

Fetch's skull pounded. "The loneliest giant is a statue?"

"Oh," Hawthorn breathed.

Beck hovered before Soledad. The statue was beautiful—elegant, even. The giantess had long, flowing hair and lithe limbs. Her eyes were made of sparkling sapphires. Her gaze was lifted as if staring at something way off in the distance.

"Why is she called the loneliest giant?" Hawthorn asked.

Gazing at Soledad, Filomena said, "Her husband left on a boating expedition and every night she waited on the cliffs, staring out at the sea, hoping he'd come home."

"He never did?" Fetch guessed.

Filomena shook her head. "She lived the rest of her life in utter solitude, but that isn't the reason she is truly called the loneliest giant."

"Then why?" Fetch asked.

"Because she guards the dead."

There was a beat of silence, something akin to reverence, before Beck asked, "Why does she have stones for eyes?"

"They were part of her wedding ring," Filomena explained. "It seemed fitting."

Fetch ran a paw over his throbbing head. "All right, so . . ."

"See that keyhole in the back of her hand?" Filomena pointed. "Try your key there."

"Is she going to give us a history lesson too?" Beck asked.

"Only rambling poets do that sort of thing," Filomena said.

Gripping the key, Fetch drew closer to the statue, to her tightly closed fist that was either showing her anger or trying to protect something.

Hawthorn exhaled, puffing her cheeks as she patted Fetch's shoulder. "If this doesn't work, I can use Enero to break through the statue."

"*That* would destroy the drum," Filomena said.

"Gently is best," added Beck.

Fetch's paw trembled as he reached out. Toward the lonely giantess. Toward the keyhole. *Please let this work. Please.*

"Not to worry you," Hawthorn whispered, "but you should hurry because someone is coming."

"No one would dare come here," Filomena growled. "First, I designed this cave to be ever-changing, so the path is never the same. Only I know the way. And second, I have not granted permission to anyone to step foot in this sacred space."

Hawthorn shrugged. "Whoever is on our tail doesn't care about the rules."

"How long do I have?" Fetch asked.

Hawthorn went still, listening. "About twelve minutes. Well, unless they pick up their speed."

"I shall head them off at the pass," Beck announced as he flew around the chamber. "Where is the pass?"

Filomena waved her hand through the air. A thick band of green light encircled the chamber.

"Make haste, Fox," Filomena insisted. "My magic won't last long."

With a tremble, Fetch inserted the key.

Then, slowly, he turned it.

Chapter Thirty-Two

Soledad's closed fist turned with a *clink* as she unclenched her hand and held it palm up.

Fetch held his breath.

Waiting. Hoping. Waiting.

"Did he do it wrong?" Hawthorn asked.

Before Filomena could answer, a nerve-grating *creeaaac-cccckkkk* sounded.

The statue split right down the middle from head to toe. Then, ever so slowly, the loneliest giant's body opened sideways.

A brilliant beam of light shone across Fetch's face, so bright he had to shield his eyes.

When he looked back, he saw a cylindrical upright drum no bigger than twelve inches high, floating in the middle of the statue. It looked to be made from a hollowed tree trunk, and carved into its dark wood were a crescent moon and a dozen stars.

"It's a thing of beauty," Beck whispered.

Fetch took the drum in hand. It was entirely weightless, as if he were holding nothing more than a single thread. Across the top of the drum was a tightly pulled skin. Sabía's words drifted into his memory:

Only a bold and worthy heart with the purest intentions can use its magic.

Fetch knew something about intention; it was the foundation of his magic. But in this moment, he felt lost. His intention was to save Violet. Was that bold enough? Pure enough? And what about the Malvada? Did the darkness now living inside him make him unworthy? But hadn't his only intention been to save Violet? Shouldn't that be what he was judged on?

Lorenzo had told him countless times that intention wasn't born in the mind, or even the heart. It had to be as much a part of you as your own skin.

Fetch asked Filomena, "What do I do? How do I use it?"

But Filomena didn't respond because she was staring down at her bird feet. "My feet," she whispered. "But I—I kept my end of the bargain."

"Maybe the act wasn't selfless enough," Beck said with so much sincerity it made Fetch's heart ache for the giantess.

The giantess's face reddened. Her eyes looked like they might pop out of her head. "I didn't turn you in! I didn't carve out your hearts!" Her face twisted. "More lies! More empty promises."

There was no more time to waste. Fetch closed his eyes, then, with a shuddering breath, he thought of Lorenzo and thumped the drum once.

A hollow, distant sound reverberated, the sound of a roaring sea. A chorus of whispers rose up.

Then everything went silent.

Fetch opened his eyes.

He was alone in the glittering Cave of Always. Gone were his friends and Filomena; gone were the statues.

"Hello?" His voice echoed across the vacant space. "León?"

There was no answer.

"You believe you are worthy to speak to the dead?" a woman's voice echoed.

"Soledad?" His voice caught on her name. He'd been hoping for his grandfather.

"You think your plight is noble?" she asked.

"I don't know if I'm worthy," Fetch said. "But my sister is, and she's been stolen from me."

"Yes," Soledad said gently. "Those we love most are too often taken from us."

Fetch brought his paws together like a prayer. "I . . . I'm sorry about your husband," he said in a low voice. "But you're my last chance. This drum . . . I need it to conjure my grandfather. He's my best shot at finding and saving her."

"Does she want to be saved?"

What an odd question, Fetch thought. "Of course."

Soledad was silent a moment. Then she said, "Well, not everyone does, you know. We just assume they do."

Her words conjured the memory of Violet telling him to stay away.

The giantess was wrong. Violet would never want to be a prisoner in the winter palace. But he didn't want to say anything to offend Soledad. He just waited, and waited some more, thinking a person could go mad in so much silence.

"Your heart is broken too," Soledad said softly.

Fetch nodded.

"Broken hearts are dangerous things, Fox. Darkness can get into the cracks. I sense a darkness in you."

Fetch stepped back. He wasn't sure what to say to that. "I've messed some things up and—"

"This is greater than your mistakes. You yourself do not feel worthy."

Fetch's shoulders slumped. He couldn't argue with Soledad. Finally he said, "But my plight *is* worthy! *My sister* is worthy."

"There is greater danger at work here than your sister's or your fate," Soledad said. "Would you ignore all that to save her?"

I already have, Fetch thought, but kept the words to himself.

Halfway through his next breath, an apparition began to

take shape. He noticed the shocking red hair first, and his heart leaped.

Lorenzo's round face materialized. His wide, curious eyes roamed the chamber.

Fetch's heart fluttered wildly.

Next came his grandfather's neck, his robust body, his strong hands. Every part of Fetch's grandfather took shape, but his form was so faint Fetch was scared a single breath would blow him away.

"León!" Fetch began to run to his grandfather.

Lorenzo held a hand up. "Stay where you are," he said in that gruff voice of his. "The space between the living and the dead is quite precarious. One wrong move and our connection will vanish."

Fetch halted, then realized that his grandfather probably didn't recognize him. He'd never seen him in fox form. "It's me," he said. "Fetch. Your grandson."

"I'm dead, Fetch. Not daft. I can see through curses, and besides," he added with a small smile, "I would know you anywhere."

"I . . . I need your help," Fetch stammered. "The winter queen's taken Violet, and I have to rescue her. Sabía said you know the palace like the back of your hand and . . ." Each word was another painful reminder of all that Lorenzo had never shared with Fetch. "Can you tell me about any secret passages to get me into the palace?"

Lorenzo's expression softened. "Fetch, you cannot save her."

"I can! And I will." The Malvada had promised! "I'm going to make this right. I'm going to bring her home."

Lorenzo studied his grandson. His eyes held a sadness that made Fetch feel defeated. "There will be no home to go to."

"What are you talking about?"

"Queen Celeste is making wicked plans. If she succeeds, all will be lost."

Everything around Fetch faded, as if only he and his grandfather existed in this between space. "What do you mean *lost*?" the fox asked.

"Even from the ghostly dimension I can only see so far."

"Is this about the trap she's setting? Maybe for the dojees?"

Fetch didn't think his grandfather's ghost could get any paler, but he did. "The dojees?"

Quickly, Fetch explained about the message Violet had threaded into Beck's dream. He expected his grandfather to hurl a million more questions at him, but he didn't. Instead Lorenzo said, "The queen was given a glimpse of her future many years ago, a future she didn't like."

"Like what?"

"I cannot be sure, but whatever it was, it made her desperate enough to put all this in motion."

Fetch understood making decisions under stress. He understood desperation. "All of what?" he asked. "How could the dojees change what they'd seen?"

"They can't."

"Then why?" The question that drove every story Fetch had ever read. "There has to be a way to find out what they told her."

Lorenzo stared at him silently, as if whatever thought was forming he didn't want to share.

"You know something," Fetch guessed.

"Only a Tangle could tell us the truth," Lorenzo whispered. "But as you know, that magic is unpredictable, and very dangerous."

Lorenzo had warned Fetch about the use of Tangles before, insisting he never *ever* attempt such Zindero magic. The spell could too easily veer out of control, growing in its own power like a storm gathering speed and force. Never mind that such an effort would drain the fox, leaving him weak and vulnerable.

"I could try," Fetch said. "You told me that Tangles are easy to get started."

"And harder to untangle!!" Lorenzo bellowed.

Fetch squared his shoulders. Maybe he couldn't manage a Tangle, but what if he could? It was the *what if* that lifted his spirits ever so slightly.

"Fetch," Lorenzo uttered softly. "I believe in you, son, but there are certain types of magic that are too monstrous to contain. And a Tangle"—he paused, his eyes filled with sorrow—"a Tangle will always ask for more than you can give. It will take pieces of you. Do you understand?"

Fetch's heart thumped wildly, as if it had decided long before his mind caught up. "I understand." His grandfather nodded curtly, as if Fetch's words were a promise. They were not.

"We don't have much time," Lorenzo said. "I will need a ghost thread."

Fetch stiffened. "I've never heard of a ghost thread."

"It is made from spirit," Lorenzo explained. "It is so light, so ethereal, only a ghost can truly manipulate it."

"How do I summon it?"

"*You* don't," Lorenzo said. He closed his eyes. His hands floated before him, and Fetch felt a shift inside his coat.

Slowly, a spool twirled up and out. The thread sparkled as it unraveled and drifted in the space between the fox and the ghost. Each turn shifted its color, from pink to orange to green, then violet.

The spectral strand landed in Lorenzo's palm. Then, inexplicably, it vanished. And yet other threads of light pulsated, brightened, and lengthened as he began to dance his hands back and forth, weaving right and left, up and down.

The air sparked silver and blue and pink and gold. Lorenzo's Zindero magic was a sight to see, as if he were stringing the stars themselves.

Then Lorenzo broke the connection, and the spool flew back into Fetch's coat.

"Do you think someday I could weave magic without thread?" Fetch asked.

"Your heart is broken, son. No great magic is ever created with a broken heart. But if you heal it—if you love unconditionally—then perhaps."

Fetch knew he'd never put his heart back together again. Not until Violet was home.

"It is there," Lorenzo said, gesturing to the spool. "The thread is invisible to all but you, and no one can sense it either. It will guide you along the right path."

The empty room felt suddenly hot. "Like a march toward death?"

"Ah," Lorenzo sighed, rubbing his chin. "You've met the girl."

Fetch nodded. "How come you never told me?"

"To tell you your destiny would be to rob it of its power. And remember, you have choices. You can change the path at any time."

Fetch didn't feel like he had the power to change anything, never mind the path of his destiny. "Please tell me what you saw," he said.

"You will come to a crossroads. And you will be forced to make an impossible decision. To save the world or save your sister."

Fetch's insides coiled tighter and tighter until he could hardly breathe. How could he, a half-cursed fox, save the world? He couldn't even keep track of his own sister. "You must have seen the wrong destiny," he said.

"Fetch, you must not close your eyes to the truth, do you hear me? If you do, thousands of innocents will die."

"I only want to save Violet!" Fetch hollered, but his heart was screaming something else. A truth he didn't want to admit.

"Sometimes what we want is less important than what is necessary."

Fetch fell to his knees. He was a monster if he didn't save Violet. He was a monster if he let thousands of innocents die. "I want a different choice," he said. "A different destiny."

Lorenzo's face sagged. "I wish it worked like that, son."

Fetch's gaze met his grandfather's. It was like a dam had broken and everything Fetch had never gotten to say to Lorenzo came spilling out. "I miss you so much, and I—I should never have taken my eyes off Violet, and it's my fault and I set the magic in motion and now our hearts and magic are going to be lost forever and—"

"Fetch."

The fox turned his gaze up to his grandfather. Tears glistened in his eyes, blurring his grandfather's image. "I wish things were different for you. And time is running out." Lorenzo glanced down at Fetch's black paws. His ghostly face darkened.

"You have been touched by a monster," he breathed.

Shame spread through Fetch like a wildfire. "I had no choice," he said. He wanted his grandfather to tell him he understood, to tell him he would have made the same choice.

But Lorenzo was barely a misty outline now. Only the red

of his hair lingered, like a magnificent fiery aura. "Do not let it hear your plans, do not let it see. Do not trust what it tells you. Keep it in the dark, and when the time comes, you must fight, Fetch. Fight."

And then his grandfather vanished into nothingness.

Malvada

The darkness lashed out against nothing. There was no fox, no fear or pain. No broken heart.

Wherever Fetch was right now, it could not follow. Was he speaking to the ghost? What did he learn?

The Malvada's fury grew. If it was to succeed, it needed to see and hear everything the fox did.

Seething, the Malvada went very still.

Ultimately, I will win. For soon the fox will release me and my power will know no end.

Chapter Thirty-Three

The chamber began to spin, faster and faster.

Fetch swayed dizzily, struggling to keep his paws rooted to the floor. He could feel the Malvada expanding inside him, cold and dark and bitter. He curled into a ball as the world around him whirled. Birds squawked. Beasts growled. Magic hummed. It was as if time was lingering between each breath, each heartbeat.

Lorenzo's words played through Fetch's mind, weaving themselves into his memory.

You will come to a crossroads. And you will be forced to make an impossible decision. To save the world or save your sister.

Fetch didn't want the choice. And yet there it was, hovering in the not-so-distant future. It was as if he could sense it coming, like the first chill of winter winding its way to his doorstep. There was no outrunning it.

The chamber came to a sudden halt.

A cacophony of voices erupted all around. "Fetch . . . go . . . now . . . no time."

His friends' hands reached for him, tugging, dragging him to his feet, but it was as if he had returned as a ghost himself. He couldn't make himself stand. He couldn't open his eyes. He couldn't move at all.

And for a blink, he didn't want to return to the land of the living. He wanted to stay in that once-silent chamber with his grandfather's ghost and pretend there was no monster inside him. No undead army hunting him, no crossroads, no impossible choices.

Fetch drifted numbly in and out of consciousness. He couldn't feel his legs, or his paws. All he could feel was the Malvada twisting inside him. Surging through his veins like lightning.

Fetch remembered what the Malvada had promised: *Do you see how powerful you can be? We will defeat the winter queen together.*

It was here, in that liminal space between then and now, that Fetch realized why the Malvada had chosen him—as a shelter, yes, but because he was broken just like Lorenzo had said, just like Soledad, a complete stranger, had seen. Her words came back to him now.

Broken hearts are dangerous things, Fox. Darkness can get into the cracks.

Was that why the monster had chosen Escarlata the witch as its last host? Because her heart had been broken over what she mistakenly assumed had been her sisters' betrayals? The more Fetch thought about it, the more it all felt real and true. Which meant the queen was also broken. And the dojees had seen it, had predicted a future she feared, just like Lorenzo had said. It was this future that Fetch needed to see. It was the only way to learn not only about her plans for the dojees, but how she intended to change their prediction.

You're exhausted, the Malvada whispered softly. *Allow me to take control now. So you can rest.*

Fetch wanted to rest. He wanted to slip into the shadows of sleep. Just for a moment. Just for . . .

No!

He struggled against the Malvada's will. But it was like fighting an avalanche of stones tumbling down, down, down, each crushing another part of him.

I don't have to stay broken.

He reached for his Zindero magic, for the invisible threads that were woven between his bones, stitched into his heart. A magic that was his birthright.

He clung to its strength, its promise.

Fetch opened his eyes to a black sky.

"Did it work?" Hawthorn asked Fetch. "Did you talk to Lorenzo?"

With a nod, Fetch got to his feet.

Beck hopped from foot to foot nervously. "What did he say? Did he give you a map?"

Fetch felt the weight of the Silver Drum in his coat. The drum that had given him a few precious moments with Lorenzo. Moments he could never let the Malvada know about.

"Where are we?" he asked.

"At the edge of Mammoth," Filomena said.

Then, remembering, he glanced down.

"No more bird feet," she said.

"She got us out of the chamber before whoever was coming arrived," Hawthorn announced, "and she brought us here at the risk of her own neck."

"Selfless," Beck said. Then, by way of explanation, the dragon added, "Because she helped us even when she thought all was lost, though her spelled bird feet remained."

Seeing the giantess restored felt like a whisper of hope. "That's amazing," Fetch said. "How much time have we lost?"

"A day," Hawthorn said matter-of-factly. "The festival is tomorrow."

Fetch felt as if the ground might swallow him whole. "How will we ever make it to Sterling in time?"

"You must go now." Filomena removed a key and twirled it before her. The key floated into the air, creating a brilliant sphere of gold.

The air pulsed and rippled with magic.

"Use this portal," Filomena said. "It will save you two days' travel." She removed a brass skeleton key with a heart-shaped bow from her belt and handed it to Fetch.

"What does this unlock?" he asked.

"The House of Invisibility."

"Invisibility?" Hawthorn frowned.

The giantess nodded. "A secret place we giants have used for eons. It is not far from Sterling."

"But if it's invisible, how will we find it?" Beck asked.

"The key will allow you to see what others cannot," Filomena said. "Once it's used to open the lock, the key will vanish and return to me."

"Thank you," Hawthorn said to Filomena as the gateway floated closer.

"We are forever grateful." Beck bowed as he and Hawthorn stepped into the sphere.

Clutching the key, Fetch's gaze fell to Esme's flowers around the giantess's neck. "You've already done so much for us, but do you think . . . can I have those?"

Just as Fetch thought the giantess would scowl or scold him, she removed the necklace. "They are of no use to me, but I hope the blooms will be helpful to you."

Fetch stared at Esme's delicate flowers in his paws, then placed the necklace over his head. His heart squeezed with hope. If anyone could tell him how to defeat the Malvada, it was his otherworlder friend, who had faced the darkness and won.

"Thank you," he said. Then he turned and stepped into the gateway.

Chapter Thirty-Four

A hot white light exploded, and the world around Fetch dissolved as he tumbled through the arctic air of the portal.

Then, *thump . . . thunk.* He plunged into a snowbank.

Above him were gnarled, leafless trees, their crowns nothing more than thorny branches stretching toward the sky.

Hawthorn was rolling to her feet next to him, gripping her lower back. "Well, that wasn't fun. A warning would have been nice."

Beck popped out of a pile of snow, shaking his head wildly to remove the excess. He tipped to the side, his tail flailing as he tried to get his balance.

Fetch stood. The only light came from a bright moon, tucked against the black sky. For as far as his eyes could see, there was nothing but rolling hills of snow and icicles hanging from blackened trees.

"I don't see a house," Hawthorn said. "Do you, Fetch?"

Filled with disappointment, he shook his head. Maybe Filomena had been mistaken, or—

The key vibrated in his paw. He looked down at the thing as it began to float up, until it hovered in front of his face. So close to his eyes he could peer through the heart-shaped bow. "I see it!"

The house was made entirely of glass—a massive structure taller than the trees. He ran toward it, followed by his friends. Just as he reached the door, the Malvada thrashed. *Where are we? What is that ghastly sound?*

What sound? Fetch asked.

The shattering of glass!

Fetch didn't hear anything except the thumping of his own heart. It was then that he remembered something Violet had told him long ago. She'd just finished another book and had been jibber-jabbering about it all day. "And the evil wizard couldn't enter the invisible realm," she'd said.

"Why not?" Fetch asked.

Violet stared at him as if it was obvious. "Because darkness can never be invisible."

Leave this place! the Malvada demanded.

"Fetch," Hawthorn said. "What are you doing?"

Beck landed on his shoulder. "Do you see a way in?"

Fetch nodded. The iron door was massive, at least twenty feet tall, and there were odd symbols carved into the wood—the language of giants.

The Malvada retreated, then went entirely still.

Could the House of Invisibility truly keep the Malvada at bay and lock it out of his thoughts? There was only one way to find out. Fetch placed the key into the brass doorknob and turned the lock. Instantly, the key vanished.

Fetch pushed the heavy door open and the trio stepped inside.

He had expected the interior to match the glass exterior, but instead found a cozy living room with stone floors and a stone hearth where a fire burned. Four green velvet sofas were arranged in a square near the fireplace with a table set in between. Three towers of iced cookies were arranged in the middle.

"Oh my," Beck gasped, flying over to stuff a cookie into his mouth.

"It's like someone was expecting us," Hawthorn said.

"Look," Beck said, pointing. "There's a note."

Fetch went over and picked it up before reading it to his friends. "'Enjoy your stay at the House of Invisibility. Here you will be afforded protection and privacy.'" He glanced up at Beck and Hawthorn. "Signed by Filomena."

"I like her!" Beck smiled and tossed another cookie into his mouth.

Fetch reached into his coat for Violet's hankie. There were still two stitches left, but for how long?

"What did Lorenzo say?" Hawthorn asked as she dropped onto a sofa.

Fetch remembered his grandfather's warning: *Do not let it hear your plans, do not let it see. Do not trust what it tells you. Keep it in the dark, and when the time comes, you must fight, Fetch. Fight.*

Was Filomena right in saying that Fetch was safe here? Even from the Malvada?

"Not much," he said to Hawthorn, holding up a paw.

Malvada? he asked silently. There was no answer. He needed to be sure. *The queen is coming.*

Not even a stirring of the darkness. Fetch could barely feel its presence. He let out a long breath.

Beck said, "Ghosts are not the best communicators. Sometimes they make up riddles just to drive the living mad. Did you know that?"

Fetch's mouth curled into a smile that was one part pride and the other part love. He really had come to love Beck. For his goodness and humor, for his shine and sparkle. His endless supply of hope.

Fetch quickly explained all that Lorenzo had told him, how he now possessed the ghost thread that would lead to Violet. But there was no way to share the entire story without telling his friends about the Malvada. So he did. With each word, his cheeks grew hotter and his heart felt the weight of his shame.

Beck's eyes went wide with astonishment, or maybe fear. Fetch couldn't tell which.

Hawthorn's mouth twisted. "You joined forces with a dark being?"

"I had to do it, to save Violet. I'm sorry for not telling you. I just . . . I didn't think you'd understand." Fetch expected Hawthorn to lose her temper, to tell him what a fool he was, but she simply sighed and said, "We have to find a way to defeat the darkness once you release it."

"I think it's why Lorenzo said the world is at risk," Fetch told his friends.

Beck scratched the side of his head. "But is it at risk because of the queen, or the dojees, or this monster inside you?"

"I think it's all connected." Fetch knew what was hanging in the balance. Somehow the dojees were a part of it all. The winter queen was luring them under false pretenses, but for what? They already served her.

"If the dojees are such good oracles," Beck said, "why can't they see their own futures?"

"It's not in their nature to serve their personal interests," Hawthorn put in. "They probably aren't even looking. But you can help them, Fetch. I saw it in your eyes."

Beck flapped his wings excitedly. "What did you see exactly?"

Hawthorn explained how she had transformed in the dungeon. "And that's when I saw that Fetch's next move should be to help the dojees."

"Ohhhh," Beck said, wide-eyed. "Perhaps stress, or near-death experiences, or tiny places force you to change."

Fetch was only half listening to his friends; he was still

stuck on what Hawthorn had just thrown at him. It didn't matter what she thought his next move should be, not when Lorenzo said he controlled his destiny. He could choose.

Hawthorn's gaze dropped to the flowers around Fetch's neck. "Why do you have those?"

He explained how one of the flowers had allowed him to communicate with Esme in the dreamworld. "She defeated the darkness once." Fetch remembered how she'd used the Daggers of Ire to kill the monster. But he didn't have any weapon as powerful as that. "She might be able to tell me how to beat the Malvada when the time comes."

Hawthorn drew closer. "Are you saying that you're going to sleep? Now?"

"What if the Malvada follows?" Beck asked. His long tail swept across the snow.

"The monster can't hear anything as long as we're in this house," Fetch said.

"That's because the dark can't ever be invisible," Beck said.

Fetch grinned, wondering if the little dragon had read the same book as Violet.

Fetch didn't know if his idea would work, but he had to try.

He shook out his paws and took a few unsteady breaths. Then he focused. He thought of Violet, of her hope and innocence. Of León, of his strength and wisdom. And of the thread that tied them together as family. As he brought the memory of each closer to his heart, he felt a wave of warmth, an indescribable power that vibrated across his very bones. And he realized that the threads that connected his family were made of only love. His Zindero magic coursed through him, as if it was waiting to be called on, waiting to be of service.

And for the first time in his life, he let go. He trusted the threads. His magic.

Soon, a pale blue thread floated up and out of his coat. Without losing focus, he removed Esme's flowers, then began to weave the shimmering thread through each bloom.

Magic to magic.

Pulse to pulse.

He held his breath. Filling himself with Violet's hope. With León's strength.

The world around Fetch narrowed to a pinpoint of light, then slowly it began to expand again until he realized he was no longer with Beck and Hawthorn.

He knew this place.

This world.

This jacaranda tree.

He was standing in Esme's front yard.

Chapter Thirty-Five

The sun slanted through the tree's branches, warming Fetch's face. Winter felt like a distant memory.

"Esme?" he called out.

Had the thread really brought him here, or was this just a dream?

"Fetch?"

The fox spun to find Esme, with her dark hair and wide, surprised eyes, right in front of him.

"Is it really you?" he whispered.

Esme smiled. She ran to Fetch and threw her arms around him. "I never thought I'd see you again!"

"I can't believe it worked."

She pulled back and looked up at him. "Where are you?

How did you call me here? I was working on an enlargement spell when, *poof*! I was suddenly here."

"I'm in trouble and I need your help."

Esme's smile faded. "Tell me everything."

And so he did, not leaving out a single detail. When he finished, Esme said, "You made a dream dragon? That's incredible!"

"Esme."

"Right." She shook her head. "I really thought I'd gotten rid of that horrid Malvada monster."

"Tell me how you did it."

"It was the Daggers of Ire," she said with a shudder, as if she didn't want to remember. "Though obviously they weren't enough to totally get rid of the Malvada," she spit. "I can't believe that wicked beast followed you and it's all my fault."

"No," Fetch said. "I'm the one who let it in. I did this." They were both silent for a moment before he added, "Is there anything else, any other detail you can remember that might help me? I mean, Esme, you *defeated* it."

"Obviously not." She began to pace. The white blooms in her hair shimmered and, for a blink, Fetch remembered what it was like to go on a quest with her, with her determination and her Chaos magic. "Let's think back. The Malvada was able to possess Escarlata because her heart was broken, but why did it want *her*?"

"She's one of the most powerful witches in history," Fetch said.

Esme pressed her lips together. "So the monster wants more power. It's using you like it used Escarlata. It possessed her too, absorbed her magic."

"Except that I have no true power," Fetch said. If anything, it was the Malvada that had expanded his Zindero magic. "Well, not like Escarlata." Why would the monster go to all this trouble when there were so many others who had way more strength than he ever could?

"Who does?" Esme asked.

It took Fetch a second to catch on. "In my world?"

Esme nodded.

A terrible weight came crashing down on the fox. A realization so awful, he didn't want to admit it. How had he not seen it before now? The Malvada needed a commanding vessel, someone with immense magic. "The queen," he whispered. "It wants her. That's why it's been helping me—to get closer to the palace and to her so that it can possess her!"

Esme's eyes went wide with fear or shock, or maybe both. "Fetch, imagine the control the darkness will have if it wears the crown."

The horror of Esme's words stole the fox's breath. The gears in his head were grinding fast and hard.

"She's the perfect vessel," Esme said.

"Broken yet powerful," Fetch said.

"You cannot let the Malvada anywhere near the queen."

"That's not possible."

She stared at Fetch for a moment. He saw the realization

dawn in her eyes. "Violet," she said quietly. "She's at the very place the Malvada wants to get to."

This was the crossroads Lorenzo had warned him about, the terrible choice he'd have to make. If the darkness possessed the queen, the world as he knew it would be forever changed, likely plummeted into a wickedness he couldn't even imagine. Fetch had the power to keep the Malvada away from the queen—but if he did that, he could never save Violet. He had to know the entire truth, and that included the queen's true motivations.

"It's more than that," Fetch said, explaining what Lorenzo had told him about the dojees and their prediction for the queen's future, one she hadn't liked, one that had set her entire wicked scheme into motion.

"But why would she need to trap those poor creatures if they can't change her destiny?" Esme asked.

"I don't know," Fetch uttered. "But there is one way to find out."

"How?"

"A Tangle." He quickly told her about the magic and its perils.

"No way," she argued. "You can't risk your magic. And what if you lost control of the Tangle? What if—"

"I have to try. It's the only way to see the whole picture."

Esme blew a long dark lock from her face. "Even if you did see the truth, that doesn't help you defeat the Malvada."

"Which is why I'm here. I was hoping you could tell me."

"But you already know that the daggers drove the monster out of Escarlata."

"Because they were made of ire?"

Esme shook her head. "More like the bond between the original witches."

"The sisters."

The world began to fade and the distance between them grew. "It was their love for each other," Esme said.

"That isn't helpful. I love my sister but that won't save her."

Esme sighed. "I wish I could tell you more, but remember that the daggers obviously didn't get rid of that horrid monster as entirely as we thought."

Fetch felt the weight of the sky on his back. "Are you saying there's no way to truly be rid of it?"

"I'm saying you'll need a force so great it can destroy the Malvada and end its darkness once and for all."

Before Fetch could utter another word, his friend blinked out of existence and he found himself back in the House of Invisibility.

Chapter Thirty-Six

"Are you okay?" Hawthorn caught Fetch by the elbow. "You were zoned out like a statue."

"Did you see Esme?" Beck asked. "Did she tell you how to beat the darkness?"

Fetch gathered himself, then after a shaky breath he said, "The Malvada wants the queen. It wants her power. Which means if I go near the palace, if I try to save Violet..."

Hawthorn's face clouded over. "The Malvada wins."

Beck tucked his wings tightly against his body. "Every story comes to this. An impossible choice. But we will prevail!"

Fetch loved Beck for his confidence, but the dragon was too new to this world, to the darkness and wickedness that seemed to fill its every crack.

Lorenzo's words were like barbed threads stitching themselves into Fetch's heart. *Sometimes what we want is less important than what is necessary.*

How could Fetch deliver evil to his world, an evil that could affect thousands and thousands of creatures? But Violet was his sister, his blood. And she was on the verge of losing her heart—and her magic.

Tears blurred Fetch's vision. But his decision was clear. "We need to stop the queen. And we need the save the dojees," he managed with a tremble in his voice.

"You can't go anywhere near the palace," Hawthorn said, echoing what Fetch already knew.

He nodded, feeling the crush of defeat.

Hawthorn pulled her fur hood over her face. "So I'll go. I'll find Violet. I'll save her for you."

"I'll help," Beck said. "I'm quite small, and no one is looking for me. Plus, I know what she looks like—I've seen her in my dreams."

Fetch's heart swelled with love for his friends, who were willing to risk their lives for him, for the dojees. Beck really was a true warrior, and it wasn't because Fetch had created him that way; it was because his heart was built that way.

"But what about the reason you wanted to go to Sterling?" Fetch asked Hawthorn. "The information you're searching for."

"Secondary" was all she said. Then, "But what will you do?"

Fetch glanced at his pocket watch. "I'll try to intercept the dojees before they get to Sterling tomorrow."

"How?" Hawthorn asked.

"I don't think they'll travel in the open—they're too important, too protected," Fetch said.

"You think they'll take the Queens' Road," Hawthorn guessed.

Fetch nodded.

"That road is forbidden to anyone but the queens!" Beck argued. "I read all about how people lose their heads and limbs and organs if they trespass there."

Fetch stood straighter, adjusting his coat. "There's no other choice." If he could warn the dojees, if Beck and Hawthorn could get to Violet, if he could keep the Malvada far, far away from Sterling and the queen . . . There were too many ifs. And then there was the biggest mystery of all—what was Celeste herself truly up to?

Lorenzo's warning swept across his memory like a harsh wind.

Fetch, you must not close your eyes to the truth, do you hear me? If you do, thousands of innocents will die.

"We should get some sleep," Fetch said.

Beck rounded up a few more cookies, then snuggled onto one of the pillows. "Maybe I can dream something about the queen's plans."

It was a maybe Fetch couldn't count on. He nodded as Hawthorn collapsed onto a sofa. He dropped onto another and pretended to sleep. It didn't take long for his friends to fall into deep slumbers. Fetch got to his feet quietly.

He summoned a sleeping thread to ensure his friends weren't awakened. Quickly, he floated it over them, creating a protective circle.

He shook out his paws and closed his eyes, wishing he could get more breath into his lungs. Bracing himself, he summoned a memory thread. Next he called up a spool of royalty, another of winter, then one of greed, and finally one of truth.

He hoped it was the right combination, one that would create the storm he needed.

The spools twisted in the firelight, waiting to be commanded. A part of him half expected the Malvada to surface, to override Fetch's power, but the monster was quiet.

Fetch swiped a paw through the air, then with his other, he spun his magic wildly. Turning, twisting the threads, intentionally entangling each.

Memory. Royalty. Winter. Greed. Truth.

The spools battered against one another, clashing with wails and screeches and hisses and howls.

The floor quaked. The walls swayed. The room blurred in a mass of shadows. All Fetch could see was the storm of magic, the tangled threads expanding into a giant angry sphere. A sphere that was trying to suck him in.

A violent current of magic took hold of him. Fetch struggled to stay on his feet as pain exploded behind his eyes. His muscles spasmed. His heart lurched.

Show me the truth of Queen Celeste's intentions.

The Tangle darkened, a blackness so deep Fetch was sure he was staring into pure evil. His legs buckled, and he collapsed to the floor.

Then everything went still.

A brittle silence stretched. He lifted his gaze. And there in the center of the fury, a thread of cold white light zipped across the air toward Fetch and straight into his chest.

His heart seized as the Tangle's spell wrapped around each beat, squeezing like a giant fist.

Fetch tore at his chest, as if he could reach his own heart, as if he could will air into his lungs.

A Tangle will always ask for more than you can give. It will take pieces of you.

He'd lost control and now he would die.

Somewhere far away he heard a scream. An explosion of light. A hurling of magic. But not his own.

Enero flew through the air, a flash of green straight into the heart of the storm. The force was so great, Fetch was thrown back. Wings beat wildly. Footsteps pounded across stone. And then everything went silent.

Fetch lay there, dazed. He was alive, and now he understood the ugly truth.

It was Hawthorn's face that came into view first—wide eyes, a grim angry line for a mouth. "What did you do!" she growled, hauling him to a sofa.

"I . . . I . . ." The words were slow, unformed. He felt weak.

Beck landed next to him. He wrapped a wing around Fetch's shoulder.

"Care to explain?" Hawthorn said.

"Would a cookie help?" Beck asked.

Fetch shook his head and caught his breath. "I—I know the queen's intentions."

"Eep," Beck squeaked.

"They . . . they were stitched into my heart." He went on to tell them about the Tangle he'd created to allow him to see the truth.

"A foolish risk!" Hawthorn snapped. "Why . . . why would you—"

Beck leaned closer to Fetch. "Tell us."

And so he did.

Chapter Thirty-Seven

"The queen is weak," Fetch said. "It's why she moved the festival up. It's why she wants the dojees' enchanted fur. So she can regain her strength and her magic, and if the Malvada possesses her, if they unite—"

Hawthorn clenched her fists. "With that kind of power she could overthrow the other queens."

Fetch could barely stomach Hawthorn's words, knowing what they truly meant. "If that's true, then Ocho Manos will exist in perpetual winter," he said. There would be no end to her power, to the Malvada's power. With Celeste's magic, who knew what cruelty the bitter darkness would inflict on every creature in Ocho Manos.

"That's not all," Fetch said. His paw went to his chest. "The dojees prophesied that the queen would die this winter."

There was a long stretch of silence before Hawthorn growled, "Serves her right."

Fetch barreled ahead, needing to get this all out. "They also prophesied someone who could change the queen's future."

Hawthorn and Beck stared mutely at Fetch in the firelight. Giving him the space and time to tell them the rest. When he didn't, Hawthorn said, "Who?"

Fetch's eyes flicked to her. "Violet."

"How?" Beck asked.

"I didn't learn the how," Fetch admitted. "But at least now we know why the queen took her."

It wasn't random after all. The queen had *chosen* Violet. Had wanted his sister's magic for her own gain, and now that Violet had come into her full power, Celeste could put the rest of her plan into place. "That's why she wanted the dojees," he said. "For their power of prophecy, so Violet can change not only the queen's future but anything else Celeste didn't like."

"Total and complete power," Hawthorn whispered. "But . . . why imprison the dojees?"

"They'd never agree to serve her under these conditions," Beck put in.

Fetch nodded. "And the queen reduced the hours of magic to distract everyone and reduce the chance that anyone might find out her plan."

What Fetch couldn't understand was why Violet would agree to such treachery. Unless she was being forced to do so.

Hawthorn frowned. "Don't ever try a sleeping spell on me again."

"How did you break it?" Fetch asked. But then he remembered that the effort of creating the Tangle had left him weak and vulnerable. Which meant his spell had been weakened too. "I have to warn the dojees," he said, seeing the path clearly now. "If I can make them aware of the truth . . ."

"They'll refuse the queen and she'll have no future to worry about," Hawthorn said with a crooked grin.

Beck stretched his wings. "I'm sure they will be most grateful."

"The Malvada will be furious to know that the vessel it wants wasn't worth the journey," Fetch said.

"Do you think the Malvada will strengthen the queen enough that she won't die?" Beck asked Fetch with a yawn.

"Even the Malvada can't change a prophecy."

Everything was falling into place. Fetch had a clear path now, a solid plan. One that would begin at the festival tomorrow. He just hoped that Violet's heart would hold on, and that the handkerchief wouldn't lose more than one stitch overnight.

They slept through the morning, and into a slice of the afternoon. The moment the fox opened his eyes, he checked the handkerchief.

One stitch. The relief was so intense he nearly cried. Still one stitch left, and one hour until the festival. He was so close.

Last night, for the first time, he'd half considered if maybe it wouldn't be the worst thing for Violet to lose her magic. She wouldn't be able to stitch the future for the queen or anyone else who would want to use her for her powers. All it would take would be a single claw to pluck the last stitch. But how could he ever steal Violet's heart and memory? He couldn't.

His friends woke a moment later and he showed them the good news.

"Such luck!" Beck cried, flapping his wings excitedly.

Hawthorn smiled—it was small, but it was real. "I guess it's time to storm the palace."

A few minutes later, the three friends stood on the threshold of the House of Invisibility. They lingered there with the door wide open and the endless forest before them. No one spoke. No one made empty promises. No one voiced their fears or doubts.

And once they left this safe haven, everything would change.

"Ready?" Fetch said, but it sounded more like a dry croak. He cleared his throat and squared his shoulders.

Beck threw a salute.

Hawthorn swept back her hood and marched into the woods. "Better get a move on," she said. "The festival is in an hour."

Fetch followed behind her, through fresh snow. Waiting for the Malvada to split him open for his treachery. But the darkness didn't so much as twitch.

Beck soared, making figure eights as he practiced his roar.

Hawthorn stopped in a small clearing. Fetch glanced around. "How will I find the Queens' Road?"

Hawthorn went over to a tree and, placing her hands on its trunk, she began to whisper in her tree language. Then, after a few moments, she nodded and turned to Fetch. "It's half a mile to the north. The trees will lead the way."

Fetch felt a searing heat spread through him. The Malvada was awake and it wasn't just stirring. It was thrashing. It was angry. And Fetch knew why. The monster didn't like being kept out of his plans.

Fetch held his friends' gazes. Oh, how he hoped the next time he saw them it was a celebration of victory.

"I'm just going to get some fresh air, then," he said to his friends, hoping to throw the Malvada off the scent of his deception. He couldn't let the darkness know he was heading *away* from the palace.

There could be no goodbyes, no offers of good luck, so Fetch turned his back on his friends and began his journey in the opposite direction, never once looking over his shoulder.

Chapter Thirty-Eight

Fetch plodded through the muddy snow as a light drizzle began. The evergreens swayed and bent toward the path every few feet, leading Fetch as Hawthorn had promised.

With each step, he felt the distance between himself and Violet growing. And the Malvada—it was growing too. Fetch could feel its darkness pressing into his bones, leaching into his blood.

You have taken us onto a different path, the Malvada said.

Tugging his coat collar higher, Fetch said, "A better path. To get us to Sterling more quickly," he lied.

You think me a fool? The beast thrashed inside him.

So the Malvada hadn't seen what had been stitched into Fetch's heart. Ignoring the beast, Fetch hurried toward the Queens' Road. He knew it by the skulls on spikes that lined the narrow path. And then there was the matter of the sign: Tʜɪs ɪs ᴛʜᴇ Qᴜᴇᴇɴs' Rᴏᴀᴅ. Tʀᴇsᴘᴀssᴇʀs ᴡɪʟʟ ʙᴇ ᴘᴜɴɪsʜᴇᴅ ʙʏ ᴅᴇᴀᴛʜ.

Fetch swallowed around the throbbing lump in his throat. Up ahead there was an enclosed thicket of trees that formed an arch of thorny branches. From here, it looked like a twisted tunnel reaching into the awful dark.

The sounds of footsteps forced him to crouch behind a prickly shrub. Carefully, he peered over the branch to find three ghostly guards with hollow eyes and grayish skin walking along the side of the road about twenty feet away.

Fetch's heart somersaulted. *Ernesh.*

The capitán was here, bringing up the rear. He stood straighter than the others, his eyes narrowed, scanning the forested terrain as if he was expecting trouble. It made sense that the queen would send her most trusted guard to ensure the dojees made it to the palace. Did that mean the fox hunt had been called off?

Fetch doubted it. The hunt would resume as soon as the festival was over.

And right now he had a much bigger problem. How would he get past the guards when the dojees came through?

The Malvada whispered again, *Do you think you can fool me?*

Fetch didn't answer.

You have kept me in the shadows, but what you don't understand is that I live in shadow. I thrive in shadow.

Just then, the sound of carriage wheels rolled along the icy road.

Fetch reached for an invisibility thread, but it didn't rise. His magic didn't so much as hum. Cold coursed through his veins.

I played fair, Fox. We had a deal—a deal you broke. And now you will suffer the consequences.

The dark carriage emerged from a patch of fog. A large man dressed in a black silk cape and a top hat steered the midnight steeds.

This was Fetch's only chance.

Do not move! the darkness warned.

Every instinct told him to turn and run away, to give up this futile effort. But then Lorenzo's voice broke through: *You have choices. You can change the path at any time.*

But for the fox, there was no choice. He would never forgive himself if he walked away, trembling in fear, the way he had so long ago. He would never make that mistake again.

Fetch bolted down the hillside and into the middle of the road, waving his arms wildly in front of the carriage. "It's a trap!"

In a flash Ernesh was there, throwing Fetch to the icy ground. Thick cobweb-like threads wrapped around the fox, tighter and tighter, slithering up his body, around his throat.

The capitán stood over him, backlit by the rising moon. The undead soldier's pale mouth curled into a sinister smile. "The prey comes to the hunter."

The carriage halted.

Chunks of snow tumbled down from the dark sky.

Fetch's heartbeat slowed, and his vision began to fade. He gasped, but there was no air. Only the cobwebs reaching into his nose, his eyes, his mouth.

He could feel the cold spreading across his lungs. The cobwebs reached farther, deeper, each thread consuming the fox.

He glanced up to see a dojee hovering over him, its fur black and shiny even in the dead of winter, warm dark eyes with a circle of light around the iris. "Let the fox go," the dojee said in a woman's voice.

Fetch wanted to leap for joy. He'd done it. He'd gotten the dojees' attention! He was going to save them from Queen Celeste's trap.

With a low growl, Ernesh released Fetch from the web.

But in the space between dread and hope, something else happened. The Malvada was devouring the cobwebs still inside Fetch—*feeding* on them. Its darkness spread faster than lightning, as the Malvada's power radiated through the fox's bones, his heart, his mind. His blood froze over.

Such power, the Malvada hissed.

Fetch battled against the darkness. But the harder he fought, the more the agony seared through him. *No!*

Everything went black and quiet, then . . . a pinprick of light. Fetch blinked slowly, bringing the winter world into view. That's when he realized he was staring through the eyes of a monster.

I am in control now, the Malvada said with a glee that tore at Fetch's heart.

The Malvada urged Fetch's body to its feet. "My apologies," it said in Fetch's voice. "I meant no harm. A foolish prank."

No! Fetch thrashed wildly, uselessly. But he was no match for the Malvada's power.

"A foolish prank," the dojee repeated with a hint of annoyance.

Even through the eyes of a monster, Fetch could see how magnificent the dojee was. Ten feet tall, maybe more, with sleek, shimmering fur and an elegant stature. The light in her eyes was soft, like a candle burning in the dark.

"We will throw him in the dungeons," Ernesh said.

"I can see that he meant no harm," the dojee said, waving a paw through the air. "Let him go." Her mouth curled slightly. Not quite enough to be a smile, but there was a kindness, a trust there that broke Fetch's heart. *No! You need to run!* he wanted to shout, but she was already returning to the carriage, which started once more down the Queens' Road directly to the palace and the trap that awaited them.

"We don't take orders from the dojees," one of the guards seethed.

The Malvada sighed. Then, before the guards could so much as flinch, Fetch felt the monster thread its energy with the dark magic of the road, weaving the two together. Sending a signal out to the undead: *There is nothing to see here. Go into the woods and stay there.*

The guards, and even Ernesh, went still, their hollow eyes glazed over. Then in unison they turned and began to march into the forest.

Now, let us finish what we began. Shall we, Fox? The Malvada moved swiftly down the icy road as snow dipped and swirled all around.

Fetch couldn't let the darkness near the palace! He willed his legs to turn, to carry his body in the opposite direction, but they wouldn't move—and the harder he fought, the weaker he grew. The Malvada was a wicked tide, pulling Fetch deeper and deeper.

Best to save your energy, the Malvada said. *You're going to want to see the show.* The Malvada took several breaths, as if luxuriating in the cold air.

Shall we check on Violet's handkerchief? the Malvada asked as it reached into Fetch's coat pocket and retrieved the hankie. *Oh my, only a single thread left. Well, we can take care of that, can't we?*

Fetch thrashed against the strength of the Malvada. If only he hadn't been weakened by the Tangle! But even then, he knew he was no match for the beast.

Fight me even an inch and I will rip this thread out with your fangs.

With a sinking despair, Fetch went still, taking an ounce of comfort from the knowledge that the Malvada had no idea the vessel he wanted to possess was dying.

See how easy that was? the monster said.

There were no words for the pain Fetch felt, the utter anguish of his failure. He retreated into the darkness, into the deepest shadows of himself.

Using Fetch's coat, the Malvada shot up into the sky. Faster than Fetch had ever floated. *Now where is that meddlesome girl?*

Within minutes, Fetch saw a streak of light. It had to be Hawthorn racing across the snow toward Sterling. But where was Beckblade? Had he vanished again?

"Hawthorn!" the Malvada called out in Fetch's voice as it landed a few feet away.

It was enough to get her attention. She came to a halt and circled back, panting. "Fetch! What are you doing here? What—where are the dojees? Did you warn them?"

"They never came," the Malvada lied. "I overhead the guards say they weren't using the Queens' Road after all."

Hawthorn narrowed her eyes.

Don't believe it! Fetch shouted from the darkness. But of course, she didn't hear him.

"Where's Beck?" the Malvada asked.

"Dreamland. But, Fetch, you can't come with me. You can't go near the palace. That's what the Malvada wants."

"But I still have to warn the dojees," the Malvada said. "We won't go anywhere near the queen. I promise."

Hawthorn didn't look convinced.

"I don't have a choice," the Malvada said. It was eerie how very like Fetch it sounded.

"*I* can warn them," Hawthorn argued.

"You can't find Violet *and* warn the dojees. I promise to stay far away from the festival and the queen. And honestly? I'm going no matter what you say. I have to."

Hawthorn glanced over her shoulder as if she sensed something. She looked back at the fox. "Okay. Fine. Do you have the ghost thread?"

Ghost thread? The Malvada spoke inwardly to the fox. *What is she talking about?* Fetch stayed silent. *Tell me now, or I'll burn her alive.*

Hate boiled over inside Fetch. He couldn't watch Hawthorn die. Begrudgingly, he spit out, *Right pocket.*

As the Malvada commanded the fox's Zindero magic, Fetch knew his only option was to try to outsmart the beast.

But how could he do that when he felt like he was drowning in the Malvada's wickedness?

The gossamer thread unwound itself and floated in the space between the two. "Now we follow it," the Malvada said.

Hawthorn tugged her fur hood lower. "Let's go."

The Malvada nodded, trying to hide the smile at the corners of Fetch's mouth. The girl had no idea what was in store. The Malvada was so close to victory, it could practically taste its sweetness. *The queen will be a powerful host, one that will feed my hunger.* A hunger that had begun to carve an endless hole inside the monster ever since it had lost the witch who had saved it.

The two traveled in silence, high-stepping through the thick snow.

Only then did the Malvada truly feel the cold on the fox's skin. The way it seeped into his bones and made his body shiver.

The Malvada followed the floating thread like a lifeline. Sometimes losing sight of it only to catch a glimpse of its sparkling light in a patch of utter darkness.

A bitter wind twisted around Fetch and Hawthorn as they pressed through the dead forest, then crept through a small graveyard scattered with crumbling headstones that couldn't be read. As they climbed an icy hill only to find themselves at the edge of a cliff.

There, a good hundred feet below, was Sterling, a dazzling beacon of light with rising stone towers, its walls choked with icy vines, lacing back and forth like a spider's web.

The Malvada could feel the darkness pulsing in every stone, every window, every tangled vine. It could practically see the dark magic rising off the walls like mist.

Such potential, the Malvada thought.

At the entrance of the palace, carriages were lining up, their wheels crunching along the snow, echoing through the hollow night.

The Malvada began to climb down the cliff when Hawthorn tugged its sleeve. "There's something I need to tell you."

"Now?" The Malvada felt a pang of irritation. "Can't it wait?"

She shook her head. "I'm not here to learn who or what I am," she said.

"You already told me that." *And I am not at all interested in your pathetic little secrets.*

"I don't care about my birth or my history or my dojee magic. It's Sabía," Hawthorn went on. "She's in trouble. The magic of the Hollow, it's vanishing. The trees are dying, and when they do . . ."

She didn't need to finish her sentence. It was clear that the tree spirit would die too. Fetch felt as if he was shrinking inside his own body, like the trees he'd seen in Scarred Hollow. They had looked so sickly, as if they were dying from the inside out.

The Malvada stared blankly, unsure how to respond, how to pretend it cared.

"There is said to be a packet of seeds in Sterling," Hawthorn explained, "kept by the winter gardener. They have the power to restore the Hollow." A tear rolled down her cheek. She swept it away with the back of her hand.

This girl is exasperating, with all her blubbering, the Malvada thought.

If the fox had control over his voice, he'd probably tell Hawthorn something reassuring, something like, *We'll find you the seeds you need.*

The girl gave a gentle nod. Her voice trembled as she said, "If something happens, if I don't make it out of here, will you take the seeds to Sabía?"

"Yes," the Malvada lied. Hope, however useless, would keep

the girl moving in the right direction until they could be rid of her once and for all.

Fetch's heart twisted. If only he could holler at his friend, tell her to run. To save herself.

Hawthorn took Fetch's paw into her hand. Her magic pulsed just below the surface, impressive but not enough to interest the Malvada.

The trill of music carried across the wintry air.

Hawthorn bristled, ever so slightly. And the Malvada sensed something within the girl sharpening to a point. It was as if she was listening for the fox's pulse, to see if his heart beat to a familiar rhythm. But that was just foolish thinking. This half dojee from Scarred Hollow who had rarely ventured out couldn't possibly know that Fetch was a prisoner in his own body.

The Malvada's gaze went to the palace. "We should go."

The girl wasn't listening. The Malvada could tell by the way her eyes darted across the night, the way her body was poised to fight or flee, that her senses were on high alert.

"Something isn't right," she said.

There was an instant tightness to the air. This girl and all her questions!

"We need to keep moving," the Malvada insisted.

She blew out a long breath, glanced around, then gave a single nod.

They followed the ghost thread down the icy cliff, slipping here and there, before regaining their balance awkwardly.

When they finally reached the bottom, they glided into the shadows of a garden brimming with black flowers—dahlias, velvet petunias, hellebores, and roses.

"All the flowers are black," Hawthorn whispered.

A garden of darkness, the Malvada thought, delighted, as the blooms bent toward the fox.

"What are they doing?" Hawthorn asked. "Why are they trying to touch you?"

The Malvada kept to the snowy pathway. "Maybe they can sense the ghost thread."

The music was louder now, blended with voices, laughter, the shifting of magic kept in check.

They used the shadows to conceal themselves. They dipped in and out of pools of darkness, plodding through the snow like ghosts.

The Malvada followed the thread to a narrow path. Several wraith guards roamed the area—their forms nearly transparent, like fine gauze.

The Malvada tugged Hawthorn into the shadows, where they squatted in wait. Oh, how the darkness wanted to be rid of this girl, to throw her to the wolves this very moment, but there was too much risk, and it still needed her.

At least until they were inside the palace walls. Once the Malvada was inside that web of darkness it would be one step closer to realizing its purpose.

The girl mouthed, *Now what?*

As before, the Malvada threaded the fox's magic and its

own with the darkness pulsing in the earth, sending a silent signal to the guards: *Look to the north.*

When the ghoulish sentries left, the fox took off with Hawthorn right behind him. They came to a tall iron fence, its spires decorated with black flowered wreaths and small bones.

"We need your spear," the Malvada whispered.

Catching on, Hawthorn summoned Enero and sliced through the barrier.

They dashed ahead, following the ghostly filament to the east side of the palace, to a wall covered in moss and black, thorny vines. There were no doors, no windows. No way to get inside.

The Malvada dragged the fox's paw down the wall. "It's spelled."

"How do you know?" Hawthorn frowned. Her gaze was locked on the fox so keenly the Malvada was sure she could see through the deception.

At the same moment, the thread pulsed, coiling into a circle of light. A circle that expanded and widened.

The stone cracked. Bits of rock crumbled to the ground. The vines swept back to expose an opening large enough to climb through.

"What just happened?" Hawthorn asked.

"The ghost thread." Just as the Malvada spoke the words, the thread vanished in a wisp of smoke that swirled into the fox's coat. It had done its job. It had led them to a secret passage.

The girl tugged Fetch's coat sleeve. "I have a bad feeling about this. It's been too easy."

"Easy?" the Malvada growled. If the girl only knew how long the journey had been, how much plotting and sacrificing the Malvada had endured to get here. "We can do this. We'll find Violet, and the dojees, and then we'll get the seeds you need."

Hawthorn nodded hesitantly.

The Malvada led her into the darkness.

Chapter Thirty-Nine

"We need Beck's light," Hawthorn whispered.

But the Malvada didn't need eyes to see through the dark. It knew the passage was five feet wide and thirty feet long. The memory of cold and pain and death echoed across the cobwebbed walls.

Fetch struggled against the Malvada's dark magic, but it was too late. The Malvada had breached the winter palace, had joined with the dark magic here. The fox would remain a prisoner until the Malvada commanded him to release it into the world.

A green light ignited instantly. The girl had awakened Enero.

The Malvada groaned inside, blinking away the wretched glare.

A blur of motion stirred at the edge of the Malvada's vision. It turned to find a twisted shadow crawling up the wall, a caged ghost.

You, the specter whispered. Then joined by another: *No trespassers.*

"Sounds inviting," Hawthorn said to the wraith, keeping her grip on Enero. As if it would do her any good against the undead.

The Malvada knew the girl could move with a rare speed. She could cut through here like a streak of light, but she wouldn't leave the fox behind. That much was certain.

We know who you are, another ghost whispered.

The Malvada urged the girl forward. "They're not in their right minds."

"Might have something to do with being locked down *here*," Hawthorn whispered.

Ghostly shadows flew across the wall, faster and faster, following the fox's every step.

Stay with us.

The Malvada and the girl rushed through the dark. Their footsteps reverberated across the stone. *Thud thud thud.*

They came to a winding set of crumbling stairs.

Hawthorn paused and looked up, her face cast in a sickly green glow that heartened the Malvada. *Soon*, it thought eagerly. *Soon I will use the voice of darkness, my true voice, and that will be the end of you and the beginning of me.*

They took two stairs at a time.

Fetch's body ached with the weight of the darkness. Struggling beneath all that mounting magic. The Malvada gripped the fox's ribs and caught its breath. *A weak body and a weaker spirit*, it thought with disgust.

"Are you okay?" Hawthorn asked, glancing over her shoulder.

"Fine. We need to keep moving." *Before this body gives out.*

They came to a wooden door, splintered and worn with age.

The Malvada pressed a black paw against the rusted latch, testing to see if it was spelled. It wasn't.

It tugged on the latch once, twice. The lock hadn't been opened in too many years. The Malvada glanced at the girl.

Her eyes softened into a pitying expression. "We'll find her, Fetch. I know it."

But the Malvada had no interest in Violet and had no intention of ever finding her. The fox's sister had served her purpose to get him here.

"I can use Enero to bust open the door," Hawthorn suggested, but finally the latch dragged across the wood with a creak, and the door swung open.

They peered out onto an outdoor stairwell. A vicious cold swept across their faces.

At the top of the stairs the path forked. To the right was a long and winding passageway leading into deeper shadows. To the left, a balcony bloomed with light.

"The right looks more promising," Hawthorn said. "If we're looking for a dungeon."

The Malvada fought the urge to smile. Yes, the dungeon

was exactly where they would go. Somewhere cold, somewhere that would contain this girl and her magic.

They hurried into a dark corridor whose walls smelled of rotting flesh. The Malvada could sense the ghostly guards just up ahead. Hawthorn grabbed the fox's arm and tugged him back. "I hear something."

The Malvada sent out a silent signal to the undead soldiers. *Come closer. We're here.*

The walls shook. The cobwebs trembled, then began to expand, stretching across the space, taking the shape of two undead soldiers.

Hawthorn's claws extended as she summoned Enero. But before she could uselessly launch the spear at the wraiths, the Malvada grabbed her arm and pinned it back.

"Fetch!" Hawthorn cried. "What are you doing?"

The Malvada gripped the girl's other hand behind her back. Its voice rolled out of the fox's mouth, deep and commanding, working its wicked spell on the soldiers. "This girl is a traitor to the crown."

Instantly, the soldiers' limbs jerked. And then they stiffened and stared hypnotically.

Hawthorn whispered words the Malvada didn't know—a spell. But for what?

The Malvada twisted her arm harder, and in that twist, the girl's claws managed to slice through Fetch's coat, slashing his forearm. Hot blood blossomed. "Who are you?" she growled. "What have you done with Fetch?"

One of the soldiers came forward stiffly. The gossamer chains around his neck stretched across the void. Hawthorn screamed as the weblike strands wrapped around her throat, silencing her.

She fell to her knees, clutching the shackle, gasping for air.

The Malvada staggered, woozy from the cut, then, with great effort, managed to straighten. Regaining focus, it stared down at her, grinning. "Not to worry, I will make sure your death is swift."

All the color drained from Hawthorn's face as she thrashed against the chains. Her face contorted in rage, or maybe agony—the Malvada couldn't be sure.

Then the Malvada gripped the wound on the fox's forearm and said to the spellbound soldier, "Take her to the dungeon."

Chapter Forty

The fox wanted to scream, but he was suffocating under the weight of the Malvada's power. His thoughts turned to Hawthorn. She still had Enero. That was good, but she was unlikely to be able to reach the spear if she was bound by spelled chains.

Just then, searing pain rang through Fetch. The slash on his arm burned with Hawthorn's fury.

He could feel her magic coursing through his veins as Sabía's words rang in his memory: *Her claws can be poisonous or healing according to her wishes.*

But what had her claws done to *him*? She had spoken a spell, words Fetch didn't recognize. And no matter how many times he replayed them in his mind, tried to rearrange them to make sense, he came up short.

The fox suddenly felt cold. And so very, very tired.

Your struggle is futile, the Malvada hissed. *But not to worry. You will have this worthless vessel back soon enough.*

Fetch willed himself to stay awake, but the Malvada's magic pressed him under. For just a moment he floated. Easily. Peacefully.

Then came a whisper.

"Fetch?"

The fox roused himself. Was it his imagination, or—

Beck? Is that you?

"I'm here."

How?

"You're dreaming quite deeply," the dragon said with a tremble. "Now I can talk to you without that dreadful beast hearing. I'd like to wring its neck but that would be your neck and I of course cannot do something so vicious, which puts me in quite a pickle."

I've made a mess, Beck. I tried to warn the dojees. But they didn't listen. And the Malvada is now controlling me and—

"You must listen, Fetch. I've dreamed a terrible truth."

Fetch heard the rumble of the beast's voice in the distance. The Malvada's darkness wrapped around his heart, threading its wickedness through his ribs.

"You must make me a promise." Beck's voice caught on something, something like fear or dread. "You must stay far away from Violet."

Fetch's pulse pounded in his ears. *Beck. I have to see her, even if it's for the last time.*

"If you don't stay away, something terrible is going to happen."

Nothing could be more terrible than her being abducted and imprisoned by the queen.

"She's not imprisoned." The little dragon's words landed like a storm. "My first dream wasn't read correctly. I'm sorry for that. But now I'm sure."

Sure of what?

"Violet's murder."

Pain and fear and grief surged through the fox all at once. He felt the Malvada's magic calling him, drawing him up and out of this prison. *No! You're wrong. I-I'll get to her in time!*

"Fetch." Beck's voice drifted away. But not before Fetch heard the horrendous truth. "You're the one who kills her."

Chapter Forty-One

The fox's body felt like a shrinking cage.

Such a pathetic vessel. But soon, my power will know no end.

The Malvada dashed down the long, cold corridors of the palace, past the windows fractured with ice, past the walls choked with cobwebs that swayed gently in its wake.

It hurried toward the festival and the merriment that would soon come to a terrifying end.

The thought delighted the darkness, urging it forward faster and—

A sharp pain took hold of the fox's body, forcing the Malvada to stop and rest against the wall. Fetch's heart pounded with determination.

Not yet, the Malvada thought. *Not yet.*

A force more powerful than the worthless fox was at work

here. A force that pressed against the darkness, trying to repel it. But what?

With a grunt, it pushed off the wall and made its way along the corridor, down four flights of wide granite steps. The last landing was adorned with a life-size ice sculpture in the likeness of Queen Celeste.

Her face was a thing of beauty by any standard, with wide, probing eyes, a full mouth, high cheekbones, and a proud tilted chin. But beneath all that beauty was the cold and heartless guardian of winter, who wore a dark crown and commanded the undead.

The Malvada pressed the wound from that beastly Hawthorn's claw against the freezing ice, relishing the bitter cold and the momentary comfort it provided.

A droplet of blood stained the ice.

The Malvada made haste, following the music down to the first floor, where it stepped into a grand hall supported with ice columns. Its black marble floors were polished to such a shine they reflected the creatures dancing across it. There were duendes, alasinders, witches, and Espíritus. Even the Maldicioneros, the curse casters, were in attendance.

Every guest was dressed for a celebration. There were long feathered gowns, multicolored fur coats, even several reptilian capes.

Undead soldiers stood at attention at the far corners of the hall, their empty stares cold and penetrating. There were no veins beneath their translucent skin, no beating hearts. Only bones, and the wraiths waiting to be commanded.

And then there were the dojees.

The fox was taking back more space, expanding in his desire to break free. But how? The Malvada had spelled him into the deepest shadows.

With a growl, the Malvada glanced down at the slashes on the fox's arm. The wound burned and throbbed with magic.

The girl! Hawthorn's wretched claws had done this, had found a way to somehow help the fox. But the Malvada's memory wasn't the fox's memory—could it have missed something about the girl's abilities?

A witch in a pink feathered ensemble snorted in the fox's direction. The Malvada looked up at her as she whispered to the others in her group. All five of the brujas turned their heads toward the Malvada with sneers.

"This is the Winter Festival," the feathered witch said. "Perhaps you should dress more appropriately."

"He looks rather familiar," another whispered.

Just then the lights flickered. A horn sounded, and then another.

The music came to a halt and the crowd went silent.

At the far end of the room was a raised dais holding a dark throne constructed of gnarled dead branches intricately woven with cobwebs.

A man's voice boomed, echoing from all sides. "Loyal

subjects," the man announced, "guests of the grand Winter Festival—" Here he paused, a pause the Malvada couldn't afford, for the fox was twisting his way to the surface. The darkness fought to hold on to the fox's form. Just a few more minutes. A few more . . .

"I present to you," the man said, "our beloved Queen Celeste, Keeper of Winter, Guardian of the Undead, ruler of the oldest season in Ocho Manos."

Silence.

The air grew ominously colder.

White breath floated from the fox's mouth.

Heads turned to the back of the room.

The Malvada followed their gazes to where Queen Celeste stood. The crowd parted, giving her a clear path.

As she glided across the marble floor, people bowed, not daring to lift their gazes.

The queen's silver gown trailed behind her like a gently moving stream. Perfectly combed white hair fell down her slender back. And her face: yes, it was beautiful, but it bore the lines of cruelty, as did her cold gaze, and the thorny black crown she wore, which was delicately woven with gossamer threads.

She didn't look sick. She looked like pure power.

Was it possible the Tangle had gotten it wrong?

The queen carried a silver staff that glittered like diamonds in sunlight, and as she passed, the fox quickly ducked behind a few other festivalgoers. The queen had cursed Fetch into this pitiful form. If she were to recognize him now, everything could be ruined.

After Celeste stepped onto the platform, she turned to her followers. "I welcome you to Sterling," she said.

"You are all here to celebrate the onset of winter," she continued, turning her staff. "The most glorious season in our realm. For without winter there can be no spring rebirth. But there has been trouble brewing, my fine subjects. Trouble I cannot divulge quite yet, but you must know that it has forced me to harbor a secret in order to protect the winter realm."

She paused and scanned the crowd, her mouth twisting.

Fetch fought his way to the surface, to hear the queen's words.

"Many years ago," she said, "I had a daughter."

Gasps filled the air.

Queen Celeste went on, urging silence. "I raised her in secret, for I feared there were those who might harm her, but now she has come into her full power, her full magic, and you are the lucky few who shall witness her debut into our winter world."

Fetch felt nothing but cold shock. He hadn't expected a princess.

Murmurs spread through the hall.

A princess?

What a delight!

We are indeed lucky.

Fetch wondered what sort of magic the princess possessed,

and how it would play into the Malvada's plan. Had the monster known about her? Or was it as surprised as everyone else?

"I present to you," the queen added, "my daughter, Amelia, princess of winter and heir to Sterling." The queen thumped her staff once upon the dais.

A column of bright light appeared from the floor. In the next breath, Amelia ascended through the opening, accompanied by two silver birds with wings made of ice. She looked just like her mother, with white hair that fell in waves around her pale face.

The princess stared straight ahead, her silvery eyes never once straying to the crowd.

The ice-winged birds fluttered around the girl, blending in with her startingly white gown gilded with silky icicles. In their beaks, each bird held one side of a tiara made of silver antlers.

As they placed the crown on the princess's head, the crowd exploded with delight. Cheers and applause filled the room.

A shadow swept across the girl's face, there and then gone as her fingers traced the sharp edge of the crown.

Fetch thrashed, clawing to take control of his body, to see through the monster's eyes. To get a better look at the mysterious princess.

It's useless, the Malvada said. *But not to worry, Fox. For the greatest crowning is yet to come.*

Fetch went still. He stopped resisting. For he felt something warm twining around him. Hawthorn's magic.

The Malvada growled, pushing back against the girl's magic as it twisted inside the useless shell of a fox. There was no more time. But it couldn't take the queen—not until it had an opening, a wound. The darkness glanced around, searching for—

There! A two-pronged brooch attached to a fairy's belt.

The Malvada inched closer, taking advantage of all eyes on the princess. With a trembling paw, it reached for the makeshift weapon. Drew it away from the fairy just as the feathered witch gasped. "You! You're that fox on the wanted posters!"

The Malvada stiffened. It hadn't come this far to be ratted out by a tired old witch. "You're mistaken."

As the witch opened her mouth to scream, the Malvada jammed a claw into her side, piercing her with dark magic.

The fox screamed, fighting to surface while the Malvada watched its evil consume the witch from the inside out. Ribbons of shadow sucked the life from her, leaving nothing but bones.

Screams sounded. The spectral soldiers marched closer.

The Malvada ducked and rushed through the now-occupied crowd, struggling to command the fox's body. Just three more steps toward the queen. Toward power.

Two.

One.

The Malvada used some of the last bits of its magic to take perfect aim and propel the pin toward the monarch. It watched as the small weapon turned through the air, as it slashed Celeste's mouth, as it drew blood.

The queen shrieked with fury, and the Malvada roared, "It is time, Fox. Release me!"

Fetch felt a surge of power, like a scream that mounted in his chest until he could no longer keep it in. He threw his head back and opened his mouth. An agonizing howl the likes of which he'd never heard flew out of him.

The Malvada spilled out in a torrent of black that rushed toward the queen.

Celeste watched as the darkness came. She didn't run. She stepped closer, her steely eyes fixated on the Malvada. Then, just as the monster reached her, she opened her mouth and swallowed the darkness whole.

Chapter Forty-Two

"*No!*" Fetch screamed.

The guards were steps away, but he couldn't move. He couldn't take his horrified gaze off the queen.

Ice-blue veins bulged on her face and neck.

Fetch watched in horror as her eyes flooded with pure black. As her face twisted in agony.

Shock waves rolled through the room. Dark magic pulsated in the cold air as the Malvada queen grinned and thumped her staff once more.

Black gossamer threads flew across the hall like spiderwebs, stitching darkness over mouths and eyes, binding hands and legs.

People fell to their knees as the threads wound tighter and tighter, choking the life, the magic, out of them.

Fetch lunged to help a writhing fairy, nearly tripping, for his legs were fixed to the floor. He sucked in a gulp of air as a single thread twisted up, floating before Fetch. He struggled to raise his paw, to fight back, but he was frozen, forced to watch the cobwebs stretching and swelling, slowly trapping everyone in their path.

He felt a terrible thrumming in his veins, hot and furious as the web wrapped around his neck, forced his gaze back to the queen. It slithered down his body and bound his legs, forcing him to his knees before her.

With the back of one vein-riddled hand, the queen wiped the blood from her mouth and smiled at Fetch.

Suddenly, the room quaked. The marble floor cracked open with a thundering blast, breaking through the thick cobwebs.

Dark soil spilled into the hall.

Then, to Fetch's astonishment, Effie and Archie wiggled up through the earth, looking vicious with slime oozing from their wide-open jaws.

But it wasn't just the brother and sister who looked like warriors out for revenge. Behind them were dozens of other angry worms. The slithering army consumed the black threads, burning through each with their poison. There was the terrible scent of rotting flesh as great spirals of smoke filled the air.

Fetch jumped to his feet. What were the worms doing here?

Magic hummed. Screams ricocheted. Fairies took flight.

Effie shouted something, but Fetch didn't catch it in all the commotion. The undead soldiers' webs whipped about the space, desperately reaching for the tree worms, but with each touch of their poison, the threads hissed and melted into nothing.

Fetch looked back to the platform at the queen, who stared blankly out across the battle.

The princess stepped in front of her mother, glaring down at him.

The pointed antlers of her crown gleamed brightly.

Then came a familiar voice.

"Fetch!" Garzo shouted across the pandemonium. The fox's heart leaped, and he scanned the commotion for the fairy, desperate for his help, but his vision . . . something was wrong. Everything grew hazy at the edges.

In the next blink, the room fell into shadow. And yet Fetch could almost make out the outlines of those in battle, like wisps of smoke.

The fox's heart pounded. He was alone with the princess and the queen, lost in this terribly cold void. Ice covered the floor, edged up the walls.

Fetch's lungs tightened. He gasped. Ice formed on his paws, his arms, his legs. His pulse slowed as if . . . as if winter itself was freezing his blood.

"Welcome to the new winter," the Malvada said. "And I have you to thank for it."

A shadow flitted past, then someone gripped Fetch's arm. Someone with familiar magic thrumming in her grasp. Hawthorn!

He felt a sharp point, something piercing his frozen paw.

"Fight," Hawthorn said, but her voice was so far away.

Hawthorn's healing magic coursed through the fox, thawing his bones and warming his blood. And just as he caught his breath, he looked up.

The Malvada queen sneered at the fox. "I have a delicious surprise for you."

"I'm not interested," Fetch said bitterly.

"Ah," the Malvada said with a grin, "but this one is quite staggering. And a promise is a promise." It then whispered something in Amelia's ear. The princess hardened her gaze and tilted her head to the side. A cloud of mist pooled around her face and as it faded, the princess transformed. Streaks of red wove through her white hair like ribbons of flame.

The door in the dais opened once more. Mist bloomed.

With a scornful smile, the queen grabbed the princess, and just as the two vanished through the doorway, Fetch spotted what the darkness had wanted him to see. The birthmark under the princess's chin. That unmistakable four-leaf clover.

Violet.

Chapter Forty-Three

Fetch bolted toward the platform.

A flash of light streaked past him.

Feet flying, legs churning, he hurtled onto the stage to find Hawthorn already there, holding the narrow passage open with Enero.

"A little faster, Fox," she grunted.

"No! You—you can't follow me."

Her cheeks reddened from the effort of holding open the gateway. "Save it, Fetch. I'm coming, and you have about four seconds to—"

Without so much as a glance, he jumped into the void, followed by Hawthorn.

Fetch tumbled through the glacial air, quickly activating his coat. As soon as he was floating, he reached out and caught his friend, who was cursing about the cold and the queen and how far down did this blasted abyss go anyway?

When the ground didn't meet them, when the dark silence closed in and chunks of snow began to fall, Fetch took a breath, and then another, trying to absorb the shock that Violet, his sister, was the princess, and that he'd led the Malvada right to her.

And now the monster had his sister, and all the queen's winter magic.

"In case we die . . ." Fetch forced the words into the freezing air. "I'm sorry about—"

"Stop it!" Hawthorn spit. "You can't die. Well, not until you rescue Violet." Fetch knew it was meant to be a joke, something light in the terrible aftermath of all they'd been through, but there was no humor in her voice, only fear.

"Okay, no dying until then," he said as they floated gently as the falling snowflakes.

Hawthorn nodded against his neck. A tremble ran through her.

In the next instant, the two landed with a thump in a bed of snow. Fetch staggered to his feet while Hawthorn readjusted her fur cape. She looked up. Her eyes went wide. "What in the spirits' name is *that*?" she asked.

A black glass tower rose out of the dense forest. Its polished onyx walls shone in the moonlight, pulsating with dark magic.

Pain flared in Fetch's chest. He glanced down at his paws.

They were no longer black. The mark of the Malvada was gone. Yet he could feel the Malvada's presence, as if they were still connected. And now the monster had his sister.

He swiftly removed Violet's handkerchief from his pocket. His heart plummeted. Half a thread hung loosely from the cloth, threatening to break away with a single breath.

Sabía's voice whispered across his memory: *When the last stitch is gone, your sister's heart will be lost forever.*

And so will mine, Fetch thought as he clung to the handkerchief Violet had dropped in the street five years ago, the one she'd thought would keep her heart safe. But it hadn't, and neither had Fetch.

Warily, he glanced up at the imposing tower. "This is all my fault," he whispered.

"Fetch—"

"I'm the one who set this all in motion when I used that locator spell to find Violet. I let the darkness in, and I carried the Malvada here. The same monster that threw you into the dungeon. *I* did this. And now the beast has my sister and . . ." He could barely get the words out. "She's the princess."

"I know," Hawthorn said. "Garzo told me when he rescued me from the dungeon. He found out during his spy mission. Apparently, the queen needed an heir and couldn't have one of her own, so she stole Violet and passed her off as her daughter, killing two birds with one stone."

"The dojees' prophecy that Violet could change the queen's future."

The fox recalled the loneliness of the last five years, how each new season had only brought more worry, more doubts, more fear.

He was sick and tired of it all.

His heart began to pound with anger, and his claws sprang forth. His magic buzzed hot through his body. A low growl sounded in his throat.

He started for the tower.

Just then, there was a spark in the air and Beck appeared, spinning wildly, as though he'd been tossed out of the dreamworld. "Oh . . . oof . . . incoming!" he called before landing on his feet.

"Beck!" Fetch dropped to his knees and pulled the dragon into his arms. "Was that really you in my dream?"

"Watch the tail!" Hawthorn warned as Beck's very long tail whipped about. The colorless world sparked green, gold, and pink.

"Yes, that was me, and I have so much to tell you!" Beck wiggled free of the fox's grasp. "So many truths and no time and . . ." The dragon huffed. "Better to let me show you."

Beck curled his tail around Fetch and Hawthorn.

The dark world fell away.

Everything grew hazy. Magic swelled. The air stilled and a vision materialized. Violet was sitting in a small pink bedroom by a large stone hearth.

Fetch studied her small form, the way her hands danced

in the firelight. She wasn't using a needle or thread—she was stitching pure magic. Just the way Lorenzo had.

The queen slipped into the room. She stood next to Violet, watching her small hands do their work. "Yes, child," the queen purred. "We will change that horrid prophecy. Surely it is wrong. No one as powerful as I could be fatally ill, but I cannot take the chance. That's why I have you. You will stitch a new future, one where I am well, whole. One that places *me* at the center of power."

A glassy-eyed Violet nodded stiffly and went back to work.

In the next breath, Fetch returned to the moment.

"Do you see?" Beck asked gently. "Violet has been bespelled."

Fetch began to pace. Tears burned his eyes. "The Malvada will never let Violet go," he muttered. "Not when she has that kind of power." The monster was hungry for domination. When Fetch had been possessed by the Malvada, he'd felt that hunger in his limbs like a spreading cold.

Beck said, "The battle with the undead is still going on and, Fetch, we're losing. The dojees were the first taken."

Hawthorn's gaze locked on the tower. Her green eyes began to glow. "I can feel them. The dojees are in there."

A tower pulsating with a wickedness that swept over the landscape in waves of shadow and terror.

"We must free them," Beck insisted.

The gears in Fetch's mind turned quickly.

He looked back at the half stitch of Violet's heart. She'd

told him to stay away, had tried to protect him. She'd tried to protect the dojees. And now she was a prisoner, forced to do the bidding of a monster.

If Fetch didn't free her before the last thread vanished, she'd lose her powers and the Malvada would no longer need her. The monster must not have known how important Violet was to the queen's plans or it would have made sure those stitches had stayed in place.

His gaze swept over the imposing black tower.

The handkerchief warmed in his paw. Violet was in there, close to the dojee prisoners. He could feel it. Just the thought of such majestic peaceful creatures being imprisoned made his stomach turn.

An idea began to take shape in Fetch's mind. One that instilled a terrible fear in him.

His grandfather had once told him that *no great magic is ever created with a broken heart*. What if he failed, and his magic wasn't enough to stand against someone as powerful as the combined forces of the winter queen and the Malvada?

What if Fetch's broken heart made him weaker?

Or what if it doesn't? he wondered.

It was true that sometimes your heart is broken because you've lost someone. Because there is no one left to love you. Fetch had lost his family, but he had friends now, loyal friends who cared about him, who were willing to face great danger to help him. He thought of Esme then, how she had helped in her own way too.

Her words came back to him. *You'll need a force so great it can destroy the Malvada and end its darkness once and for all.*

He turned to Hawthorn. "You said the Atotolin eat souls for breakfast. Is that true?"

"Well, they eat souls, but I have no idea if it's a breakfast thing. Why?"

"I think I know how to get rid of the Malvada," he said. "It's a long shot, and I'll need both of you to pull it off." He quickly shared his idea.

Hawthorn narrowed her gaze. "How are you going to contact the Atotolin? The king birds aren't exactly hanging around here, Fetch."

"The drum," he said.

"Seriously?" Hawthorn looked from the dragon to the fox like she was waiting for someone to tell her it was just a bad joke. But their blank stares must have told her there was no joke because in the next breath, she asked Fetch, "How do you know it will even work?"

"I don't."

"But it did call Lorenzo from the dead," Beck said brightly. "Which means it could work again."

Hawthorn gripped her forehead. "So you want us to hope that you can call the great king birds from the Land of the Dead and that they'll have an appetite for monster."

Fetch nodded. "Precisely."

Hawthorn exhaled and shook out her hands. "Okay. Where do we start?"

Fetch took in a lungful of icy air, gathered his friends close, and whispered, "Here's what we're going to do."

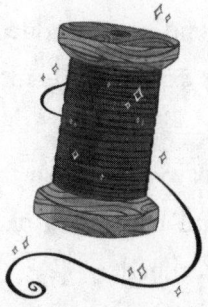

Chapter Forty-Four

After Fetch laid out the plan, Hawthorn turned to Beck. "Are you sure you didn't dream how this all ends?"

The dragon's face fell as he shook his head. "I'm sorry to not have more answers."

Hawthorn glanced back at the tower. With her distracted, Beck lowered his voice and said to Fetch, "Remember my dream?"

The one where Fetch killed Violet.

Fetch nodded. "I'd never hurt her." Beck had to have read the dream incorrectly.

So much could go wrong, and for this to work, everything had to go exactly right—there couldn't be even an inch of error.

"Beck," Fetch said, "please don't disappear. Not until . . ."

"I won't let you down," Beck promised. Except that the dream dragon could hardly control when the dreamworld was going to haul him away. "I will be the mightiest dragon ever."

"And a mightier friend," Fetch added.

Beck didn't smile as expected. He merely nodded and whispered, "Always."

Fetch held out his paw. "Together," he said as Beck planted a wing in his palm and Hawthorn placed a hand on Beck's wing. "Together," she echoed.

Fetch felt a tug in his heart, like the tightening of a stitch.

Then they turned and walked toward the black tower.

The closer they got, the taller it grew, like a black gemstone polished to a shine. If it wasn't so imposing, it might have been beautiful.

Stopping in her tracks, Hawthorn said, "Do you hear that?"

Fetch heard nothing. "What is it?"

"The dojees," she said shakily, "I can hear them. They're afraid."

Fetch's heart plummeted. "We need to keep moving." Snow swirled violently, lashing at them as they continued on.

For the millionth time in the last minute, he touched the Silver Drum inside his coat, making sure it was still there, hoping his plan to use it would work.

They came to an iron door. Long shadows crept up, sliding across the surface like dark ghosts.

Fetch's pulse pounded in his ears as he reached for the

handle, but it was Beck who thrust his mighty tail against the door, forcing it open with a loud groan.

Together, they stepped inside the massive chamber.

Violet's handkerchief warmed and curled in his grasp. She was close, he could feel it.

The air buzzed with dark magic and was so cold, Fetch had a hard time drawing in breath. He tugged his coat around him tighter.

"The dojees are right above us," Hawthorn whispered.

They climbed a set of winding icy stairs that ended in another frosty chamber. Torches flickered along the walls, throwing shadows across the frosted stone.

Fetch's gaze lifted. He gasped. Ten dojees were suspended a good fifteen feet off the ground, each enveloped in a delicate silver web, shimmering with frost. Their eyes were closed as if they were hibernating.

In a flash of light, Hawthorn summoned Enero. Just as she thrust her arm back to launch the spear and free the dojees, she froze as if someone else's will was pinning her in place. A terrible *cracccckkkk* sounded.

A web of ice grew up her legs, then her body, until she was encased in cold.

"Thorn!" Beck cried.

The queen's laughter echoed. "Did you really think you could take what is mine?"

Fetch sniffed the air, trying to catch the Malvada's scent, but there was nothing other than the wicked cold. "You're a coward who won't show your face!" For his plan to work, he needed the queen to make an appearance.

Beck flew straight for the dojees, his tail whipping. Bursts of fire flew from his mouth.

"Beck, no!"

Instantly, the dream dragon froze in midair. Icicles formed beneath his wings and across his tail. His small face contorted painfully.

Fetch held his ground. Any sudden moves would bring the Malvada's wrath down on him like an avalanche. If he was going to be of any use to his friends, to Violet and the dojees, he had to get the queen to come out of the shadows.

"You have done me a great favor coming here," the Malvada said. "Now I can end you once and for all."

"I want to make a deal," Fetch shouted.

"I don't need anything you have to offer," the Malvada said. "I have your sister, a crown jewel. She is the more powerful Zindero, isn't she? It was a delightful surprise to learn that she can weave the future. But not to worry, Fox, I will make your death swift."

Fetch's magic dipped and rose in waves of frustration. "But she can't weave that future without Zindero thread." This was a lie if Beck's vision had been accurate, but the Malvada didn't know that. He just hoped the beast didn't see the bluff.

"Let me guess," the Malvada said. "You will provide that thread if I free your friends."

"Yes." Fetch could feel his Zindero magic rising, pulsing beneath his fur.

"Or I could kill you and take the spools," the monster suggested.

"They can't be stolen," Fetch said. "Only given freely or their magic dies with me."

Silence engulfed the chamber. Fetch's heart pounded in his ears as panic bloomed.

The Malvada said, "I have seen your heart, Fox. I know its contents. You will never leave here without trying to free your sister. So what is your plan? To kill me?" The queen's laughter reverberated across the icy room.

Fetch held up the hankie. "Remember this? If this last stitch vanishes, then Violet's magic will too. The body you stole is ill, and if you want to change that, then you can't risk losing my sister, can you?"

Fetch felt a ripple of power move through him, hot and buzzy. It was the Malvada's fury. Was it some strange aftereffect of having been possessed by the darkness? If the monster had seen into Fetch's heart, maybe it was possible that he could see into the Malvada's.

"I will free your friends," the Malvada finally said. "After you have given me the spools."

Fetch shook his head. He knew he could never trust such an evil creature. "Free them now and I will bring you the spools. You have my word."

Fetch felt the Malvada shifting, its cold darkness spreading through his muscles and bones.

"Very well," the beast said. "But do not attempt to free the dojees again."

Black shadows slithered up the chamber's walls, and hissing whispers filled the space. Hawthorn's and Beck's icy prisons melted, and the Malvada said in a low voice, "Come to the top of the tower. Alone."

Chapter Forty-Five

After Fetch made sure his friends were all right, he whispered, "We stick to the plan."

Then he ran from the chamber and raced up the steps. His coat fluttered behind him with a snapping sound. Shadows upon shadows crawled up the icy walls, slithering across them like serpents.

Fetch bolted up fifteen flights of stairs until he reached a door that led him out onto the roof.

Wind howled, shoving him back.

The arctic air ripped the breath from his lungs as he searched the space for the queen, but the snow was coming faster, *too fast*, and Fetch couldn't see two feet in front of him.

He tugged his coat tighter around his body, sensing Violet

was here too. The hum of her Zindero magic was strong, as if it was calling him.

Just then, the storm quieted. The air cleared.

And there, a few feet away, stood the queen. A sinister smile curved her mouth, chilling Fetch to the bone. "Change of plans, Fox," she said slowly, making each word count. "I'd rather kill you now."

She flew toward him.

Fetch pivoted, twisting through the air. He tripped and landed on his back. The queen was on him in a blink, her freezing hand grasped his jaw, turning his face to ice. The cold was pure agony, spreading through the fox like poison.

Why was the only question that came to his mind. Why had the queen chosen to kill him before he could give her the spools? The realization dawned too late.

Because she knew Fetch would never give up the magic; he'd never leave here without his sister.

He struggled against the impossibility of her strength, trying to reach the drum. It was there, so close, resting against his heart. His spine was a column of ice, freezing him from the inside out.

But he couldn't reach the drum. His mind was slipping, deeper and deeper into the cold.

No. NO!

"Submit," the queen hissed.

Fetch broke a single arm free. He dug his claws into the queen's gut.

The queen gasped, clutching her bloody stomach. With a whimper she collapsed to the ground. Darkness swelled, pooling around the body. Shadows rose, swirling like snow around her fallen form. And then her face transformed.

Fetch stared in horror.

He'd stabbed his sister.

Chapter Forty-Six

"Violet!" Fetch fell to his knees beside her now-human form.

She grimaced, her eyes rolling to the back of her head.

Fetch looked up as the Malvada queen appeared in a cloud of frost. "Please," he cried.

"So easily fooled," the Malvada said. "I was sure you'd see through my illusion, but you saw what you wanted to see, didn't you?"

"Save her," Fetch cried, clinging to his sister. "You need her magic!"

Beck's words circled his memory: *You're the one who kills her.*

The Malvada laughed. "Oh, little fox. Don't you see? Violet is a greater prize to me than even the winter queen, and now she will be mine to control forever."

Fetch pressed his paws to Violet's wound, trying to stop the bleeding. Her magic flowed in rivers of gold and silver and blue. If the queen wanted her so badly, then why wasn't she taking control of Violet? Why was she letting her die?

The world tilted beneath the fox and all he could think of was Violet, bleeding, dying in his arms. *I did this.*

Fetch reached for the Silver Drum inside his coat. A streak of green light blazed by.

"NO!" he screamed as Enero zipped through the air. Faster than lightning, directly toward the queen. She opened her arms as the spear pierced her heart.

The Malvada shrieked.

A black cloud flew out of the queen's body. With a horrific moan, the shadow expanded, taking the shape of something monstrous, with a massive head and a bulging body and thick hairy legs. So many legs.

Fetch stared into the spider's red eyes.

The beast's legs seized Fetch.

Cold engulfed his arms. His vision dimmed. *You'll never win*, the Malvada whispered.

Unbearable pain surged through him as he thrust out his paws and took hold of the evil. As he gasped for air.

Enero flew toward the beast, but the spear ran right through it without injury.

Fetch sprang out of the monster's grasp, rolled across the roof, and launched to his feet in time to see Beck's enormous tail enveloping the Malvada.

"Now, Fetch!" Hawthorn yelled.

Fetch grasped the drum, but a leg broke free of Beck and knocked the instrument out of Fetch's paws and across the glass roof.

He stumbled after it just as the Malvada howled, morphing into a bulbous sac of quivering flesh with four tentacles. Beck's tail thrashed about, trying to control the splitting darkness, but each time he secured one, another sprang up.

The darkness rushed toward Violet.

Fetch's Zindero magic exploded inside him. Threads of light burst from his paws, unraveling wildly.

He wove the thread back and forth, creating a protective web over Violet. The Malvada beat itself against the magic with terrifying shrieks.

Fetch couldn't hold off the monster much longer.

Hawthorn rocketed across the roof, grabbed the drum, and tossed it to Fetch.

The fox caught it. *Please, please work.*

The Malvada broke through the web. A black tentacle grabbed Violet—and Fetch pounded the drum, and shouted, "Atotolin!"

Nothing happened. There were no king birds, no magic to consume the monster.

Behind his eyes, Fetch drew the image of the Atotolin, as if he could will them to appear.

The tentacle was squeezing Violet now. Fetch managed a

focused breath. The hum of his Zindero magic coursed through him. Then with every ounce of hope and love he had, he thumped the drum again and whispered, "I call on the Atotolin."

The drum vibrated.

And a dragon-sized beast with magnificent red feathers bursting with fire appeared.

The flaming bird shrieked, its eyes ablaze as they landed on the Malvada. A roar of fire as it clutched one of the Malvada's tentacles with a golden talon, then another.

The Malvada thrashed with fury and hate.

But it was too late. With its scorching wings, the great king bird engulfed the rest of the monster in fire, consuming every last shred of its darkness.

Fetch held the drum up to the bird. Streams of fire poured into it, the heat so searing Fetch nearly lost his hold. But he clung to the instrument until every last part of the Malvada had been trapped inside.

The air crackled. Bits of ash fell from the sky.

The king bird blinked its golden eyes at Fetch. Then the bird grabbed the drum and released a battle cry that echoed through the night before it vanished into a raging inferno.

Hawthorn rushed to Violet's side.

"She's losing so much blood." Fetch lifted his sister's head into his arms, trying to make her more comfortable.

"Violet," he managed, "please don't die. Please."

Hawthorn placed a single claw to the girl's wound. She drew in a shaky breath. Violet shuddered once, twice, and then she went stiff and cold all over.

"Her pulse," Fetch said, "I can't feel it."

"Just give it a moment," Hawthorn said.

Beck sat next to Fetch. He placed a wing on the fox's paw as they waited seconds, minutes, forever.

Finally, the girl's body softened. She opened her eyes.

She blinked at Fetch. "Who are you?"

His heart plummeted. Had she been spelled to forget him? Then he realized that Violet had never seen him in fox form. "It's me—Fetch," he managed, heart racing. "Your . . . your brother."

The girl sat up. "I don't have a brother."

Beck drew closer, curling his tail around the girl. "You do, and I can show you."

It took only moments for Beck to show Violet the truth, and in those moments, Fetch felt all the relief and terror of what had just happened. He had defeated the monster, he'd saved Violet, and he'd weaved magic without threads. Lorenzo had said it was possible if he loved unconditionally. He looked back at Violet and felt his heart swell. He loved her wholly. No strings attached.

"You okay?" Hawthorn asked.

"I am now," he said with a small smile. "This time the Malvada is really gone."

"Using the Silver Drum was brilliant."

"I couldn't have done it without you. Thank you."

Hawthorn gave a nonchalant shrug. "I guess Enero came in handy."

"That spear took out the queen," Fetch said.

"That's what the Malvada wanted, right?" Hawthorn asked. "For the queen's body to die so that it could escape?"

"I think it must have sensed that the queen was sick," Fetch said, "and the monster needed the queen to agree to let it go." *The way I promised to release the darkness when it commanded.*

"And the queen liked the Malvada's power," Hawthorn guessed. "So, basically, it was willing to let her die so it could escape and take over Violet."

Goose bumps broke out along Fetch's spine just thinking about how wrong things could have gone.

Just then, Beck uncurled his tail. Fetch held his breath, waiting, hoping.

Then Violet turned to her brother and ran into his arms. "Fetch! You came. You really came! And you're a fox." Her body heaved with small sobs.

Fetch held on to her, afraid that if he let go too soon, she'd drift away like a midnight dream. "I'm sorry," he whispered. Then, in a rush, more words tumbled out of his mouth. "I've missed you so much and I should never have let you out of my sight. It's all my fault and can you ever forgive me?"

"I shouldn't have run away." Then, as if processing his words for the first time, she said, "Really? You missed me?" Her voice took on a teasing tone. "How much? Were you terribly miserable or just a teeny bit lonely?"

"Terribly miserable!"

"Me too," she said, wiping another tear. "And even when I was bespelled, there was a part of me that hoped you'd come, that you hadn't forgotten me."

Fetch hugged her again. "I'd never ever forget you." His voice was barely a whisper and he wasn't sure she'd even heard him, but it was okay because they had plenty of time for apologies and stories and magic.

She pulled back. Her gaze swept across Fetch and his friends. "So about this princess business."

Chapter Forty-Seven

Three Nights Later

Fetch sat near the fire in Violet's room while she readied herself for the coronation ball. They'd spent the last three days hardly sleeping, too eager to reconnect, to talk and laugh and stitch together memories, to fill in gaps and make decisions about the future. Together.

And then there was the cleanup after the battle. Every creature had pitched in to help. Garzo directed most of it, complaining that his back hurt from all his fighting and could they hurry up and reestablish beauty in the palace.

Now Fetch tossed a log into the hearth. "Are you sure about this?" he asked Violet. "You could always change your mind." *We could go back home, pretend none of this ever happened.* But he knew better. Once one's destiny was mapped, it was no easy thing to change it.

"Are you scared I'm going to boss you around?" Violet chuckled as she tied a ribbon in her red hair.

Beck landed on Violet's shoulder. "Well, I think you will make a wonderful winter queen."

"Or you could toss the crown in the trash," Hawthorn said, fidgeting with her emerald-green gown. "Is this dress really necessary?" she muttered.

Fetch chortled.

Beck said, "You look quite marvelous, Thorn."

"I agree," Violet said with admiration. "Emerald really brings out your eyes."

Hawthorn grunted. "Fine, but I'm wearing my boots and don't even try to talk me out of it."

Beck twirled in the air. His wings sparkled gold and green. His massively long tail glowed a brilliant blue. "How about me? Do you like the bow tie?"

"You look quite handsome," Violet said. "Even regal."

Beck lifted his chin and grinned from ear to ear.

Violet turned her attention to her brother. "Your suit is a perfect fit."

"That's because you made it," he said.

"Does it do anything magical like his coat?" Beck asked.

Violet smirked. "I may have added a surprise thread here and there."

It had only been three days since Fetch had almost lost his

little sister forever, so it was hard to believe he was sitting in her chambers with his friends, watching her prepare to become queen. She was so young and would have so much responsibility. His mind buzzed with worry that she must have sensed, because she walked over to him. Her white feathered gown floated behind her like a drift of snow. "Why are you so nervous?" she asked.

"I just want you to be sure," the fox said.

"Fetch," Beck said. "She is the rightful heir. I've dreamed about her reign, and it was a good dream."

Violet sighed. "I owe it to Ocho Manos to ensure harmony, to explain to the other queens that they aren't in any danger. And not only that, but so many of this kingdom's subjects need protection, like the dojees." Her eyes flicked to Hawthorn. "Now they can continue keeping the peace."

"And you can lift the rule that they cannot mix with other creatures," Fetch said.

"Well, the first thing you should do as queen," Beck said, "is create a massive library here at the palace with only the most sensational stories."

Violet patted Beck's head. "Brilliant idea, Beck. Can you help me select the books?"

Beck grinned. He turned to Fetch. "If it's all right with . . ."

Fetch laughed. "You'll make an amazing librarian, Beck." Leaning closer, he whispered, "About this dream . . ."

"I saw myself too," Beck whispered back. "I am going to grow rather large."

Fetch grinned. "Sounds perfect."

"The library should be second," Hawthorn put in. "Violet, you need to create a new army now that those horrible ghostly soldiers disappeared when Celeste died."

Deaths no one mourned once they were made aware of her plans to overthrow the other queens and skin the dojees for their magical fur.

"Armies mean violence," Violet said.

Fetch shook his head. "They mean protection."

Garzo threw open the door and blew in, wearing a bright blue silk vest. "Hello, Your Majesty," he said, bowing. "The party is growing restless down there. They are eager to see their new winter queen. Oh, and everyone is here. Every species, every creature. Even the giants came. They all have so many questions, especially about my heroic involvement in the great mission, which people are now calling Winter's Dark Quest, and while I have done my best to regale them with unparalleled stories, they want you."

"I'm glad you're here, Garzo," Violet said.

The fairy looked flustered. His wings beat unnaturally fast.

"I'm glad you're *all* here," Violet added. "And before we go downstairs and make this official, I just wanted to . . ." She took a deep breath, reached into her dress pocket, and tugged free a small packet. "These are the seeds you're looking for, Hawthorn. The ones that will restore Scarred Hollow."

Hawthorn rushed forward and took them. "You're sure? I mean, they'll work?"

"The palace gardener assured me. And if you change your mind and want to see your birth records—"

Hawthorn shook her head. "Maybe someday. But right now I have all the family I need."

"I do have one request," Violet said.

"In exchange for the seeds?" Hawthorn asked.

"No, the seeds are yours. But, if you're willing, I would like you to lead my new army. To be my new capitán."

Hawthorn's eyes went wide. "I . . ."

"You and Enero are perfect for the job," Beck said, saluting her.

Fetch nodded. He couldn't think of anyone more loyal and steadfast than Hawthorn. Plus, she did possess the great godly spear. And then there were those claws of hers.

Hawthorn's cheeks brightened. "Yes, okay . . . I accept."

Fetch caught her gaze, about to suggest she become a chocolatier. Then, as if she could read his mind, she wrinkled her nose and whispered, "I'd much rather command an army, Fox."

Violet turned to Garzo. "You are a brave fairy indeed, and to honor your heroism, I would like to erect a statue in your honor."

Garzo tugged on his vest. "Life-size?"

Violet laughed. "Of course."

"I have one other request," the fairy said. "Do you think . . . maybe I could curate a new garden for you?"

Fetch smiled, thinking it was appropriate that Garzo's childhood dream of creating dazzling gardens come true.

Violet clapped her hands together. "Of course!"

Finally, Violet turned to Fetch. "I want you to stay here in the palace, both as my brother and as my adviser."

"Adviser?" Fetch asked. "I'm not that much older than you. Shouldn't someone more mature and, you know . . . wise be your adviser?"

With a small grin, Violet tilted her head to the side. "But, Fetch, you have a wisdom beyond your years. Think of all you've seen and done and all you've battled. You're the perfect adviser. Plus, there is no one I trust more."

Fetch's heart expanded with so much love and joy he thought it might pop right out of his chest. Yes, this was where he belonged. With his friends and his sister. "I'm not going anywhere," he said.

Beck leaped into the air, pumping his little arms. "I just love happy endings!"

Hawthorn smiled and Garzo sighed. "Fine, fine," the fairy said, "bestow your wishes on us all et cetera, et cetera, but right now can we please get to the ball?"

Beck flew over to the dressing table and picked up Violet's silver crown with its single diamond.

The dream dragon carried it to Fetch, who had agreed to do the honors. The fox took it in his paw. "It's perfect."

A few minutes later, Fetch and Violet stood outside the closed doors of the great hall that had been the site of a terrible battle only days before.

Before the doors opened, before Violet entered to be crowned, Fetch looped his arm in hers. "What future will you weave?"

She tugged him closer. "I want the future to unfold as it's supposed to . . . for now."

Fetch smiled. "For now sounds perfect."

A horn sounded. The doors flew open.

And Fetch walked into his new future with his sister by his side.